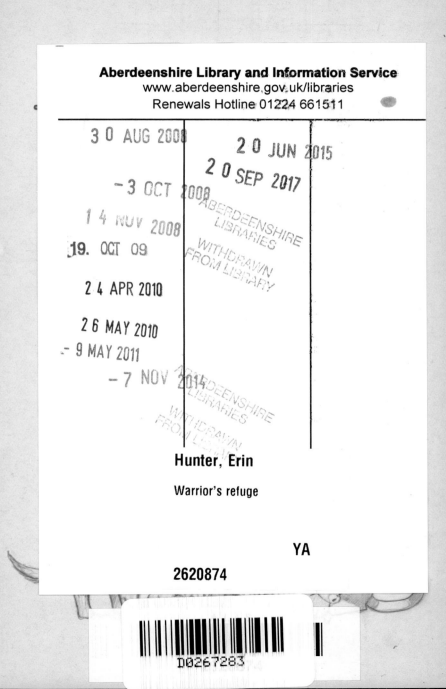

WARRIOR'S REFUGE

CREATED BY
ERIN HUNTER

WRITTEN BY
DAN JOLLEY

ART BY
JAMES L. BARRY

HAMBURG // LONDON // LOS ANGELES // TOKYO

HarperCollins *Children's Books*

Warrior's Refuge
Created by Erin Hunter
Written by Dan Jolley
Art by James L. Barry

Lettering - John Hunt
Cover Design - Anne Marie Horne

Editor - Lillian Diaz-Przybyl
Digital Imaging Manager - Chris Buford
Pre-Production Supervisor - Erika Terriquez
Art Director - Anne Marie Horne
Production Manager - Elisabeth Brizzi
VP of Production - Ron Klamert
Editor-in-Chief - Rob Tokar
Publisher - Mike Kiley
President and C.O.O. - John Parker
C.E.O. and Chief Creative Officer - Stuart Levy

A  Manga

TOKYOPOP Inc.
5900 Wilshire Blvd., Suite 2000
Los Angeles, CA 90036

E-mail: info@TOKYOPOP.com
Come visit us online at www.TOKYOPOP.com

First published in the United States by HarperCollins Publishers 2008
First published in Great Britain by HarperCollins Children's Books 2008
HarperCollins Children's Books is a division of HarperCollinsPublishers Ltd
77-85 Fulham Palace Road, Hammersmith, London W6 8JB

The HarperCollins Children's Books website address is
www.harpercollinschildrensbooks.co.uk

1

Text copyright © Working Partners 2008
Illustrations © TokyoPop Inc. and HarperCollins Publishers 2008

The author and illustrator assert the moral right to be identified as the author and illustrator of this work

ISBN-13 978-0-00-726968-6
ISBN-10 0-00-726968-4

Dear readers,

So, we know where Graystripe is, and that he's safe and healthy. But he's a long, long way from his Clan—even farther than he realizes, if you think about what's happening in the forest at this time. He has the toughest journey of his life ahead of him, but it looks as if he's found a brave and loyal traveling companion. Millie may have lived as a kittypet all her life, but she's a fast learner and there's no doubting how she feels about Graystripe! In WARRIOR'S REFUGE, she has the chance to prove that being a kittypet can sometimes be a lot more useful than Clan cats understand. And once again, the medium of manga brings the stories to life in a way that reaches out and grabs you from the very first page!

Are you ready to join Graystripe and Millie as they leave their familiar Twolegplace and set off into unknown territory in search of the Clans? Then let the adventure begin...

Sincerely,
Erin Hunter

WARRIORS

WARRIOR'S REFUGE

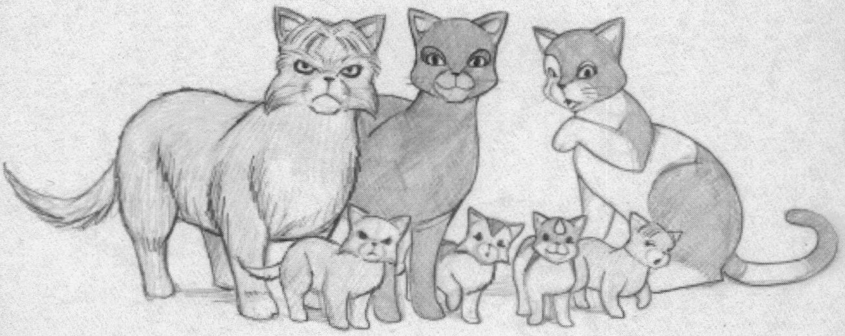

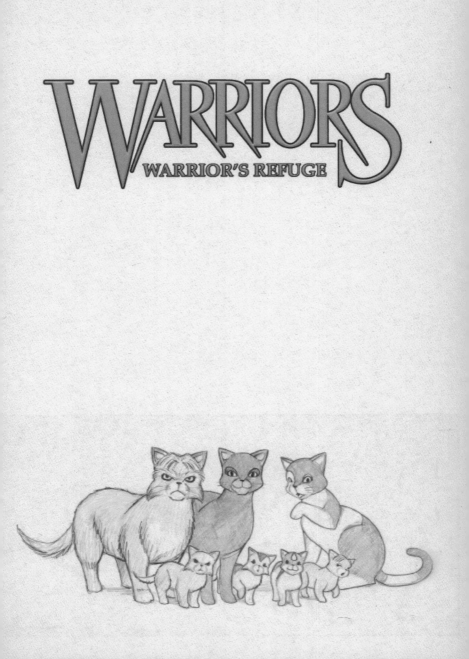

CHAPTER 1

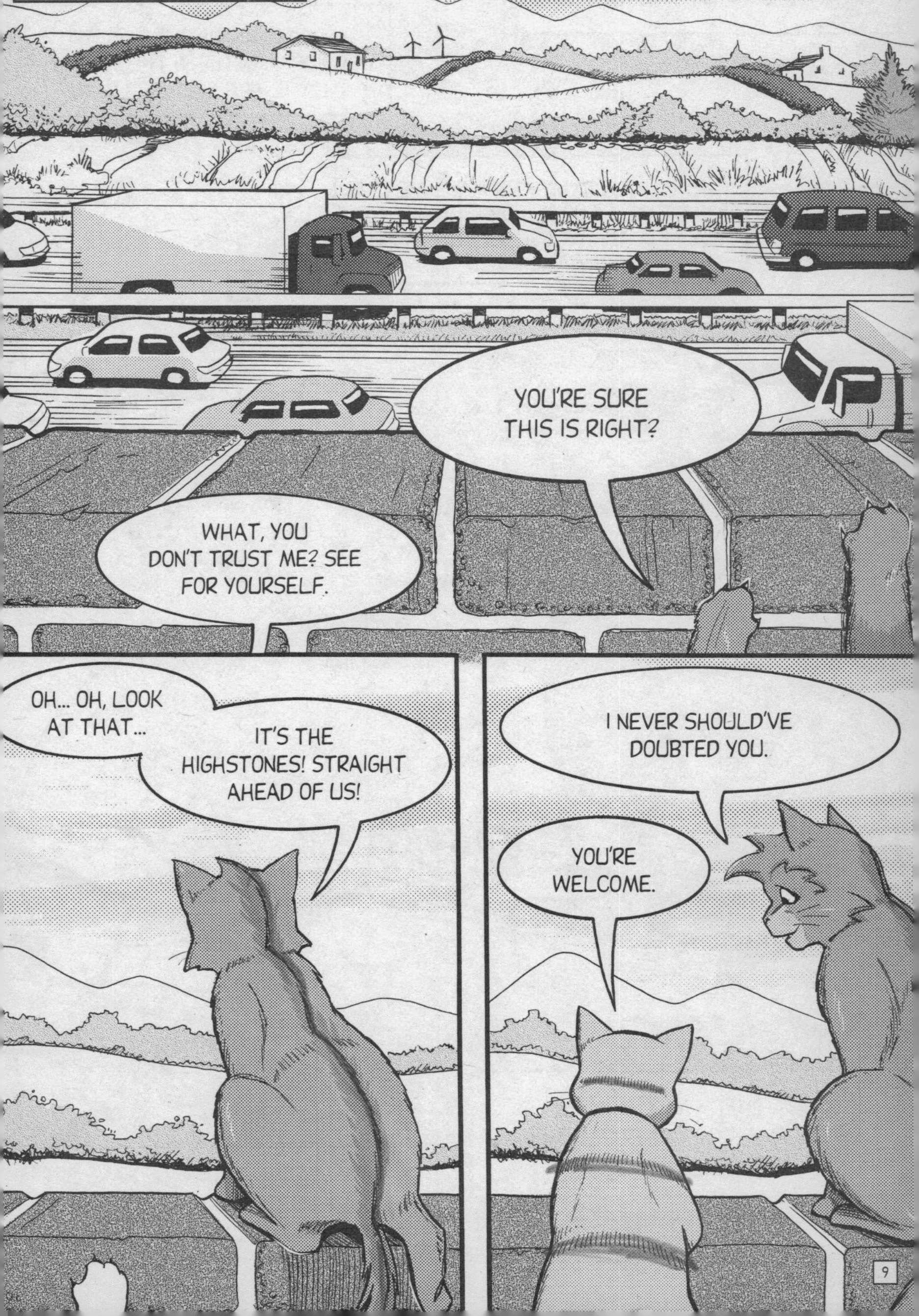

YOU'RE SURE THIS IS RIGHT?
WHAT, YOU DON'T TRUST ME? SEE FOR YOURSELF.
OH... OH, LOOK AT THAT...
IT'S THE HIGHSTONES! STRAIGHT AHEAD OF US!
I NEVER SHOULD'VE DOUBTED YOU.
YOU'RE WELCOME.

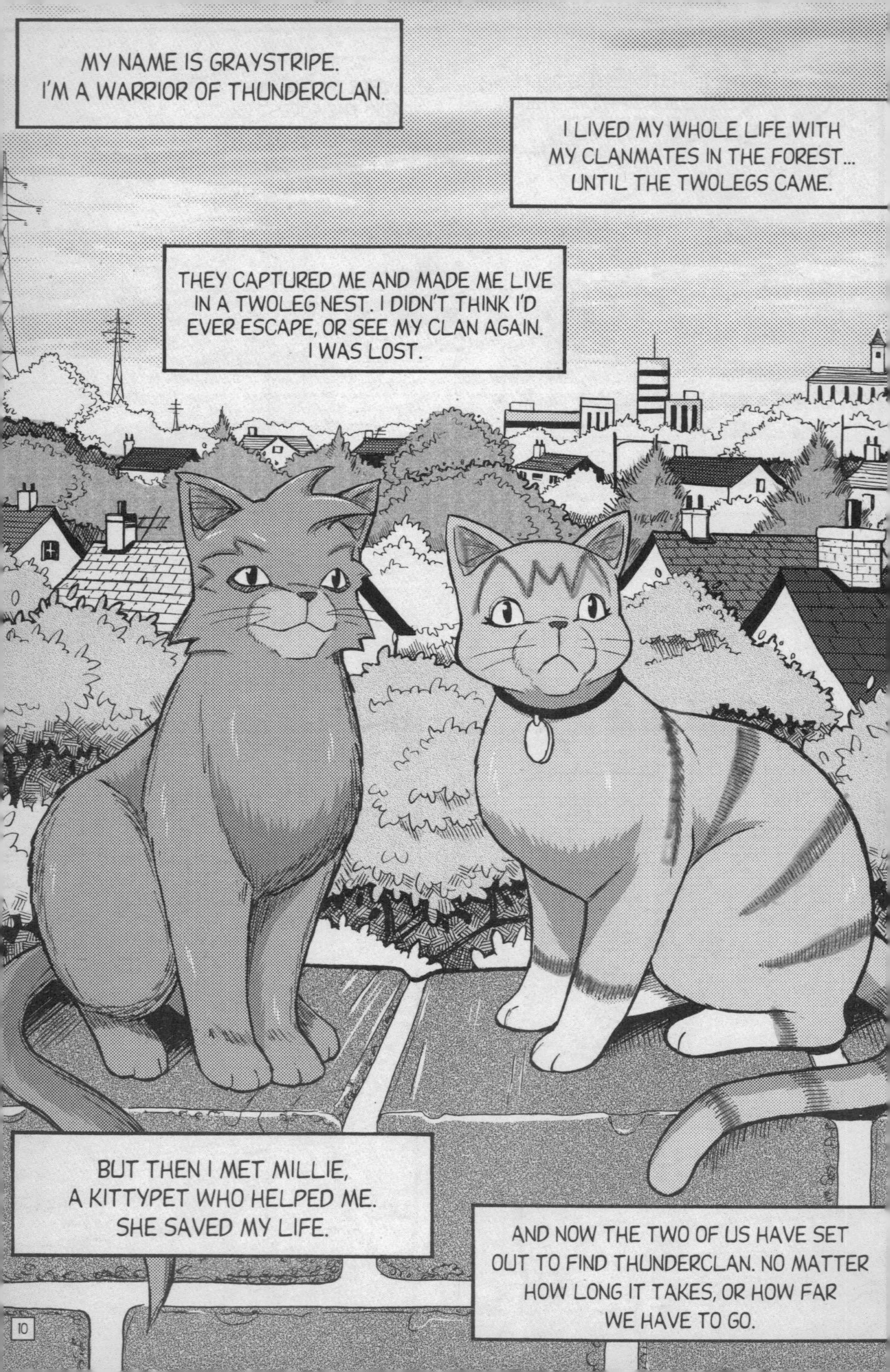
MY NAME IS GRAYSTRIPE. I'M A WARRIOR OF THUNDERCLAN.
I LIVED MY WHOLE LIFE WITH MY CLANMATES IN THE FOREST... UNTIL THE TWOLEGS CAME.
THEY CAPTURED ME AND MADE ME LIVE IN A TWOLEG NEST. I DIDN'T THINK I'D EVER ESCAPE, OR SEE MY CLAN AGAIN. I WAS LOST.
BUT THEN I MET MILLIE, A KITTYPET WHO HELPED ME. SHE SAVED MY LIFE.
AND NOW THE TWO OF US HAVE SET OUT TO FIND THUNDERCLAN. NO MATTER HOW LONG IT TAKES, OR HOW FAR WE HAVE TO GO.

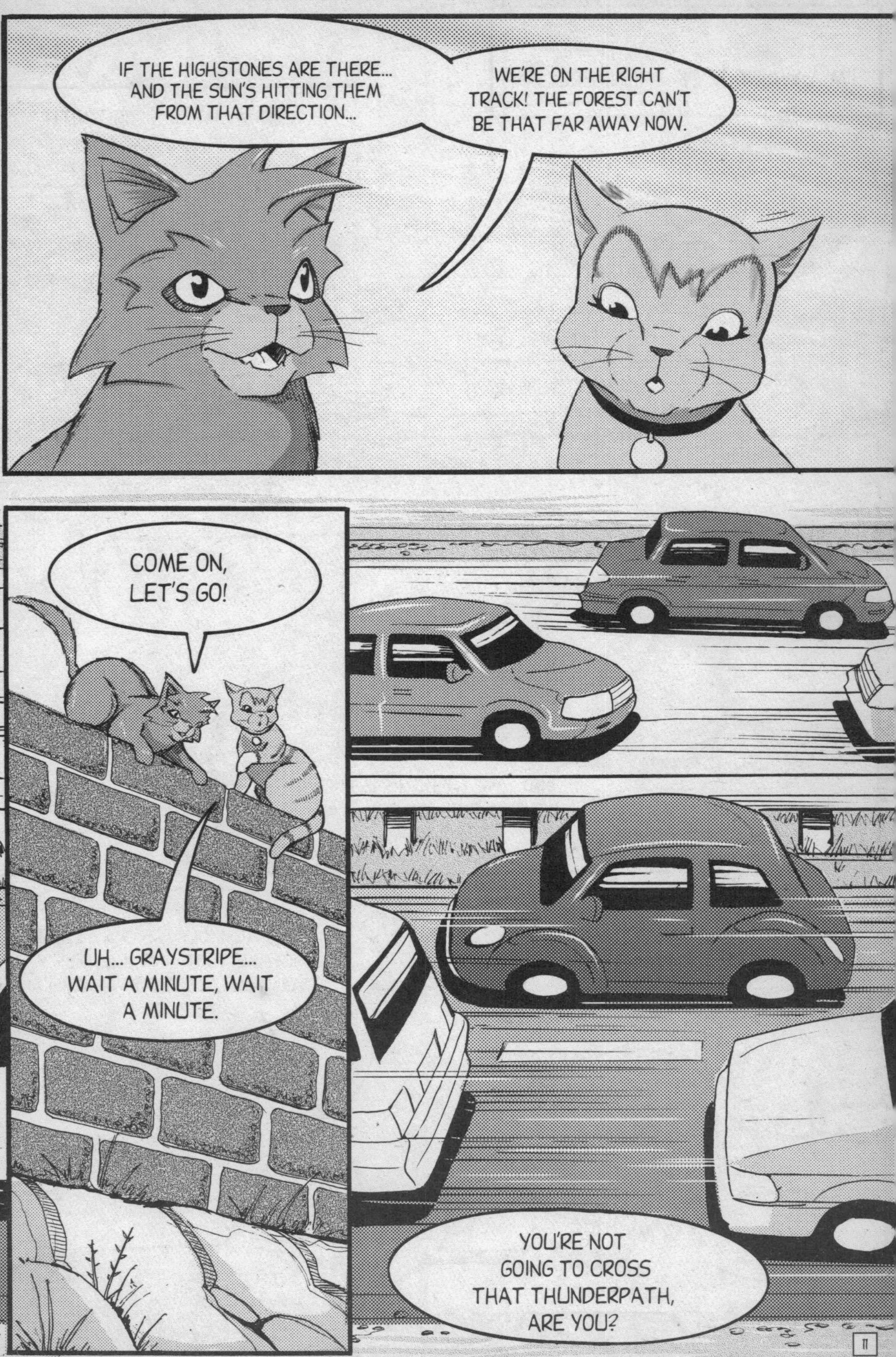
IF THE HIGHSTONES ARE THERE... AND THE SUN'S HITTING THEM FROM THAT DIRECTION...
WE'RE ON THE RIGHT TRACK! THE FOREST CAN'T BE THAT FAR AWAY NOW.
COME ON, LET'S GO!
UH... GRAYSTRIPE... WAIT A MINUTE, WAIT A MINUTE.
YOU'RE NOT GOING TO CROSS THAT THUNDERPATH, ARE YOU?

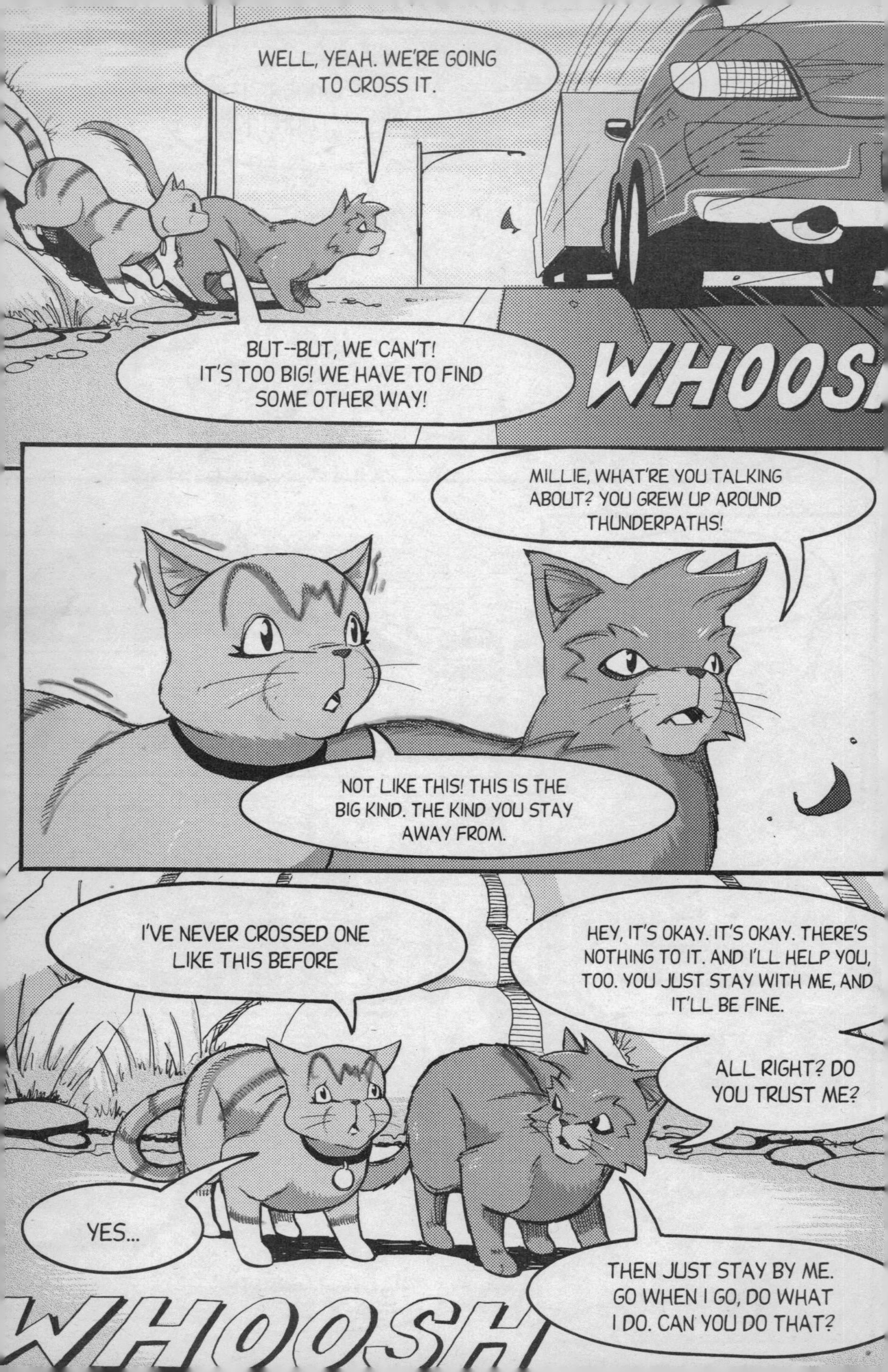
WELL, YEAH. WE'RE GOING TO CROSS IT.
BUT--BUT, WE CAN'T! IT'S TOO BIG! WE HAVE TO FIND SOME OTHER WAY!
WHOOS
MILLIE, WHAT'RE YOU TALKING ABOUT? YOU GREW UP AROUND THUNDERPATHS!
NOT LIKE THIS! THIS IS THE BIG KIND. THE KIND YOU STAY AWAY FROM.
I'VE NEVER CROSSED ONE LIKE THIS BEFORE
HEY, IT'S OKAY. IT'S OKAY. THERE'S NOTHING TO IT. AND I'LL HELP YOU, TOO. YOU JUST STAY WITH ME, AND IT'LL BE FINE.
ALL RIGHT? DO YOU TRUST ME?
YES...
THEN JUST STAY BY ME. GO WHEN I GO, DO WHAT I DO. CAN YOU DO THAT?
WHOOSH

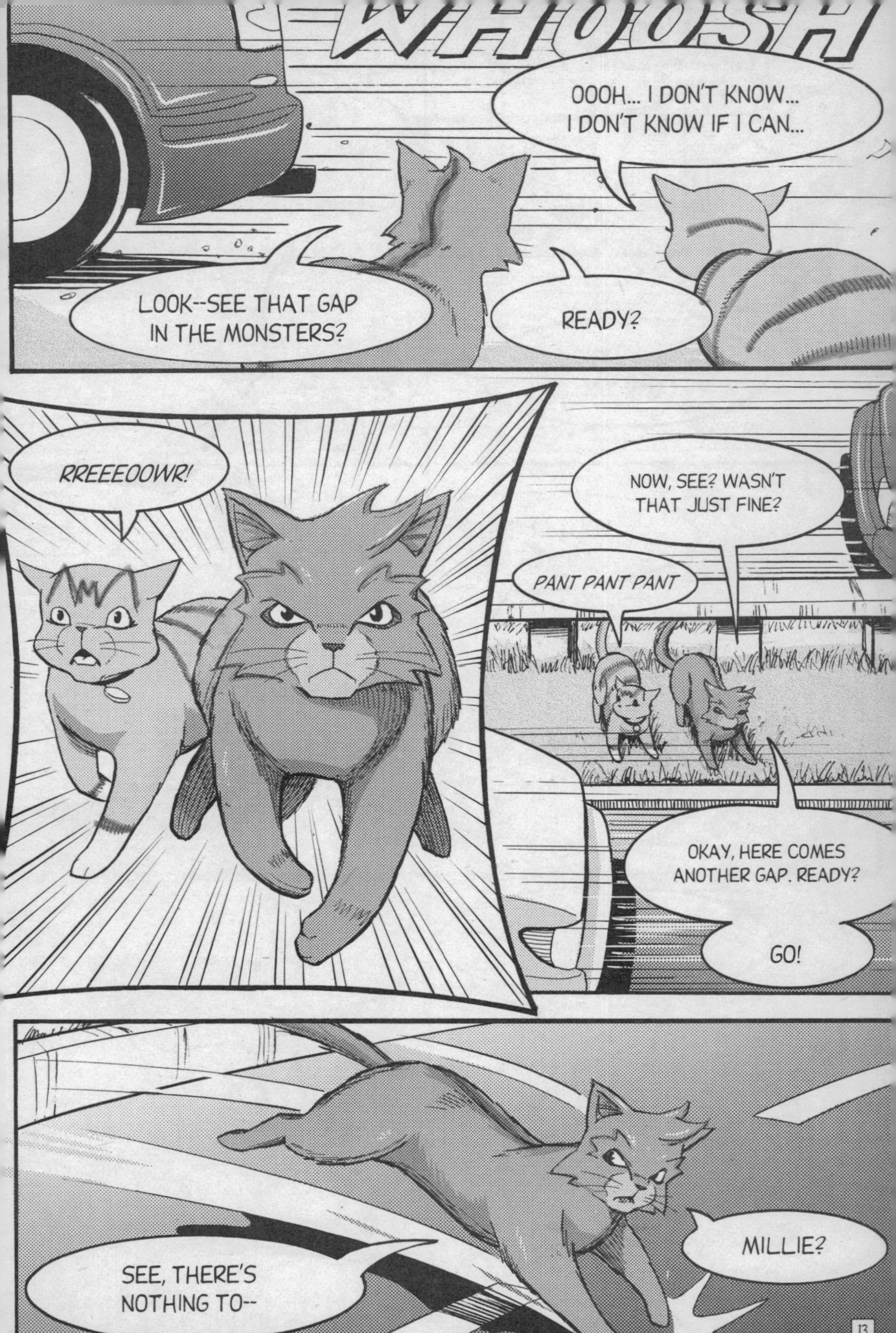
WHOOSH
OOOH... I DON'T KNOW...
I DON'T KNOW IF I CAN...
LOOK--SEE THAT GAP
IN THE MONSTERS?
READY?
RREEEOOWR!
NOW, SEE? WASN'T
THAT JUST FINE?
PANT PANT PANT
OKAY, HERE COMES
ANOTHER GAP. READY?
GO!
SEE, THERE'S
NOTHING TO--
MILLIE?

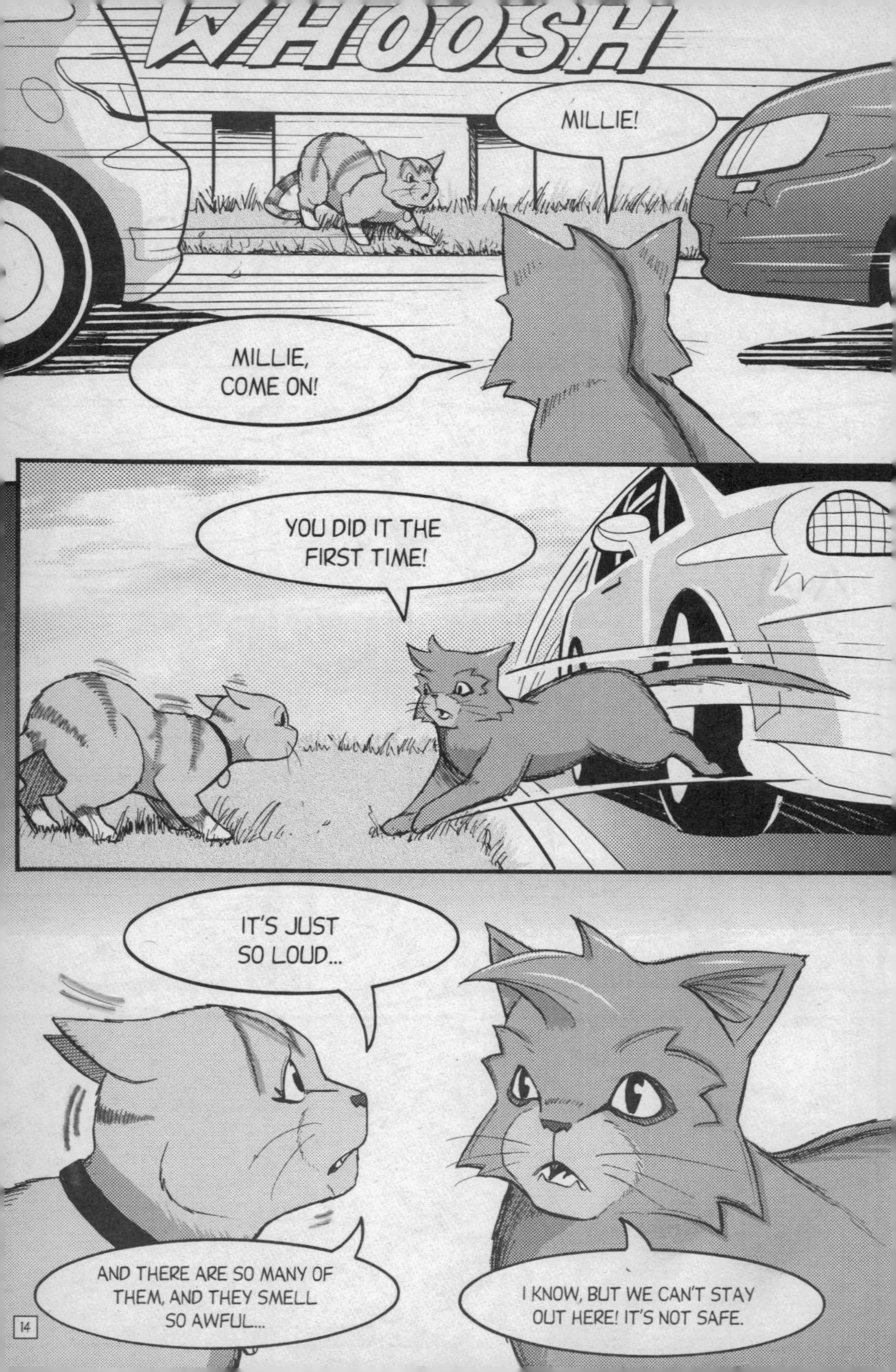
WHOOSH
MILLIE!
MILLIE, COME ON!
YOU DID IT THE FIRST TIME!
IT'S JUST SO LOUD...
AND THERE ARE SO MANY OF THEM, AND THEY SMELL SO AWFUL...
I KNOW, BUT WE CAN'T STAY OUT HERE! IT'S NOT SAFE.

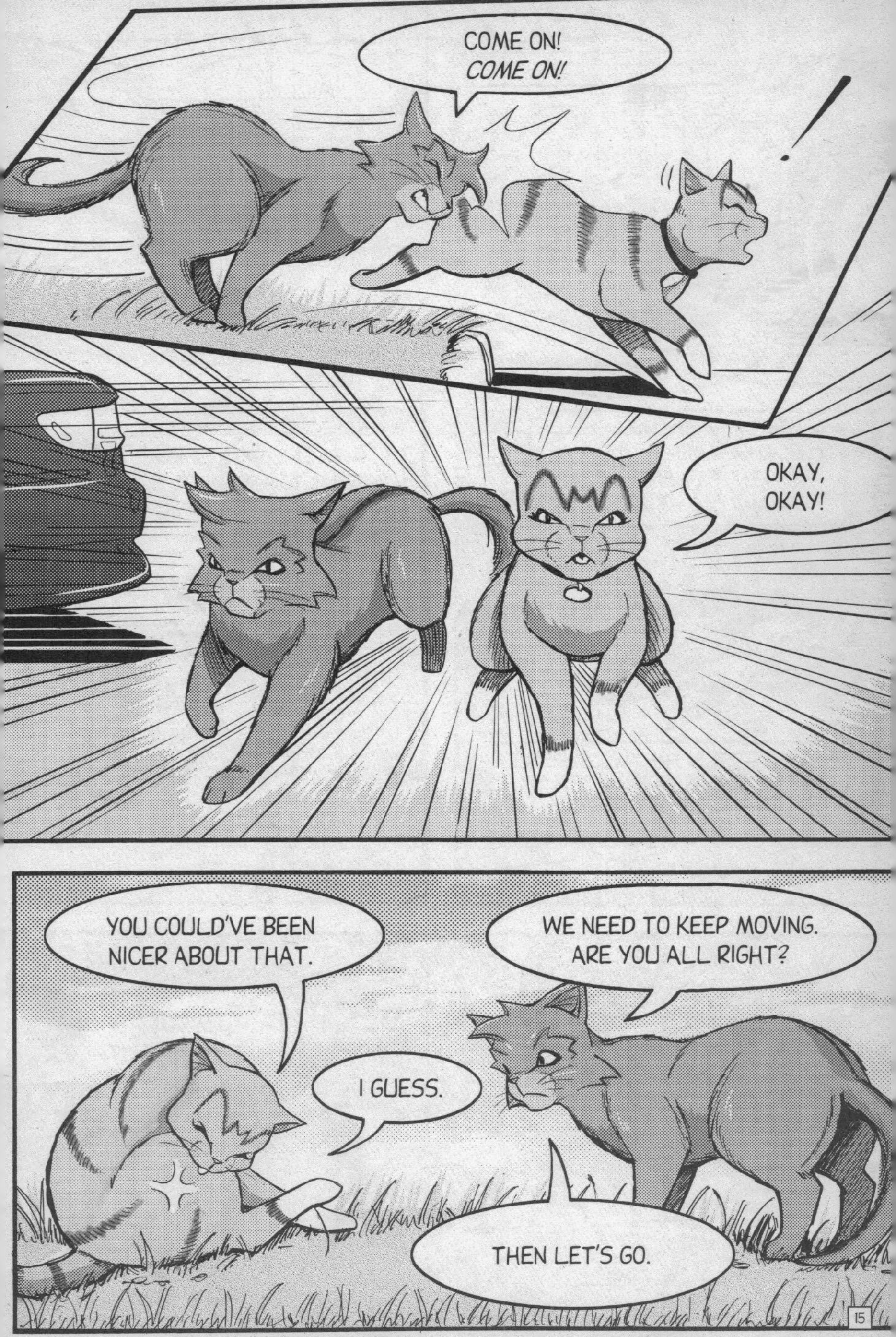
COME ON!
COME ON!
!
OKAY, OKAY!
YOU COULD'VE BEEN NICER ABOUT THAT.
WE NEED TO KEEP MOVING. ARE YOU ALL RIGHT?
I GUESS.
THEN LET'S GO.

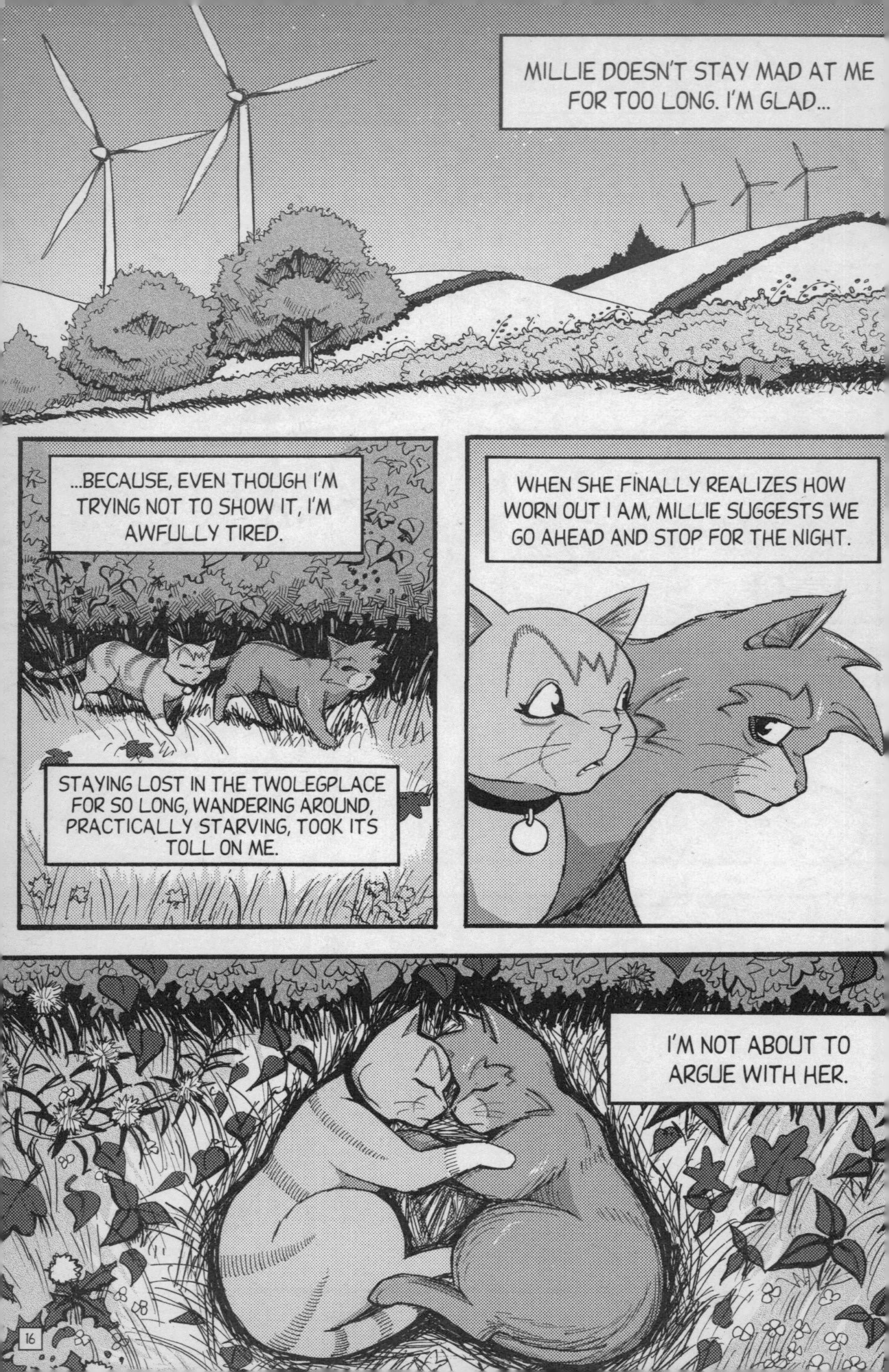
MILLIE DOESN'T STAY MAD AT ME FOR TOO LONG. I'M GLAD...
...BECAUSE, EVEN THOUGH I'M TRYING NOT TO SHOW IT, I'M AWFULLY TIRED.
STAYING LOST IN THE TWOLEGPLACE FOR SO LONG, WANDERING AROUND, PRACTICALLY STARVING, TOOK ITS TOLL ON ME.
WHEN SHE FINALLY REALIZES HOW WORN OUT I AM, MILLIE SUGGESTS WE GO AHEAD AND STOP FOR THE NIGHT.
I'M NOT ABOUT TO ARGUE WITH HER.

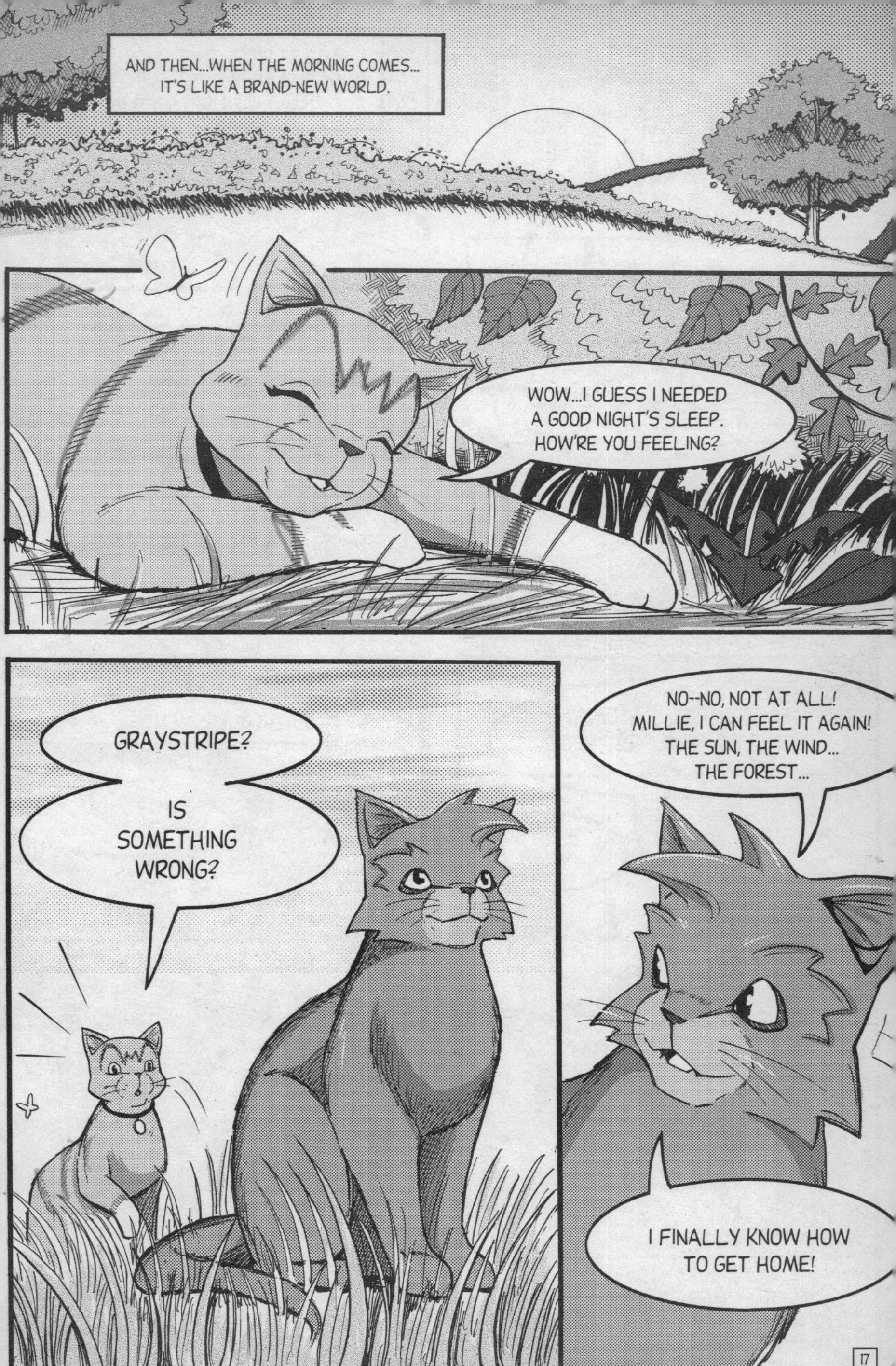
AND THEN...WHEN THE MORNING COMES... IT'S LIKE A BRAND-NEW WORLD.
WOW...I GUESS I NEEDED A GOOD NIGHT'S SLEEP. HOW'RE YOU FEELING?
GRAYSTRIPE?
IS SOMETHING WRONG?
NO--NO, NOT AT ALL! MILLIE, I CAN FEEL IT AGAIN! THE SUN, THE WIND... THE FOREST...
I FINALLY KNOW HOW TO GET HOME!

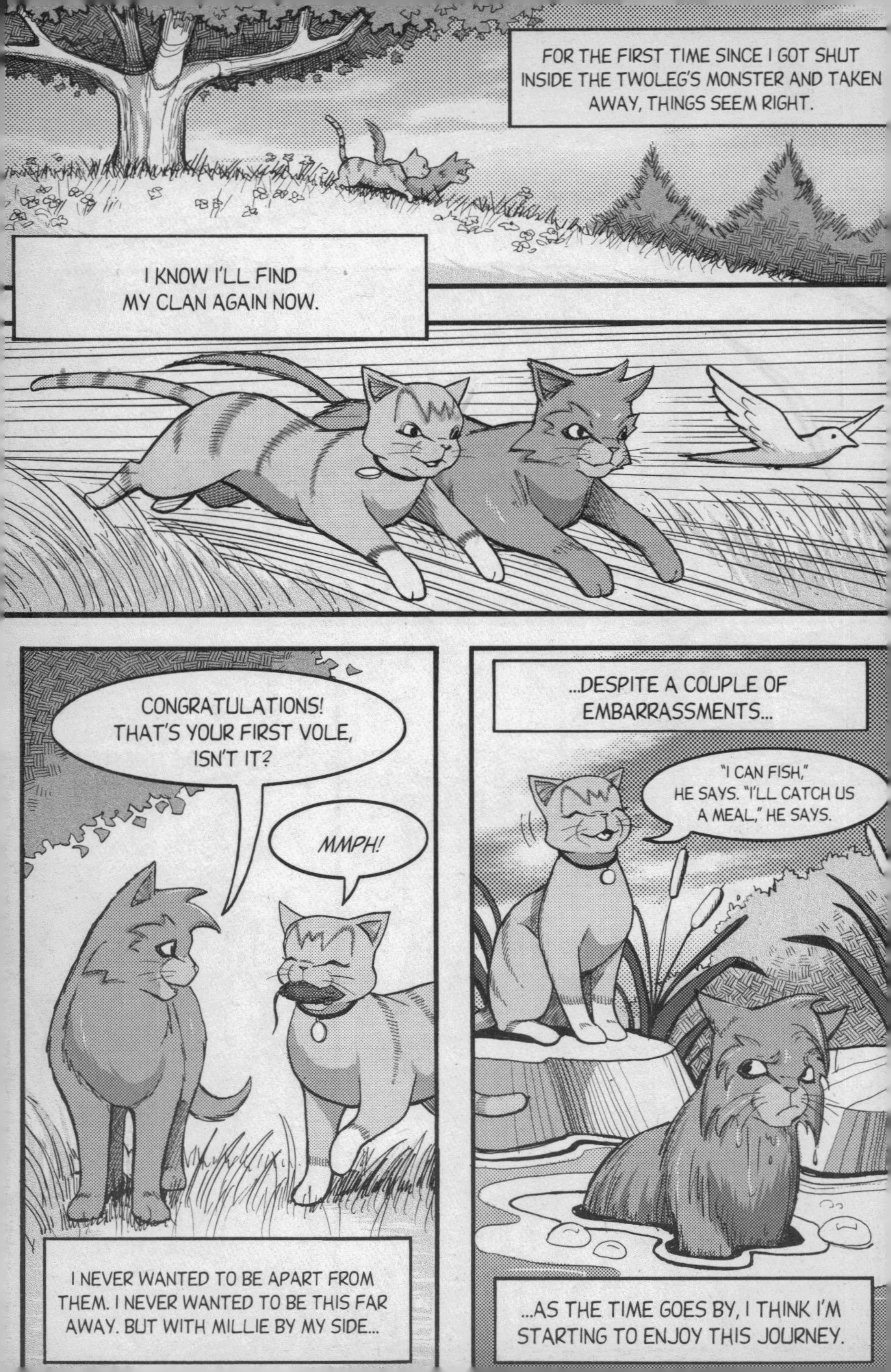
FOR THE FIRST TIME SINCE I GOT SHUT INSIDE THE TWOLEG'S MONSTER AND TAKEN AWAY, THINGS SEEM RIGHT.
I KNOW I'LL FIND MY CLAN AGAIN NOW.
CONGRATULATIONS! THAT'S YOUR FIRST VOLE, ISN'T IT?
MMPH!
I NEVER WANTED TO BE APART FROM THEM. I NEVER WANTED TO BE THIS FAR AWAY. BUT WITH MILLIE BY MY SIDE...
...DESPITE A COUPLE OF EMBARRASSMENTS...
"I CAN FISH," HE SAYS. "I'LL CATCH US A MEAL," HE SAYS.
...AS THE TIME GOES BY, I THINK I'M STARTING TO ENJOY THIS JOURNEY.

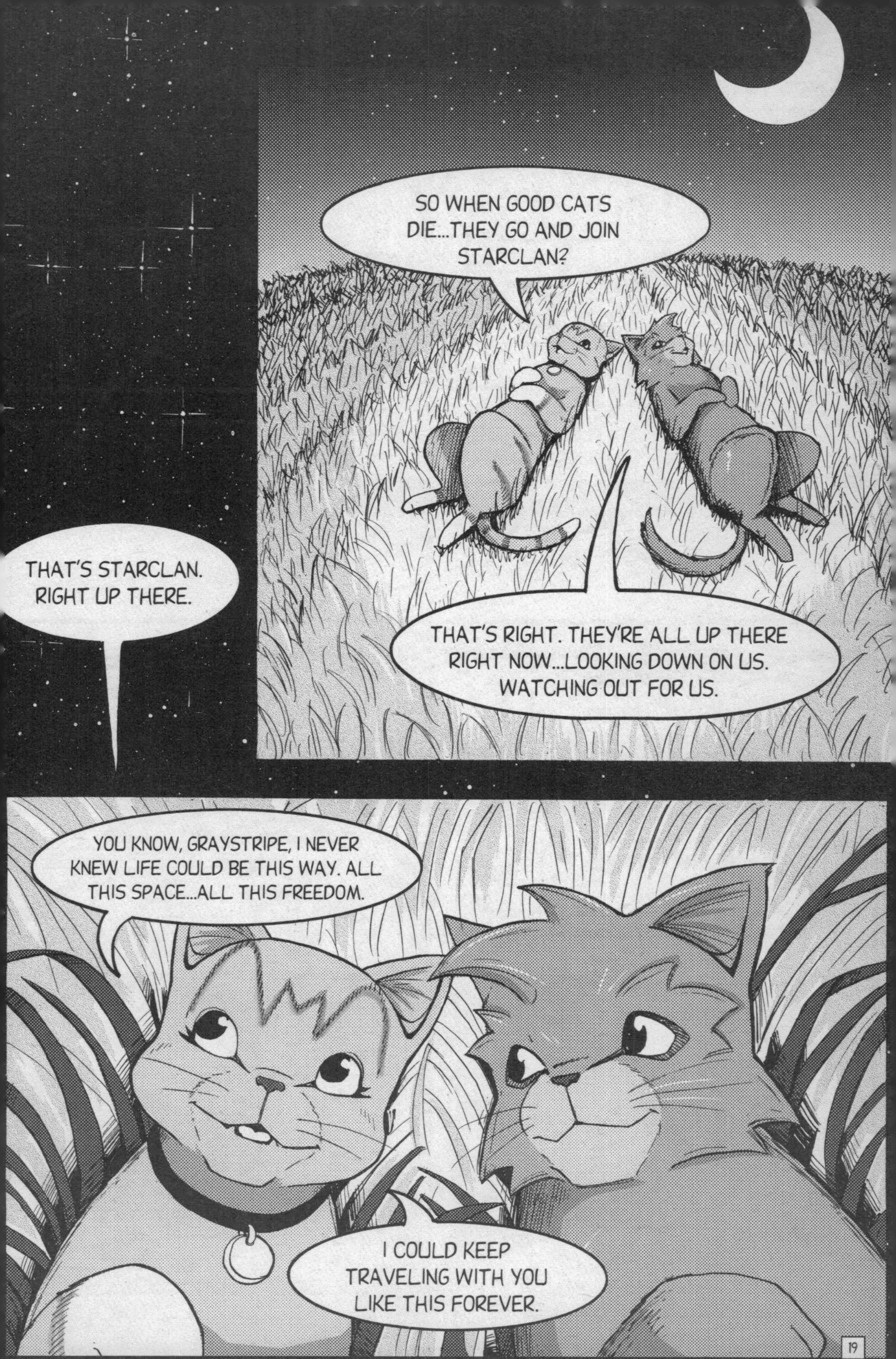
SO WHEN GOOD CATS DIE...THEY GO AND JOIN STARCLAN?
THAT'S STARCLAN. RIGHT UP THERE.
THAT'S RIGHT. THEY'RE ALL UP THERE RIGHT NOW...LOOKING DOWN ON US. WATCHING OUT FOR US.
YOU KNOW, GRAYSTRIPE, I NEVER KNEW LIFE COULD BE THIS WAY. ALL THIS SPACE...ALL THIS FREEDOM.
I COULD KEEP TRAVELING WITH YOU LIKE THIS FOREVER.

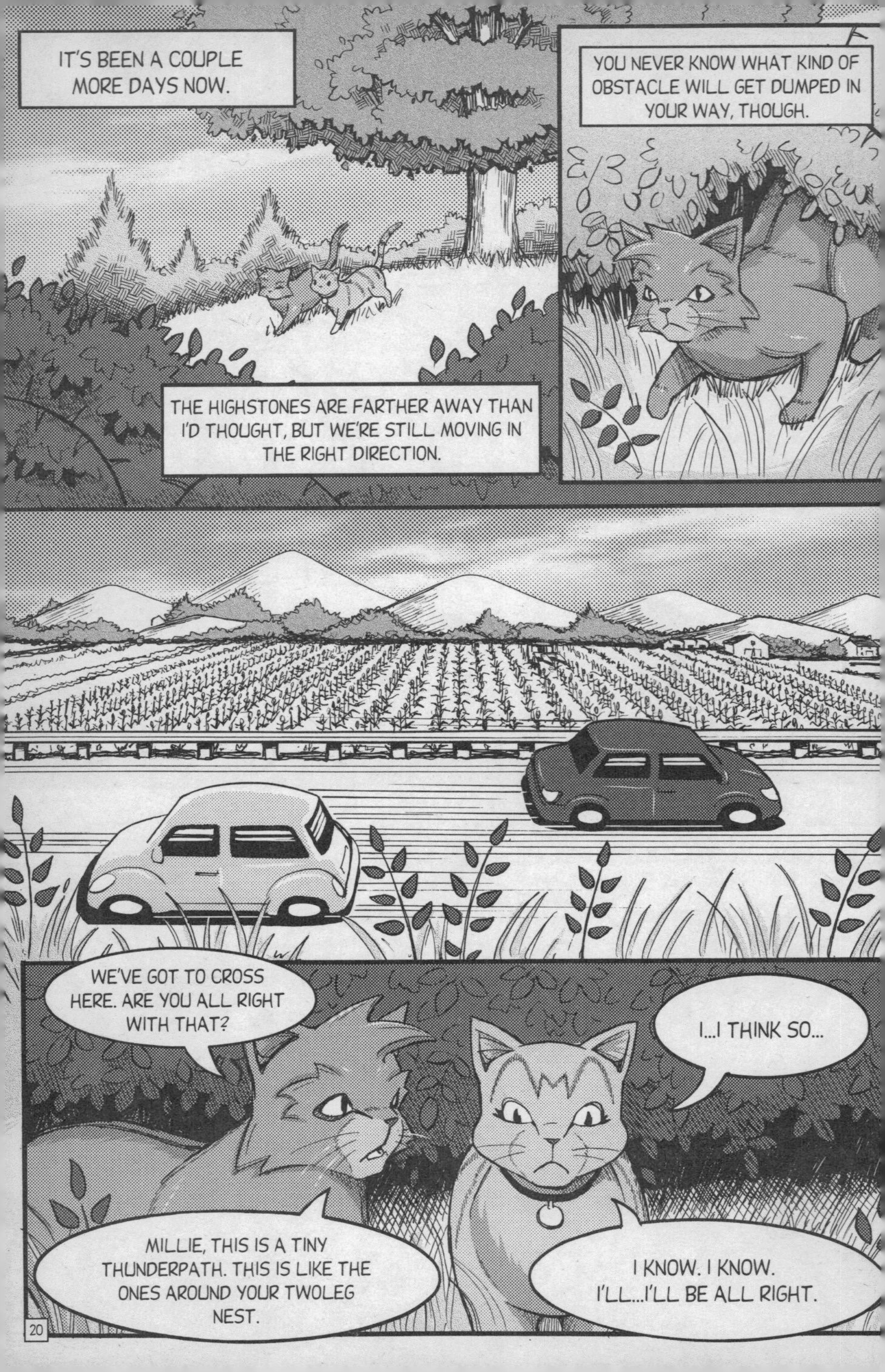
IT'S BEEN A COUPLE MORE DAYS NOW.
THE HIGHSTONES ARE FARTHER AWAY THAN I'D THOUGHT, BUT WE'RE STILL MOVING IN THE RIGHT DIRECTION.
YOU NEVER KNOW WHAT KIND OF OBSTACLE WILL GET DUMPED IN YOUR WAY, THOUGH.
WE'VE GOT TO CROSS HERE. ARE YOU ALL RIGHT WITH THAT?
I...I THINK SO...
MILLIE, THIS IS A TINY THUNDERPATH. THIS IS LIKE THE ONES AROUND YOUR TWOLEG NEST.
I KNOW. I KNOW. I'LL...I'LL BE ALL RIGHT.
20

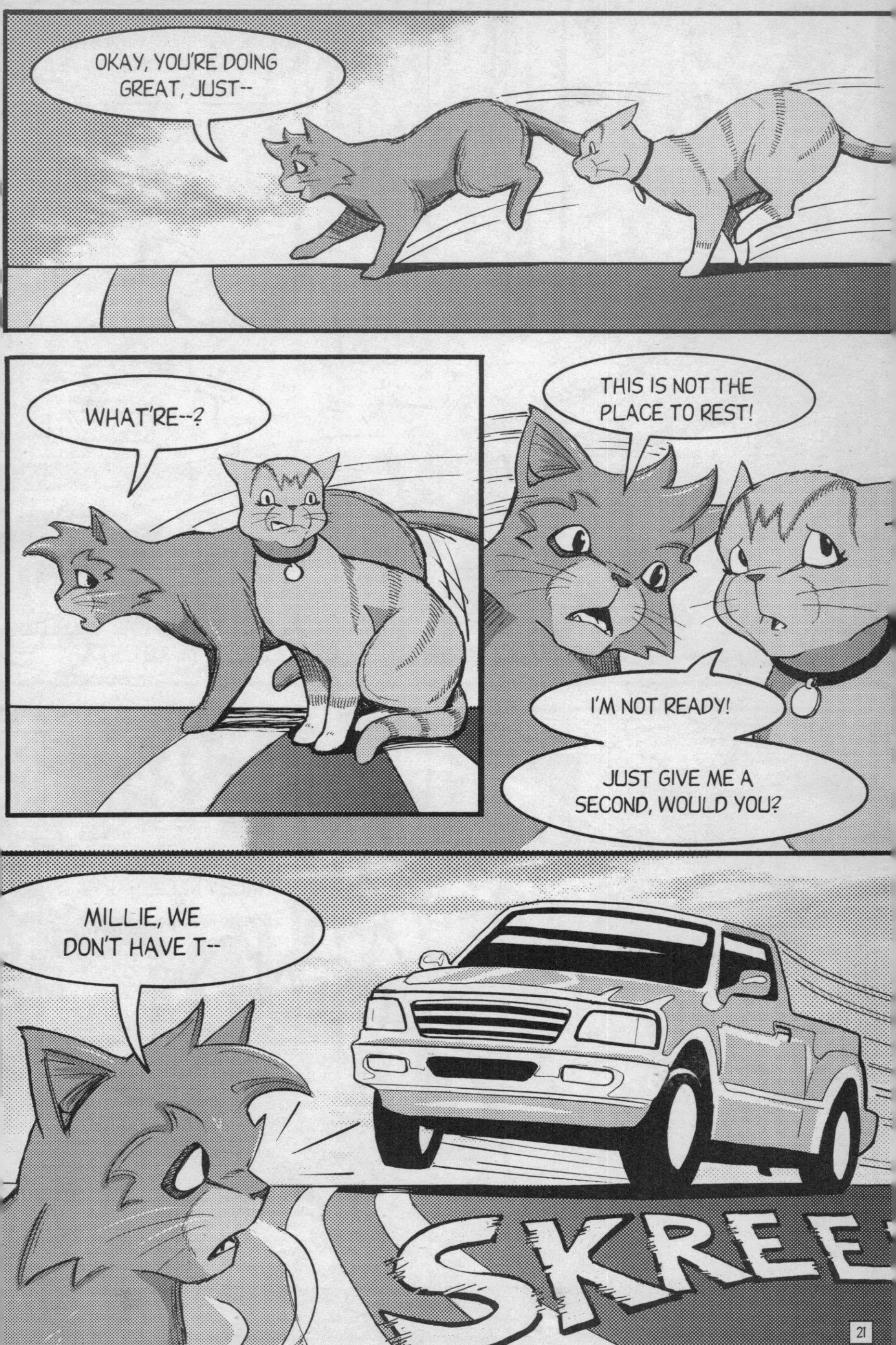
OKAY, YOU'RE DOING GREAT, JUST--
WHAT'RE--?
THIS IS NOT THE PLACE TO REST!
I'M NOT READY!
JUST GIVE ME A SECOND, WOULD YOU?
MILLIE, WE DON'T HAVE T--
SKREE

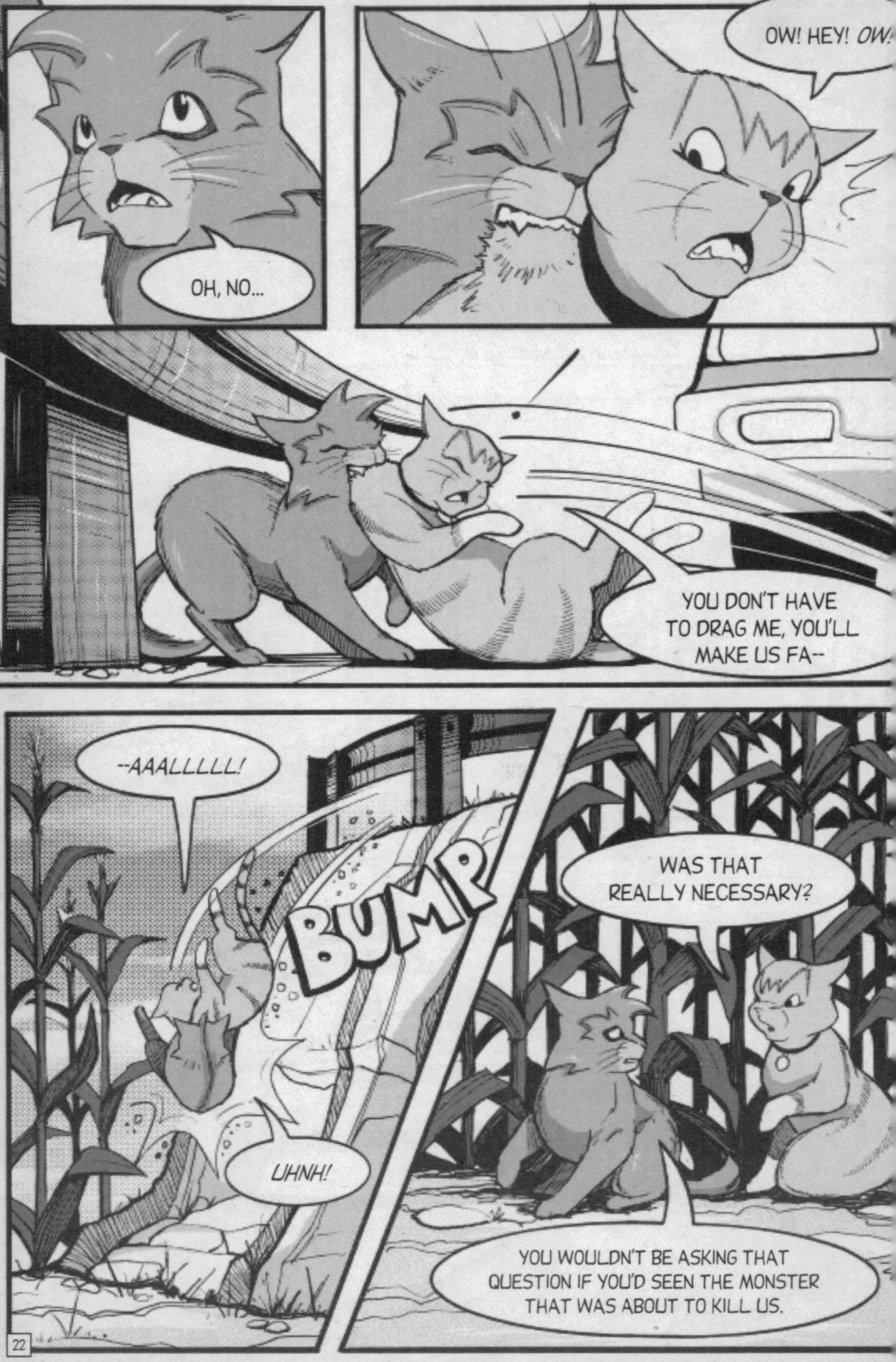
OH, NO...
OW! HEY! OW!
YOU DON'T HAVE TO DRAG ME, YOU'LL MAKE US FA--
--AAALLLLL!
BUMP
UHNH!
WAS THAT REALLY NECESSARY?
YOU WOULDN'T BE ASKING THAT QUESTION IF YOU'D SEEN THE MONSTER THAT WAS ABOUT TO KILL US.

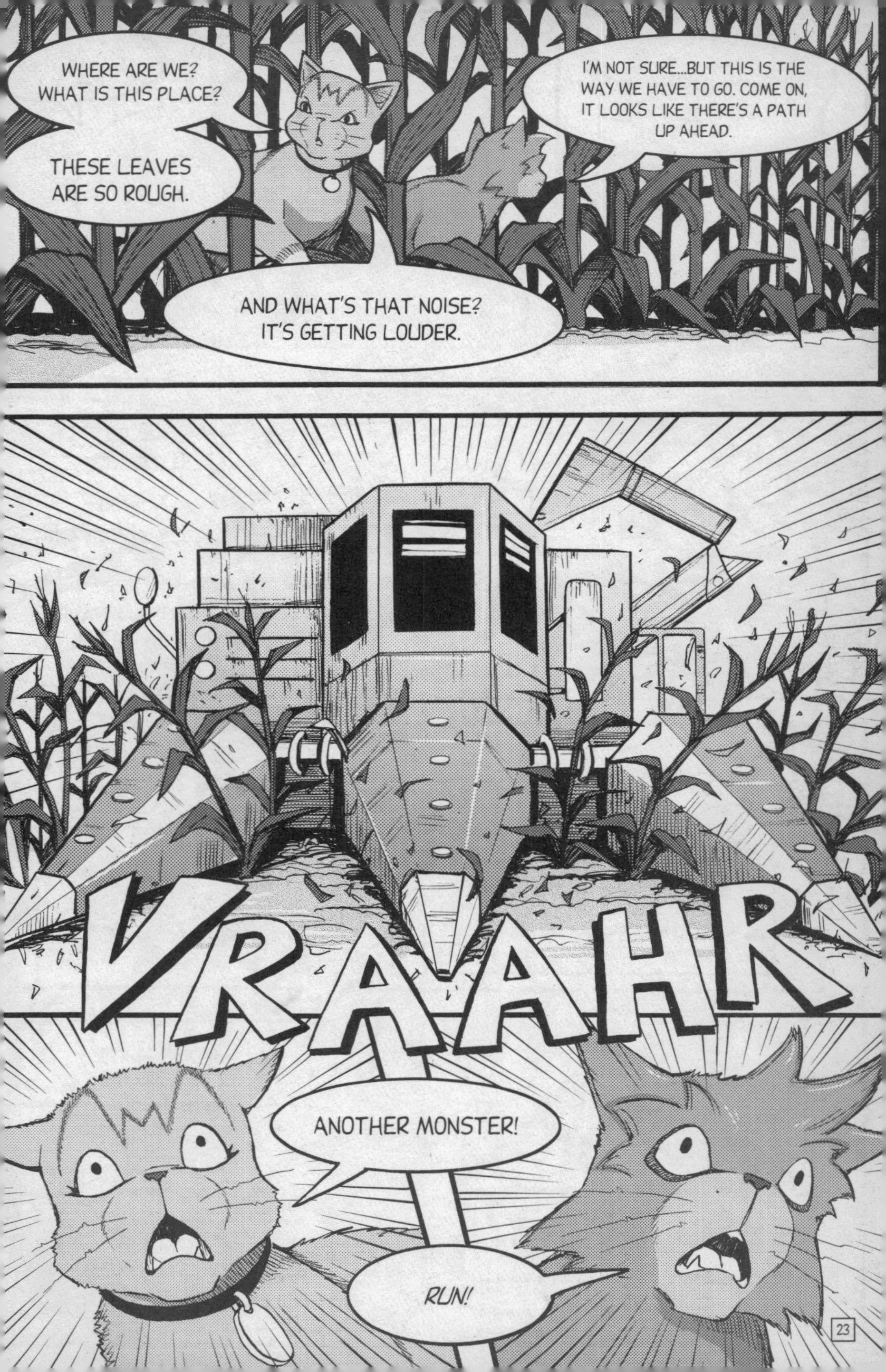
WHERE ARE WE? WHAT IS THIS PLACE?
THESE LEAVES ARE SO ROUGH.
I'M NOT SURE...BUT THIS IS THE WAY WE HAVE TO GO. COME ON, IT LOOKS LIKE THERE'S A PATH UP AHEAD.
AND WHAT'S THAT NOISE? IT'S GETTING LOUDER.
VRAAHR
ANOTHER MONSTER!
RUN!

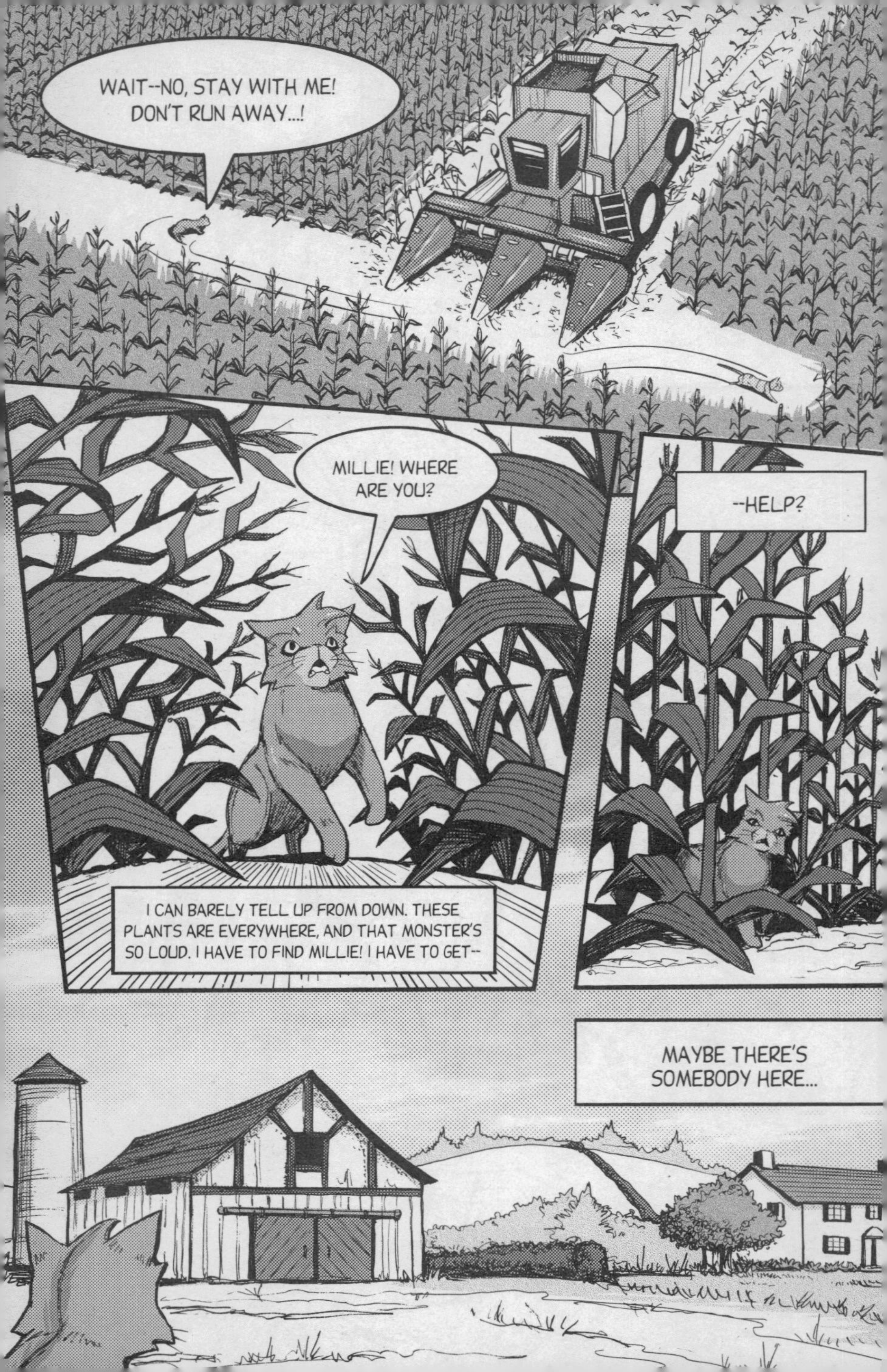
WAIT--NO, STAY WITH ME! DON'T RUN AWAY...!
MILLIE! WHERE ARE YOU?
I CAN BARELY TELL UP FROM DOWN. THESE PLANTS ARE EVERYWHERE, AND THAT MONSTER'S SO LOUD. I HAVE TO FIND MILLIE! I HAVE TO GET--
--HELP?
MAYBE THERE'S SOMEBODY HERE...

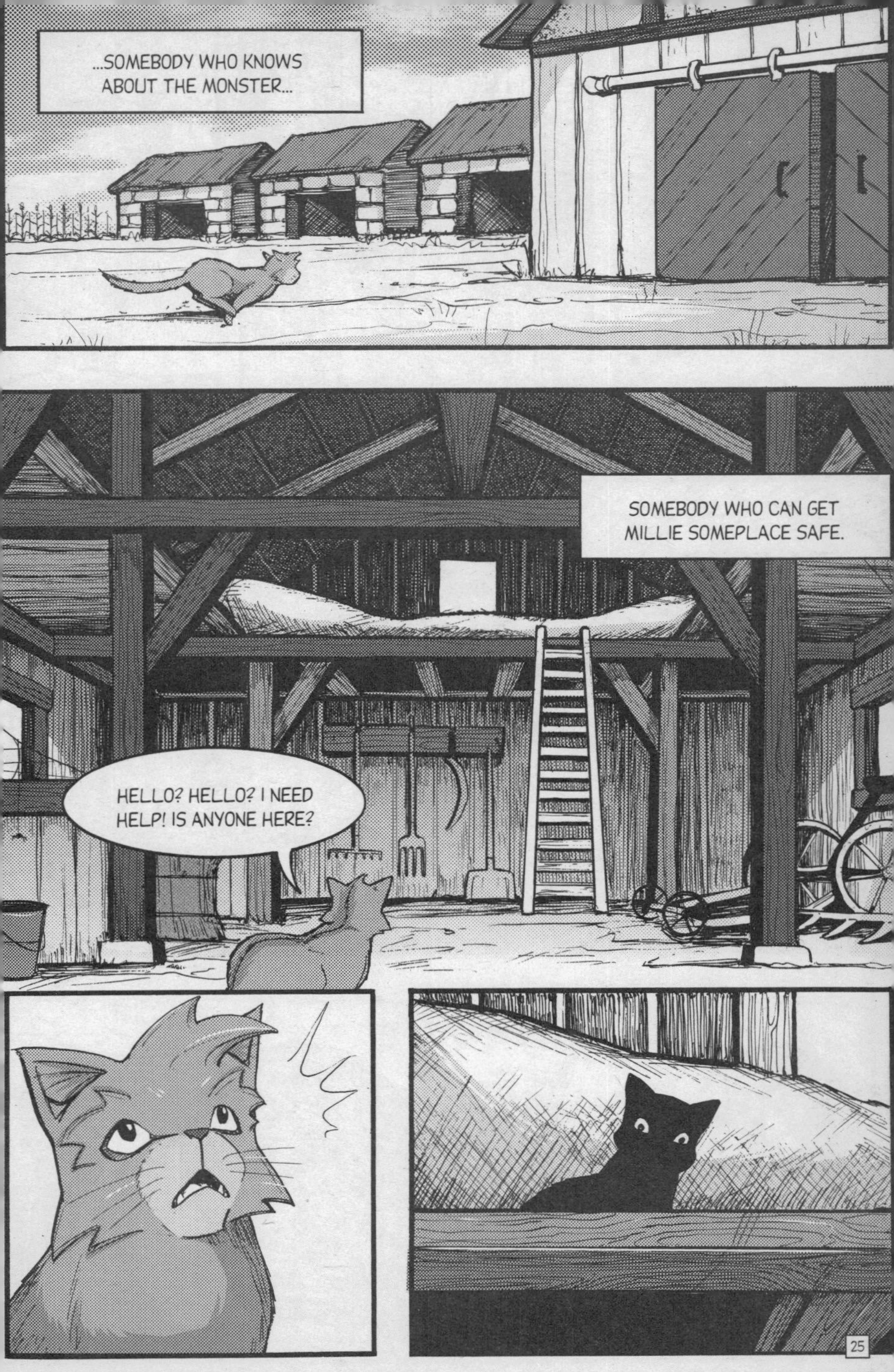
...SOMEBODY WHO KNOWS ABOUT THE MONSTER...
SOMEBODY WHO CAN GET MILLIE SOMEPLACE SAFE.
HELLO? HELLO? I NEED HELP! IS ANYONE HERE?

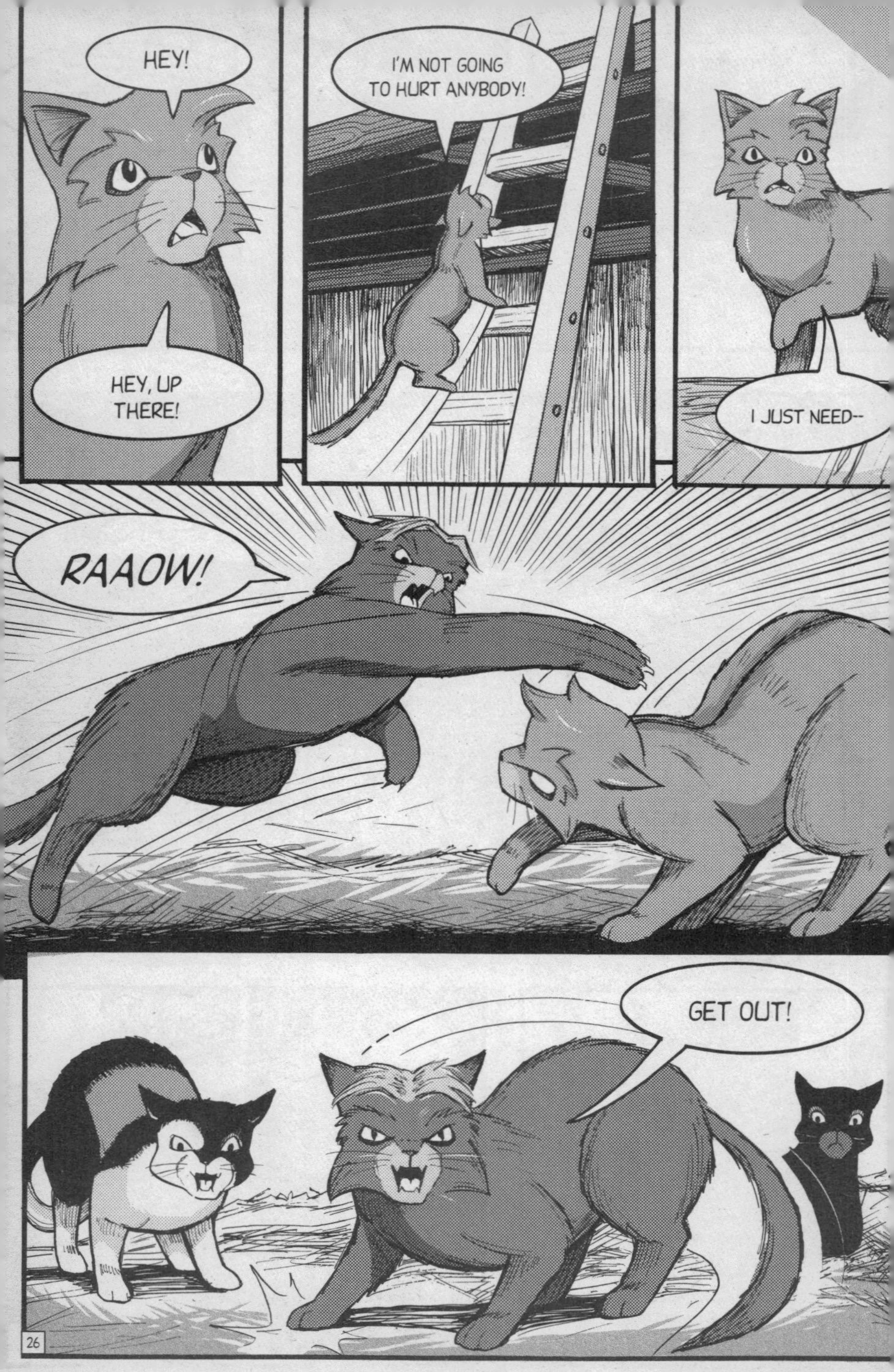
HEY!
HEY, UP THERE!
I'M NOT GOING TO HURT ANYBODY!
I JUST NEED--
RAAOW!
GET OUT!

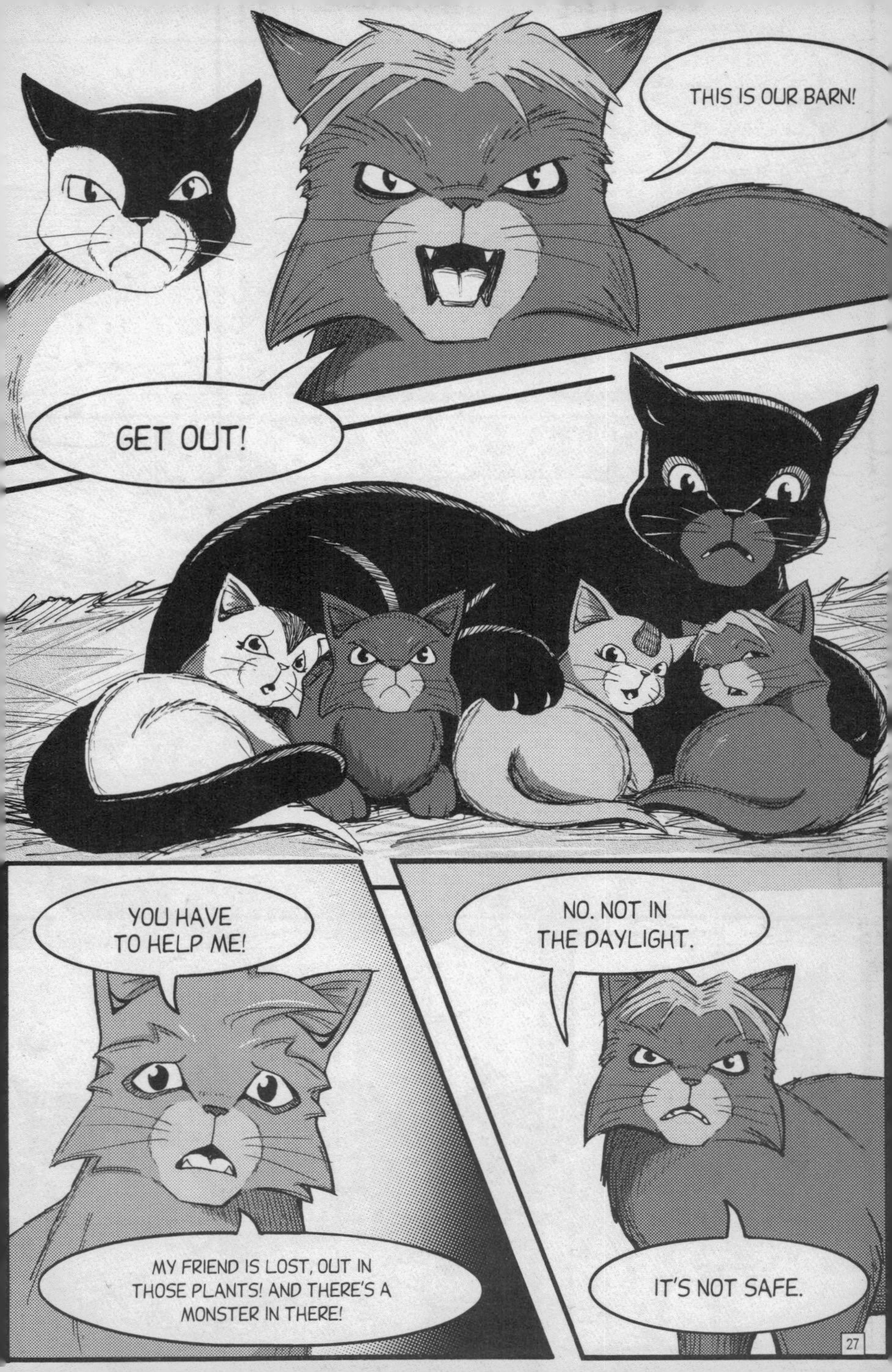
THIS IS OUR BARN!
GET OUT!
YOU HAVE TO HELP ME!
MY FRIEND IS LOST, OUT IN THOSE PLANTS! AND THERE'S A MONSTER IN THERE!
NO. NOT IN THE DAYLIGHT.
IT'S NOT SAFE.

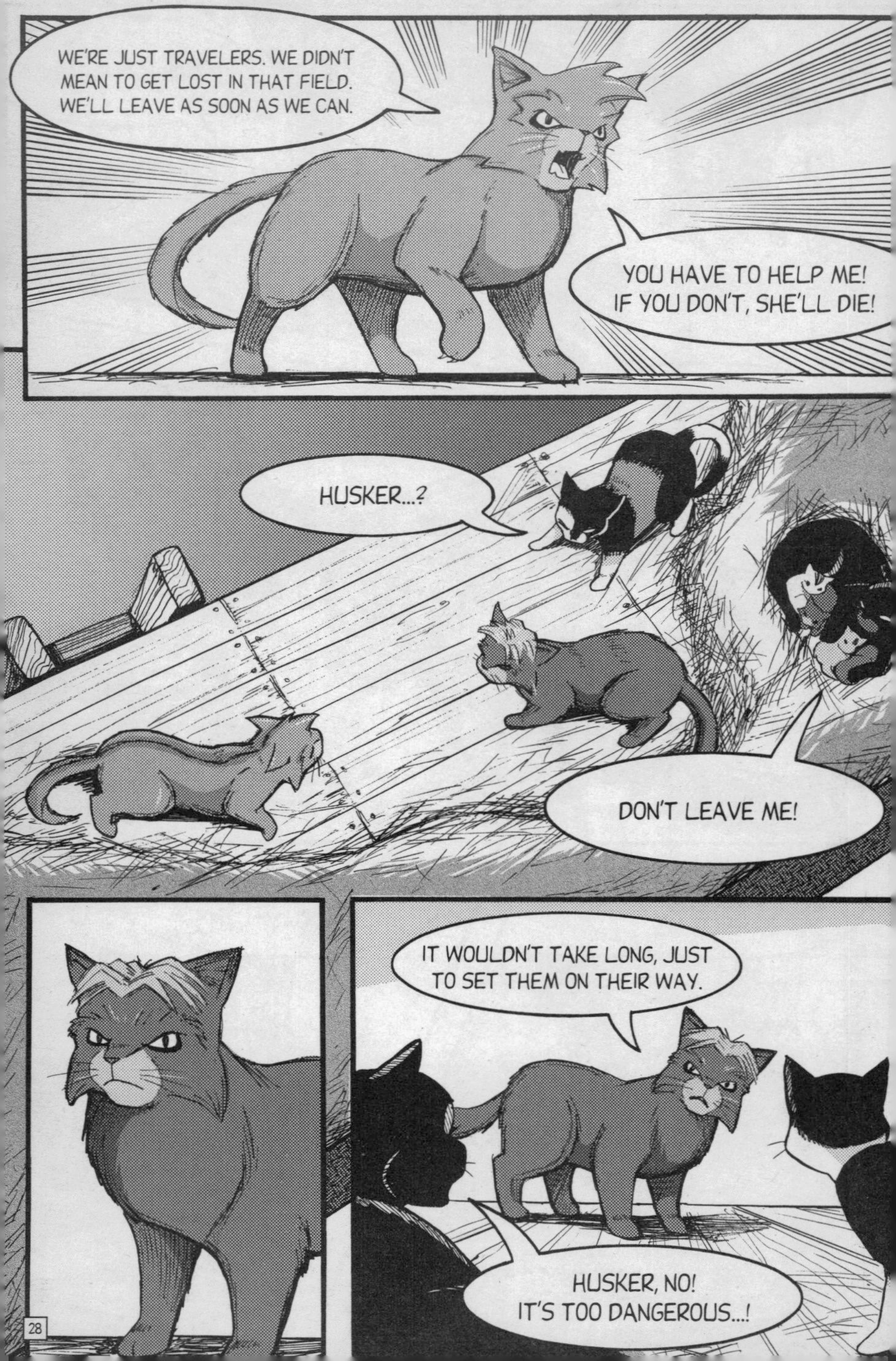
WE'RE JUST TRAVELERS. WE DIDN'T MEAN TO GET LOST IN THAT FIELD. WE'LL LEAVE AS SOON AS WE CAN.
YOU HAVE TO HELP ME! IF YOU DON'T, SHE'LL DIE!
HUSKER...?
DON'T LEAVE ME!
IT WOULDN'T TAKE LONG, JUST TO SET THEM ON THEIR WAY.
HUSKER, NO! IT'S TOO DANGEROUS...!

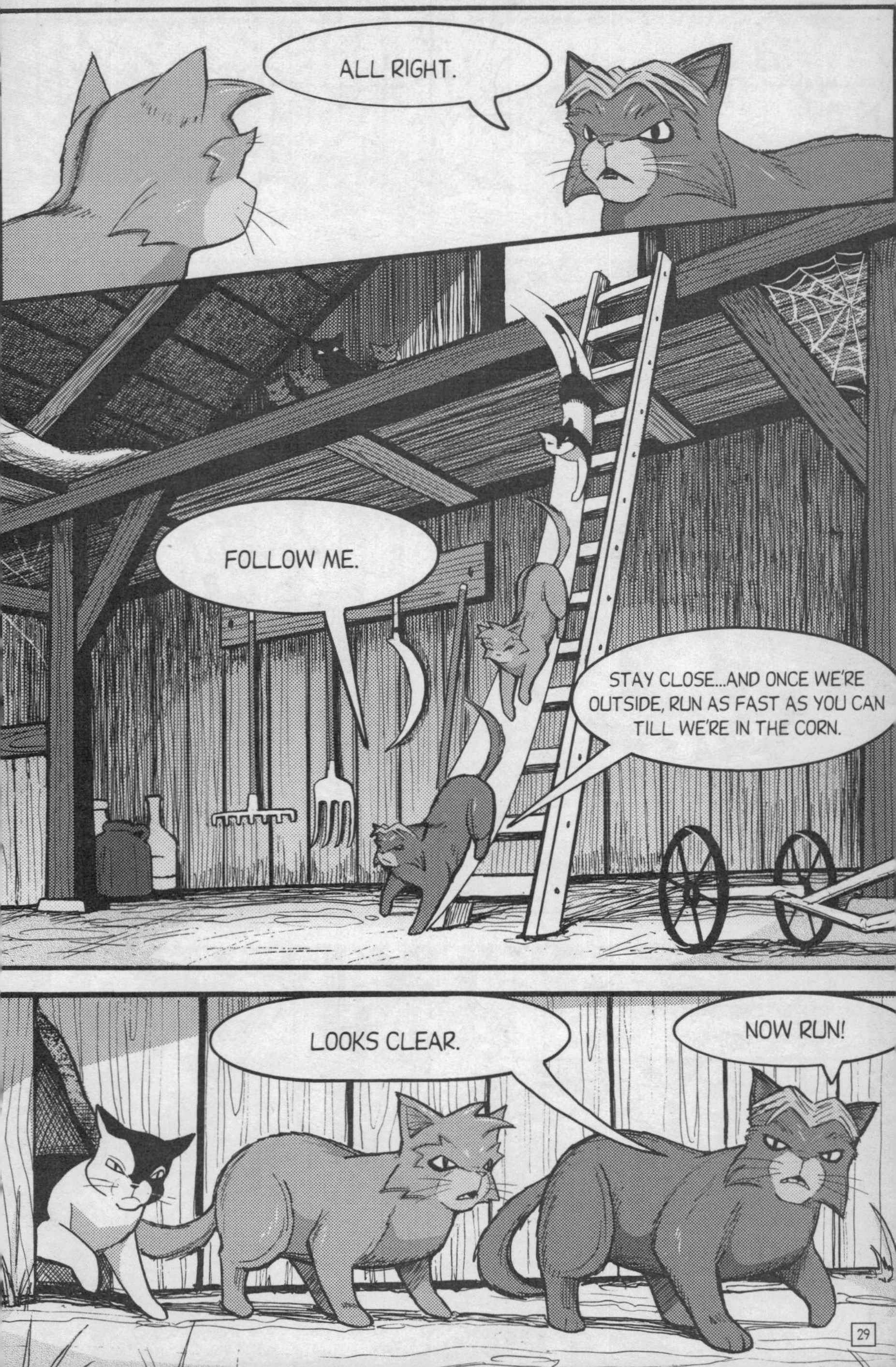
ALL RIGHT.
FOLLOW ME.
STAY CLOSE...AND ONCE WE'RE OUTSIDE, RUN AS FAST AS YOU CAN TILL WE'RE IN THE CORN.
LOOKS CLEAR.
NOW RUN!

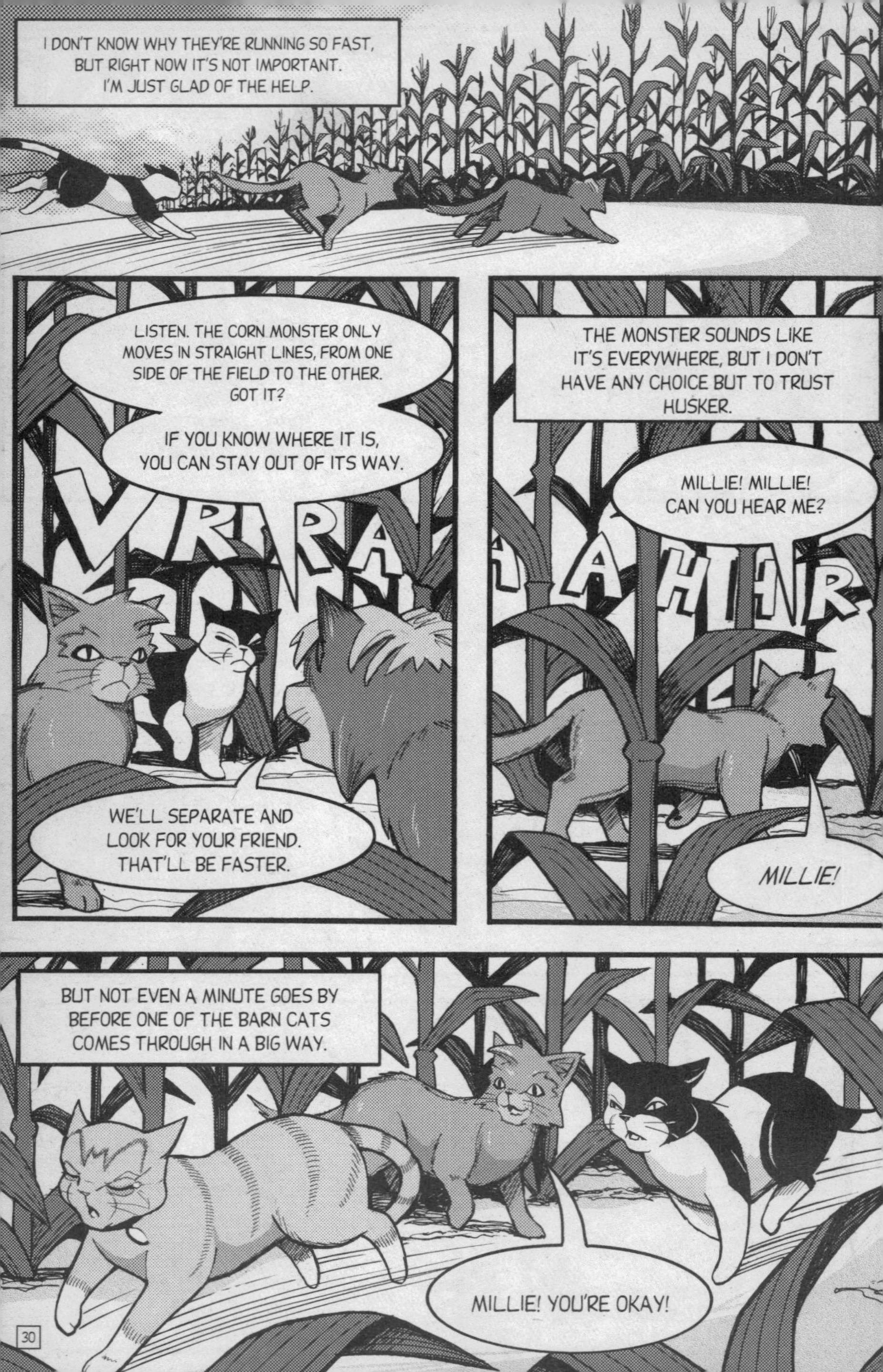
I DON'T KNOW WHY THEY'RE RUNNING SO FAST, BUT RIGHT NOW IT'S NOT IMPORTANT. I'M JUST GLAD OF THE HELP.
LISTEN. THE CORN MONSTER ONLY MOVES IN STRAIGHT LINES, FROM ONE SIDE OF THE FIELD TO THE OTHER. GOT IT?
IF YOU KNOW WHERE IT IS, YOU CAN STAY OUT OF ITS WAY.
VRRRA
WE'LL SEPARATE AND LOOK FOR YOUR FRIEND. THAT'LL BE FASTER.
THE MONSTER SOUNDS LIKE IT'S EVERYWHERE, BUT I DON'T HAVE ANY CHOICE BUT TO TRUST HUSKER.
MILLIE! MILLIE! CAN YOU HEAR ME?
AAHHRR
MILLIE!
BUT NOT EVEN A MINUTE GOES BY BEFORE ONE OF THE BARN CATS COMES THROUGH IN A BIG WAY.
MILLIE! YOU'RE OKAY!

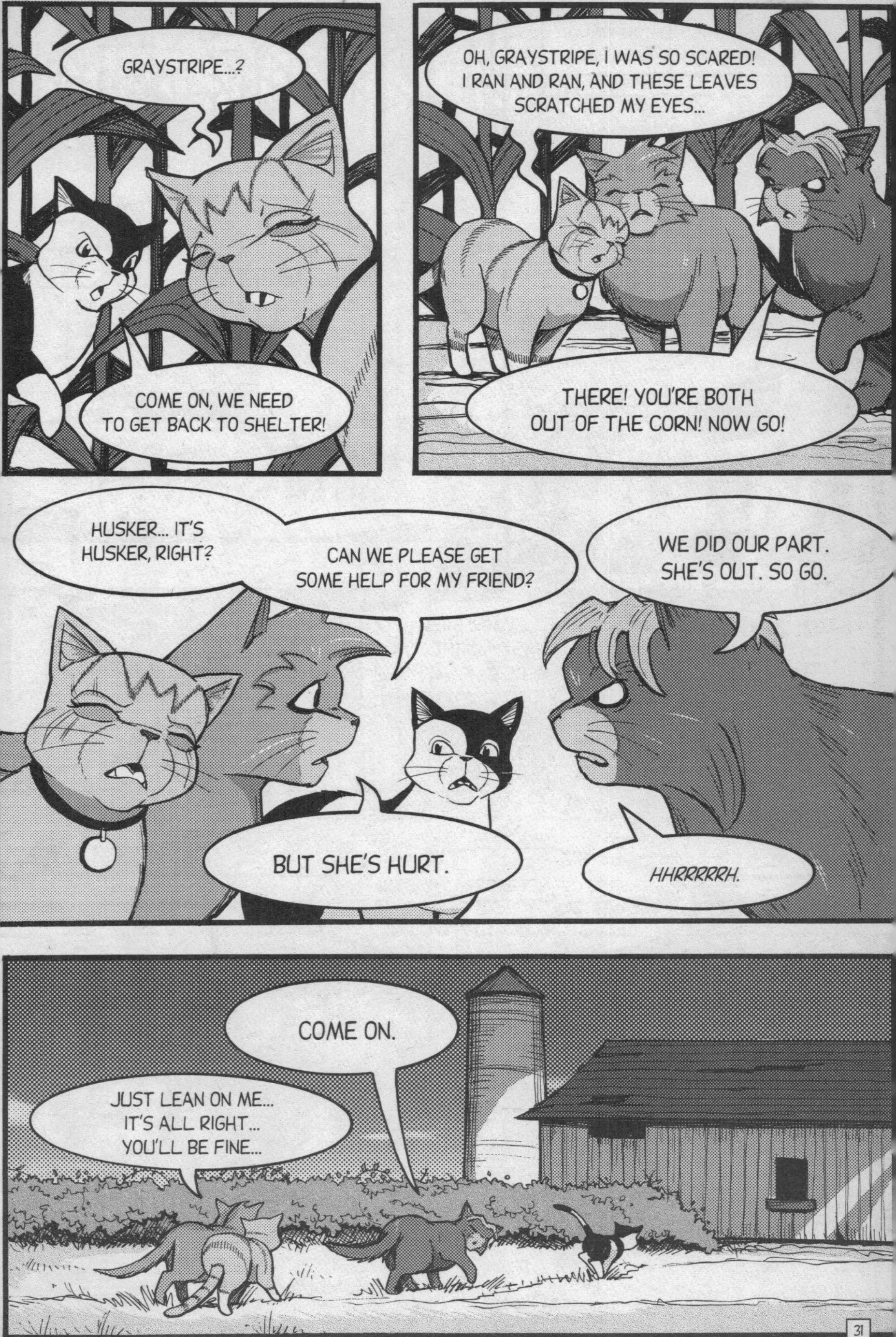
GRAYSTRIPE...?
COME ON, WE NEED TO GET BACK TO SHELTER!
OH, GRAYSTRIPE, I WAS SO SCARED! I RAN AND RAN, AND THESE LEAVES SCRATCHED MY EYES...
THERE! YOU'RE BOTH OUT OF THE CORN! NOW GO!
HUSKER... IT'S HUSKER, RIGHT?
CAN WE PLEASE GET SOME HELP FOR MY FRIEND?
WE DID OUR PART. SHE'S OUT. SO GO.
BUT SHE'S HURT.
HHRRRRRH.
COME ON.
JUST LEAN ON ME... IT'S ALL RIGHT... YOU'LL BE FINE...

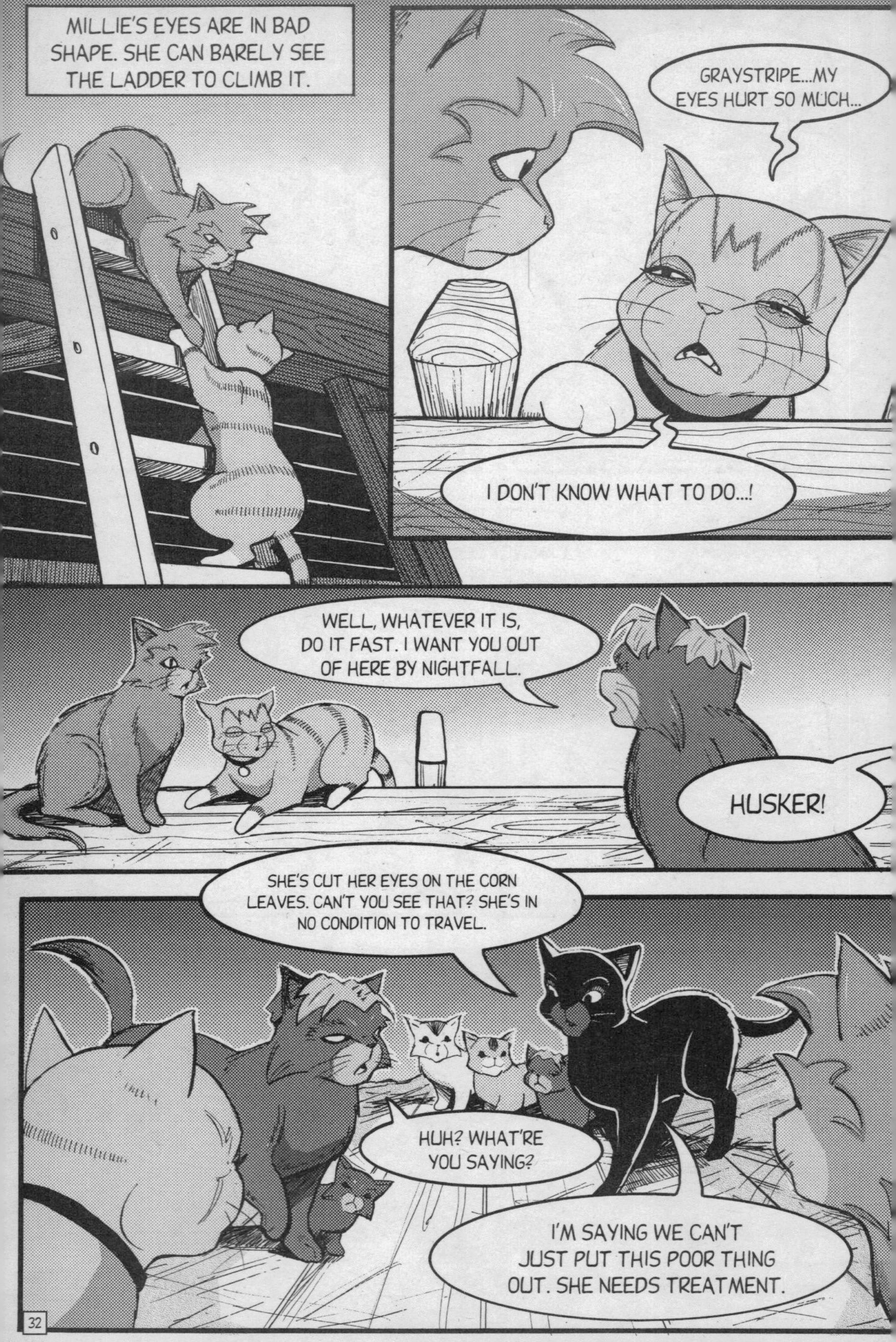

MILLIE'S EYES ARE IN BAD SHAPE. SHE CAN BARELY SEE THE LADDER TO CLIMB IT.
GRAYSTRIPE...MY EYES HURT SO MUCH...
I DON'T KNOW WHAT TO DO...!
WELL, WHATEVER IT IS, DO IT FAST. I WANT YOU OUT OF HERE BY NIGHTFALL.
HUSKER!
SHE'S CUT HER EYES ON THE CORN LEAVES. CAN'T YOU SEE THAT? SHE'S IN NO CONDITION TO TRAVEL.
HUH? WHAT'RE YOU SAYING?
I'M SAYING WE CAN'T JUST PUT THIS POOR THING OUT. SHE NEEDS TREATMENT.

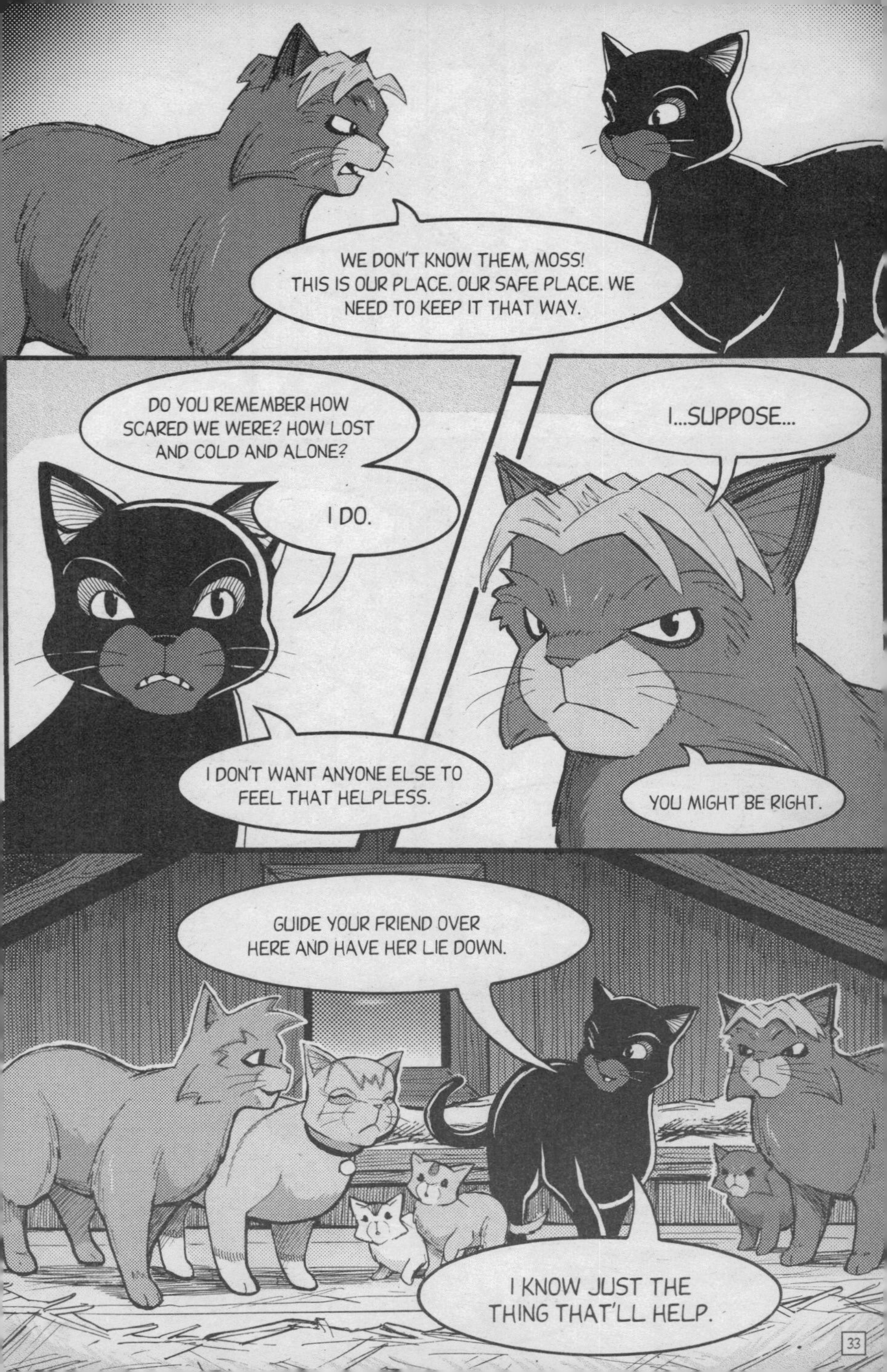
WE DON'T KNOW THEM, MOSS! THIS IS OUR PLACE. OUR SAFE PLACE. WE NEED TO KEEP IT THAT WAY.
DO YOU REMEMBER HOW SCARED WE WERE? HOW LOST AND COLD AND ALONE?
I DO.
I DON'T WANT ANYONE ELSE TO FEEL THAT HELPLESS.
I...SUPPOSE...
YOU MIGHT BE RIGHT.
GUIDE YOUR FRIEND OVER HERE AND HAVE HER LIE DOWN.
I KNOW JUST THE THING THAT'LL HELP.

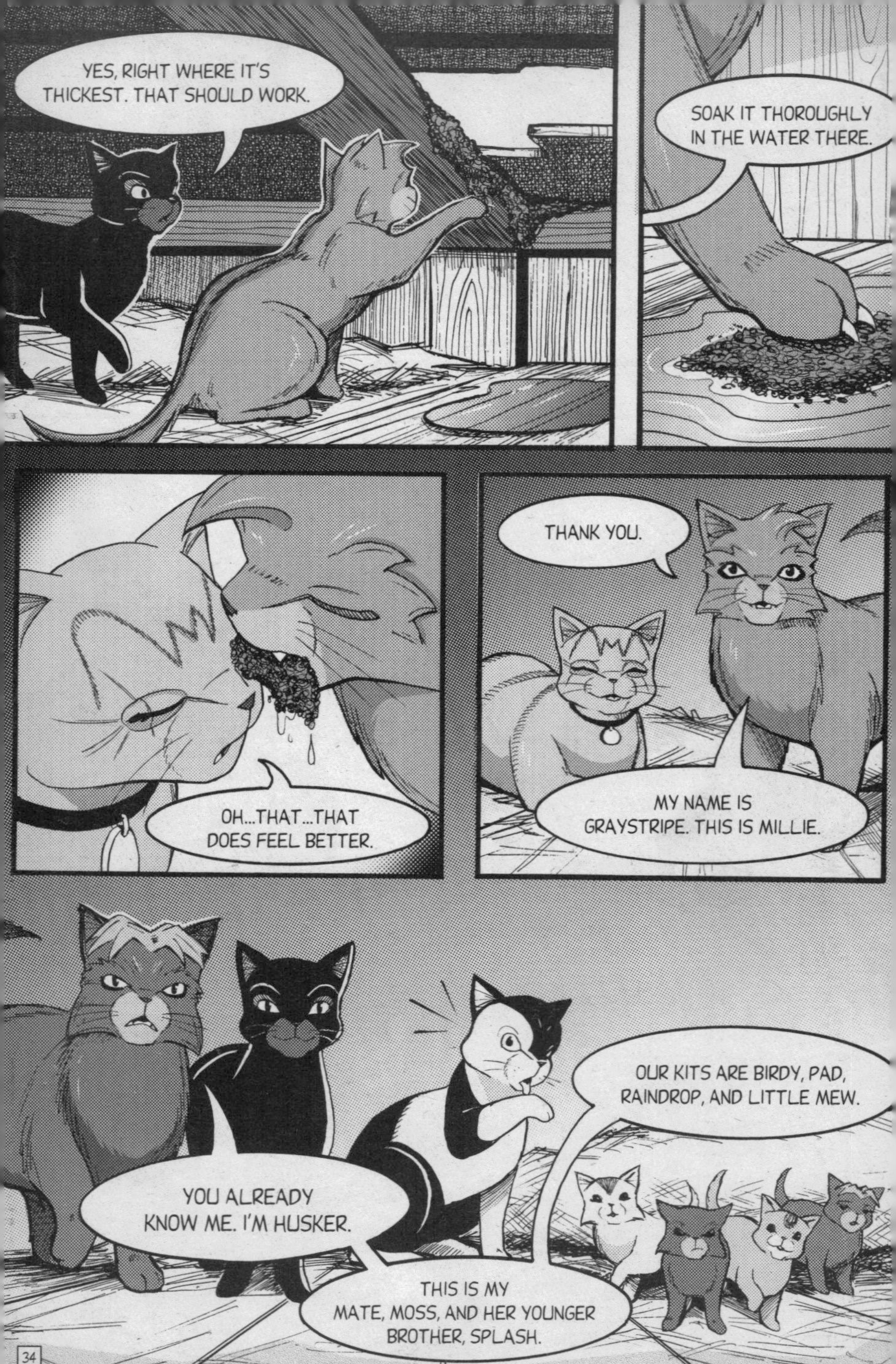
YES, RIGHT WHERE IT'S THICKEST. THAT SHOULD WORK.
SOAK IT THOROUGHLY IN THE WATER THERE.
OH...THAT...THAT DOES FEEL BETTER.
THANK YOU.
MY NAME IS GRAYSTRIPE. THIS IS MILLIE.
YOU ALREADY KNOW ME. I'M HUSKER.
THIS IS MY MATE, MOSS, AND HER YOUNGER BROTHER, SPLASH.
OUR KITS ARE BIRDY, PAD, RAINDROP, AND LITTLE MEW.

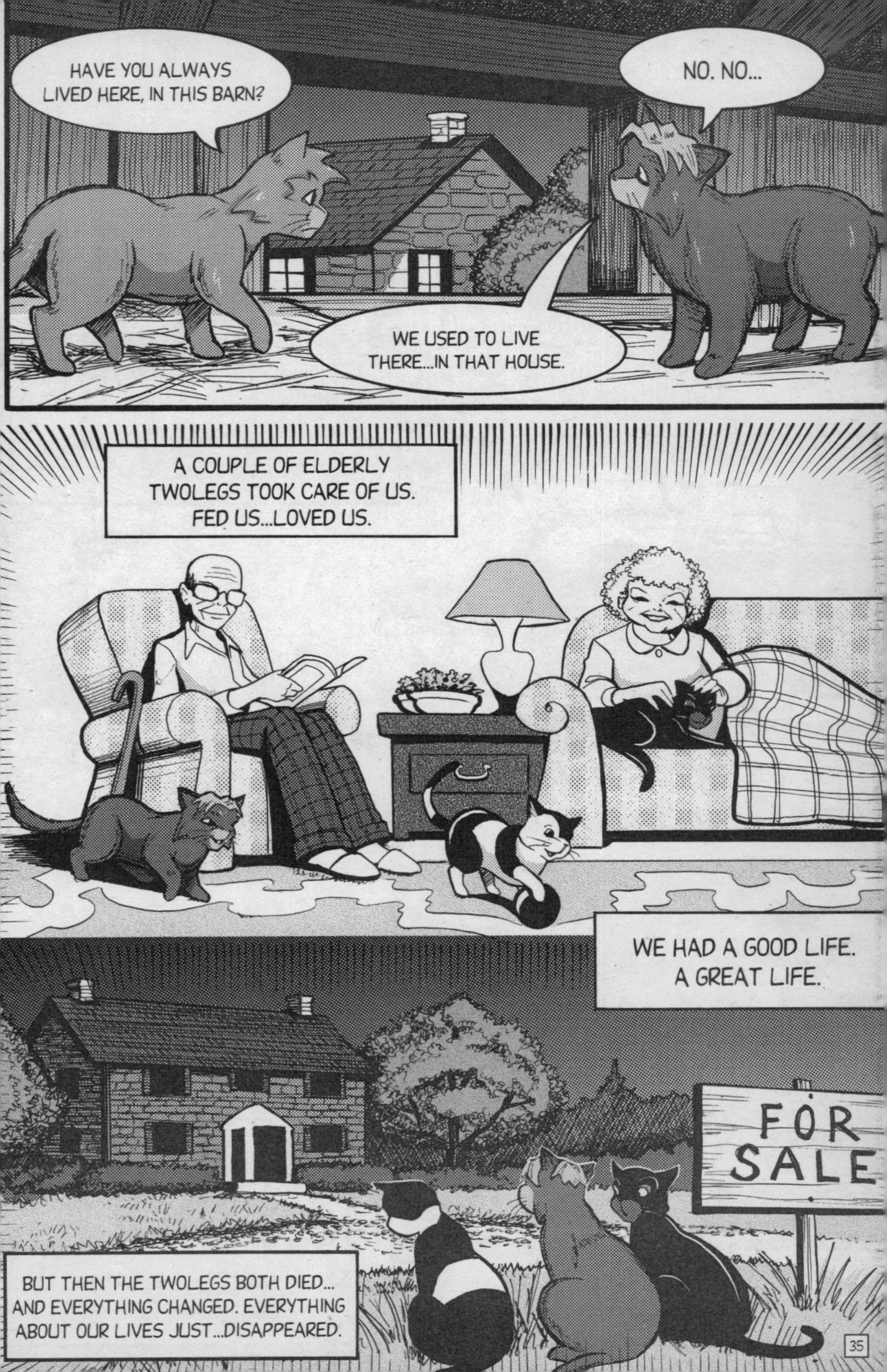

HAVE YOU ALWAYS LIVED HERE, IN THIS BARN?
NO. NO...
WE USED TO LIVE THERE...IN THAT HOUSE.
A COUPLE OF ELDERLY TWOLEGS TOOK CARE OF US. FED US...LOVED US.
WE HAD A GOOD LIFE. A GREAT LIFE.
FOR SALE
BUT THEN THE TWOLEGS BOTH DIED... AND EVERYTHING CHANGED. EVERYTHING ABOUT OUR LIVES JUST...DISAPPEARED.

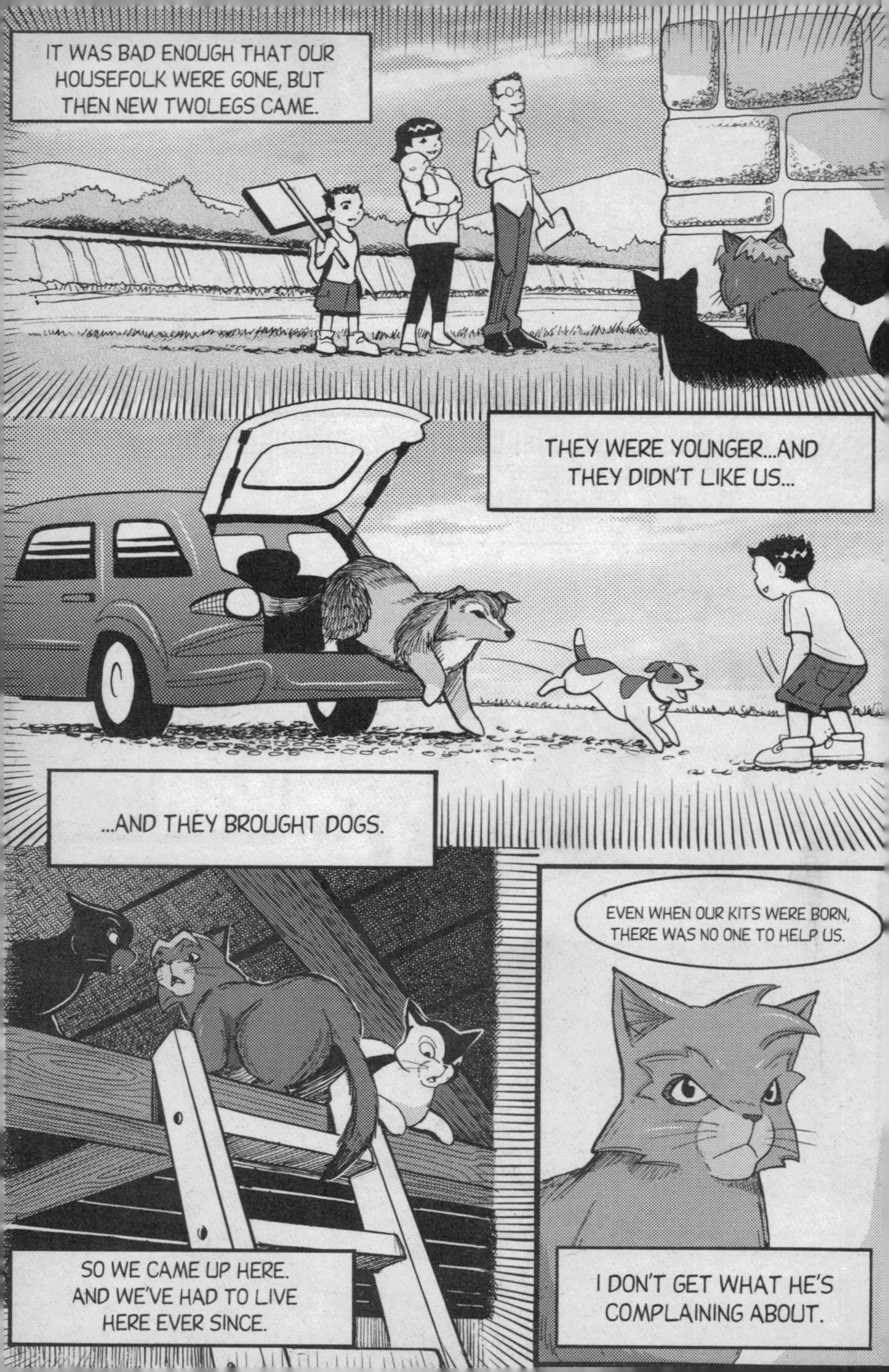
IT WAS BAD ENOUGH THAT OUR HOUSEFOLK WERE GONE, BUT THEN NEW TWOLEGS CAME.
THEY WERE YOUNGER...AND THEY DIDN'T LIKE US...
...AND THEY BROUGHT DOGS.
SO WE CAME UP HERE. AND WE'VE HAD TO LIVE HERE EVER SINCE.
EVEN WHEN OUR KITS WERE BORN, THERE WAS NO ONE TO HELP US.
I DON'T GET WHAT HE'S COMPLAINING ABOUT.

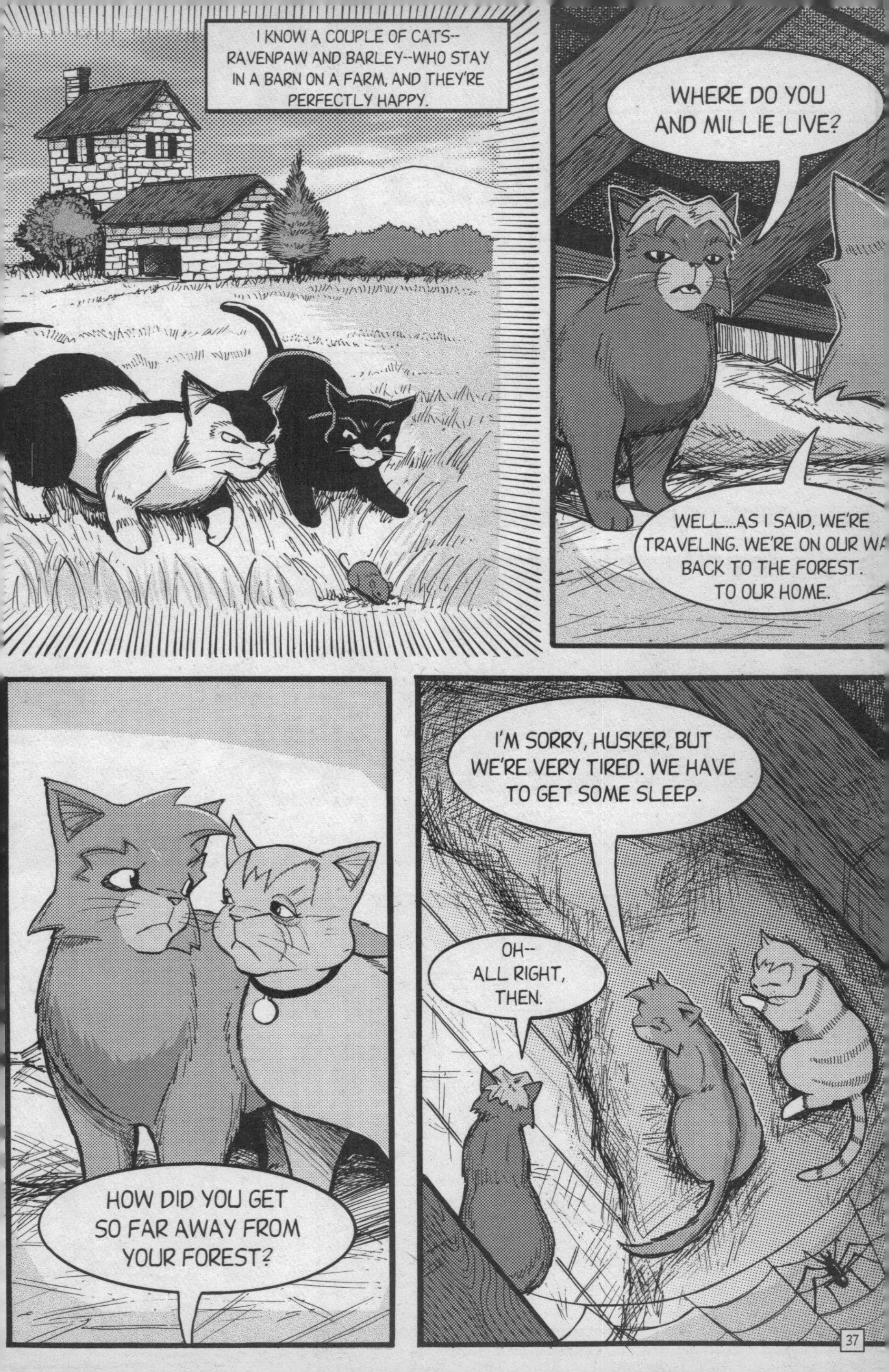
I KNOW A COUPLE OF CATS--RAVENPAW AND BARLEY--WHO STAY IN A BARN ON A FARM, AND THEY'RE PERFECTLY HAPPY.
WHERE DO YOU AND MILLIE LIVE?
WELL...AS I SAID, WE'RE TRAVELING. WE'RE ON OUR WA BACK TO THE FOREST. TO OUR HOME.
HOW DID YOU GET SO FAR AWAY FROM YOUR FOREST?
I'M SORRY, HUSKER, BUT WE'RE VERY TIRED. WE HAVE TO GET SOME SLEEP.
OH--ALL RIGHT, THEN.

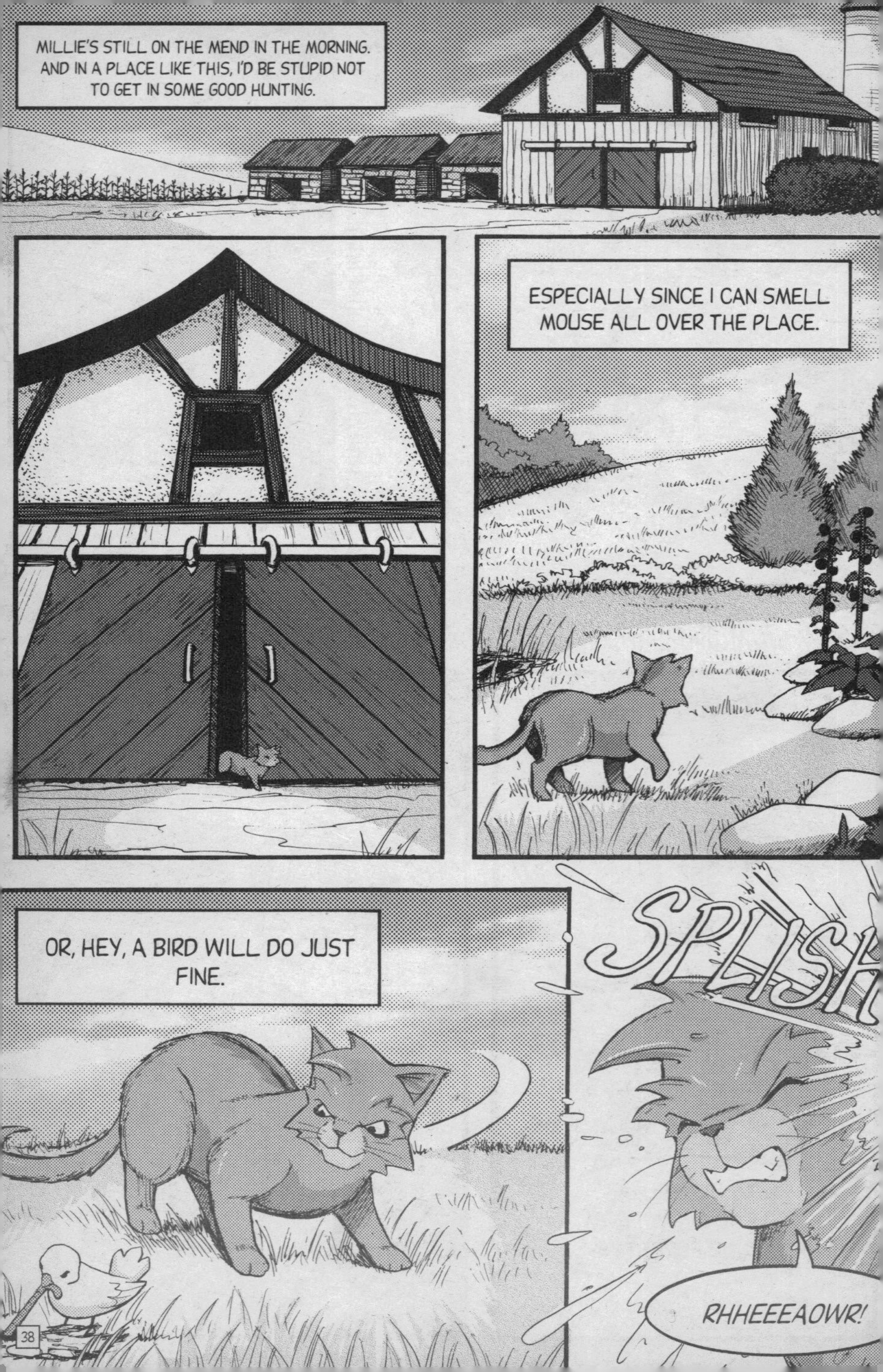
MILLIE'S STILL ON THE MEND IN THE MORNING. AND IN A PLACE LIKE THIS, I'D BE STUPID NOT TO GET IN SOME GOOD HUNTING.
ESPECIALLY SINCE I CAN SMELL MOUSE ALL OVER THE PLACE.
OR, HEY, A BIRD WILL DO JUST FINE.
SPLISH
RHHEEEAOWR!

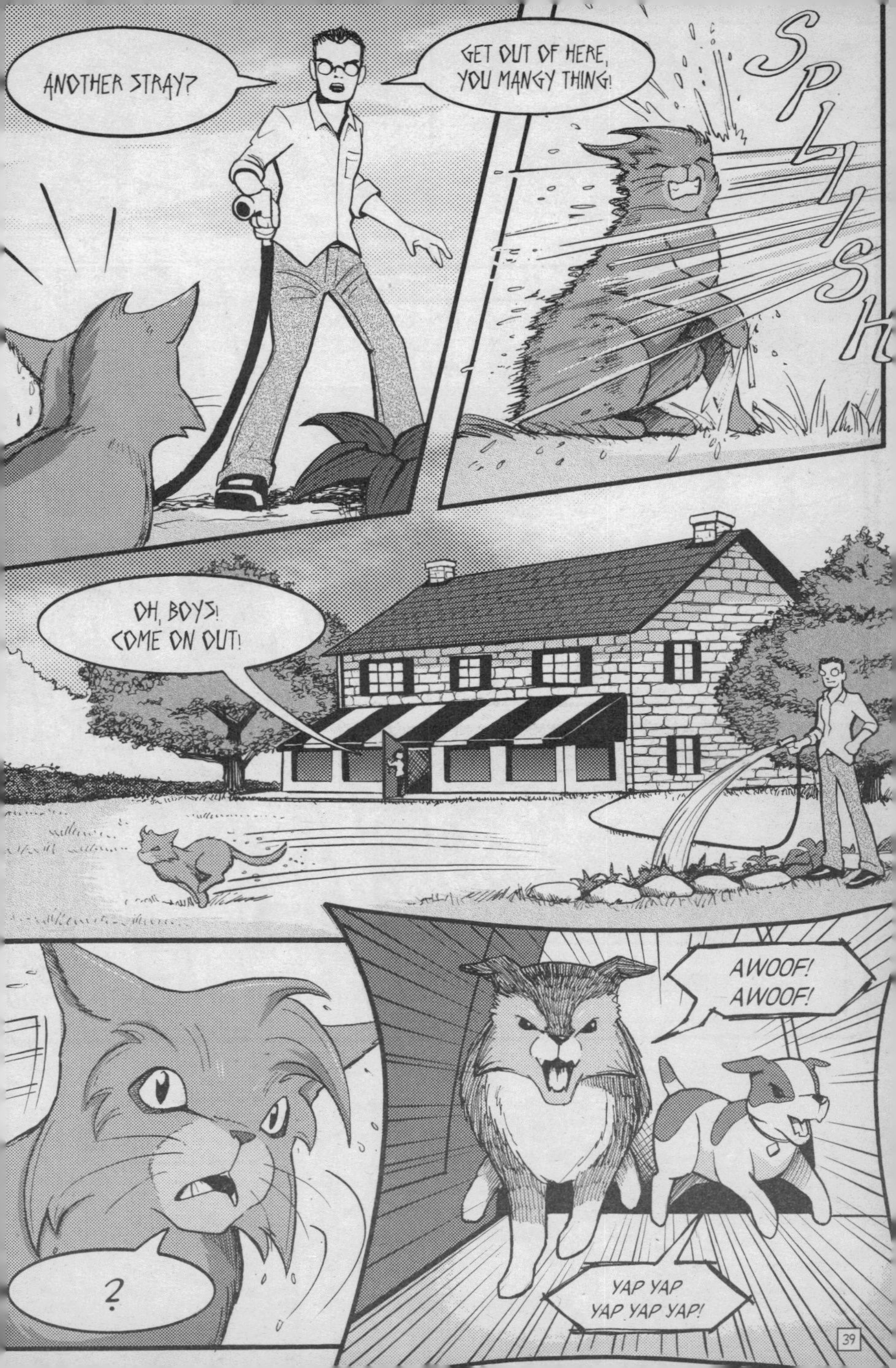
ANOTHER STRAY?
GET OUT OF HERE, YOU MANGY THING!
SPLISH
OH, BOYS! COME ON OUT!
?
AWOOF! AWOOF!
YAP YAP YAP YAP YAP!

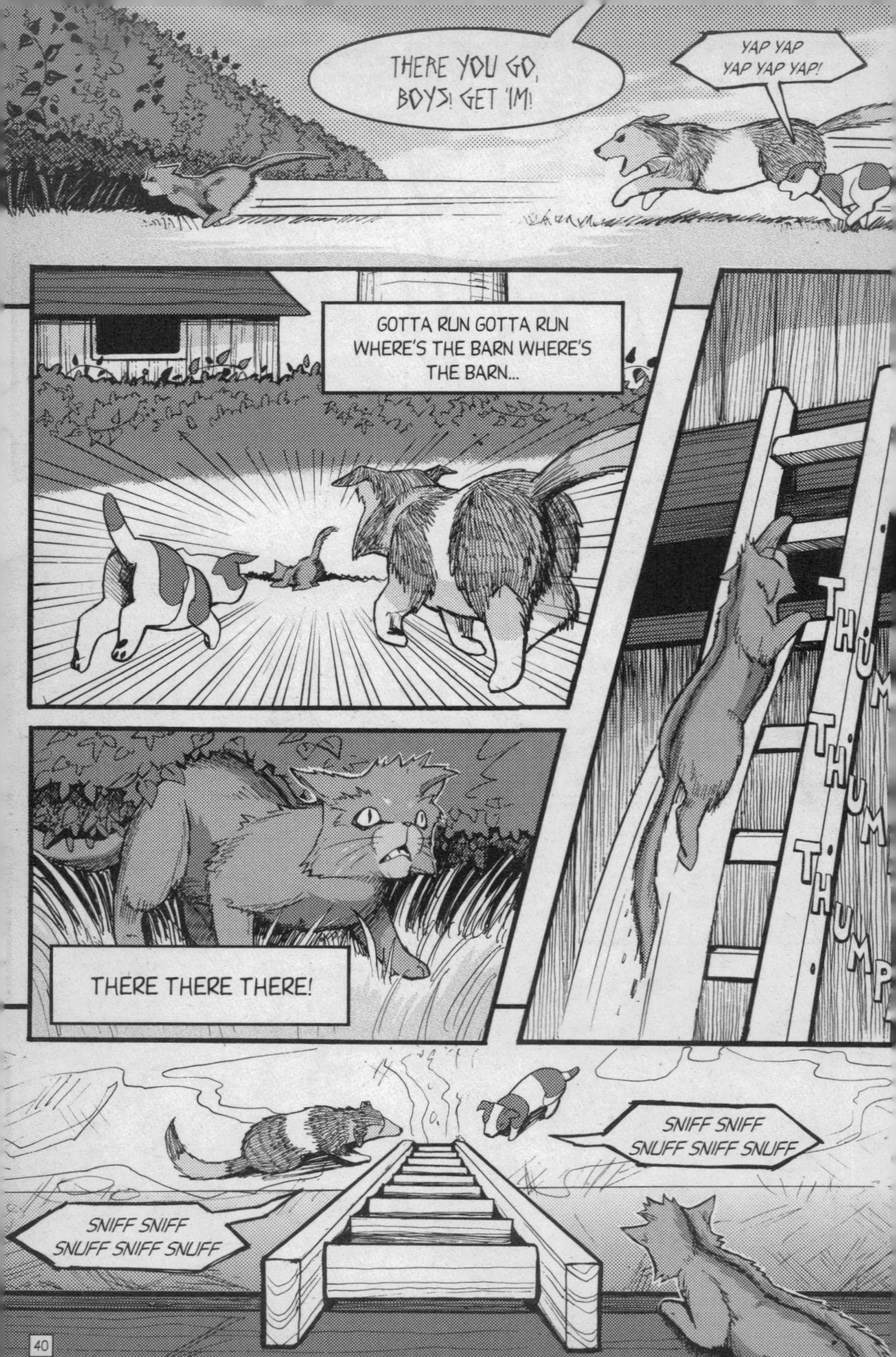

THERE YOU GO, BOYS! GET 'IM!
YAP YAP YAP YAP YAP!
GOTTA RUN GOTTA RUN WHERE'S THE BARN WHERE'S THE BARN...
THUMP THUMP THUMP THUMP!
THERE THERE THERE!
SNIFF SNIFF SNUFF SNIFF SNUFF
SNIFF SNIFF SNUFF SNIFF SNUFF

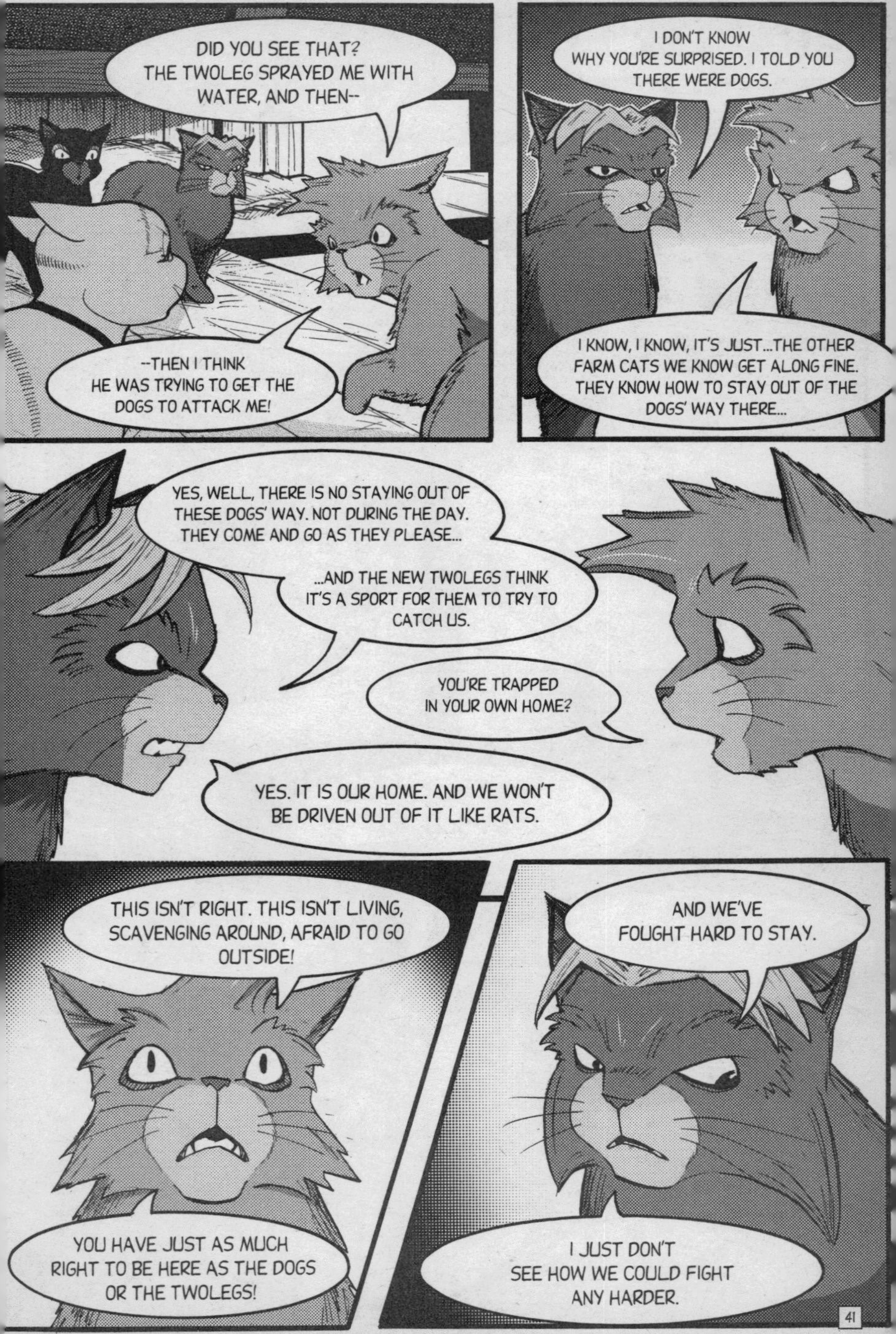
DID YOU SEE THAT? THE TWOLEG SPRAYED ME WITH WATER, AND THEN--
--THEN I THINK HE WAS TRYING TO GET THE DOGS TO ATTACK ME!
I DON'T KNOW WHY YOU'RE SURPRISED. I TOLD YOU THERE WERE DOGS.
I KNOW, I KNOW, IT'S JUST...THE OTHER FARM CATS WE KNOW GET ALONG FINE. THEY KNOW HOW TO STAY OUT OF THE DOGS' WAY THERE...
YES, WELL, THERE IS NO STAYING OUT OF THESE DOGS' WAY. NOT DURING THE DAY. THEY COME AND GO AS THEY PLEASE...
...AND THE NEW TWOLEGS THINK IT'S A SPORT FOR THEM TO TRY TO CATCH US.
YOU'RE TRAPPED IN YOUR OWN HOME?
YES. IT IS OUR HOME. AND WE WON'T BE DRIVEN OUT OF IT LIKE RATS.
THIS ISN'T RIGHT. THIS ISN'T LIVING, SCAVENGING AROUND, AFRAID TO GO OUTSIDE!
YOU HAVE JUST AS MUCH RIGHT TO BE HERE AS THE DOGS OR THE TWOLEGS!
AND WE'VE FOUGHT HARD TO STAY.
I JUST DON'T SEE HOW WE COULD FIGHT ANY HARDER.

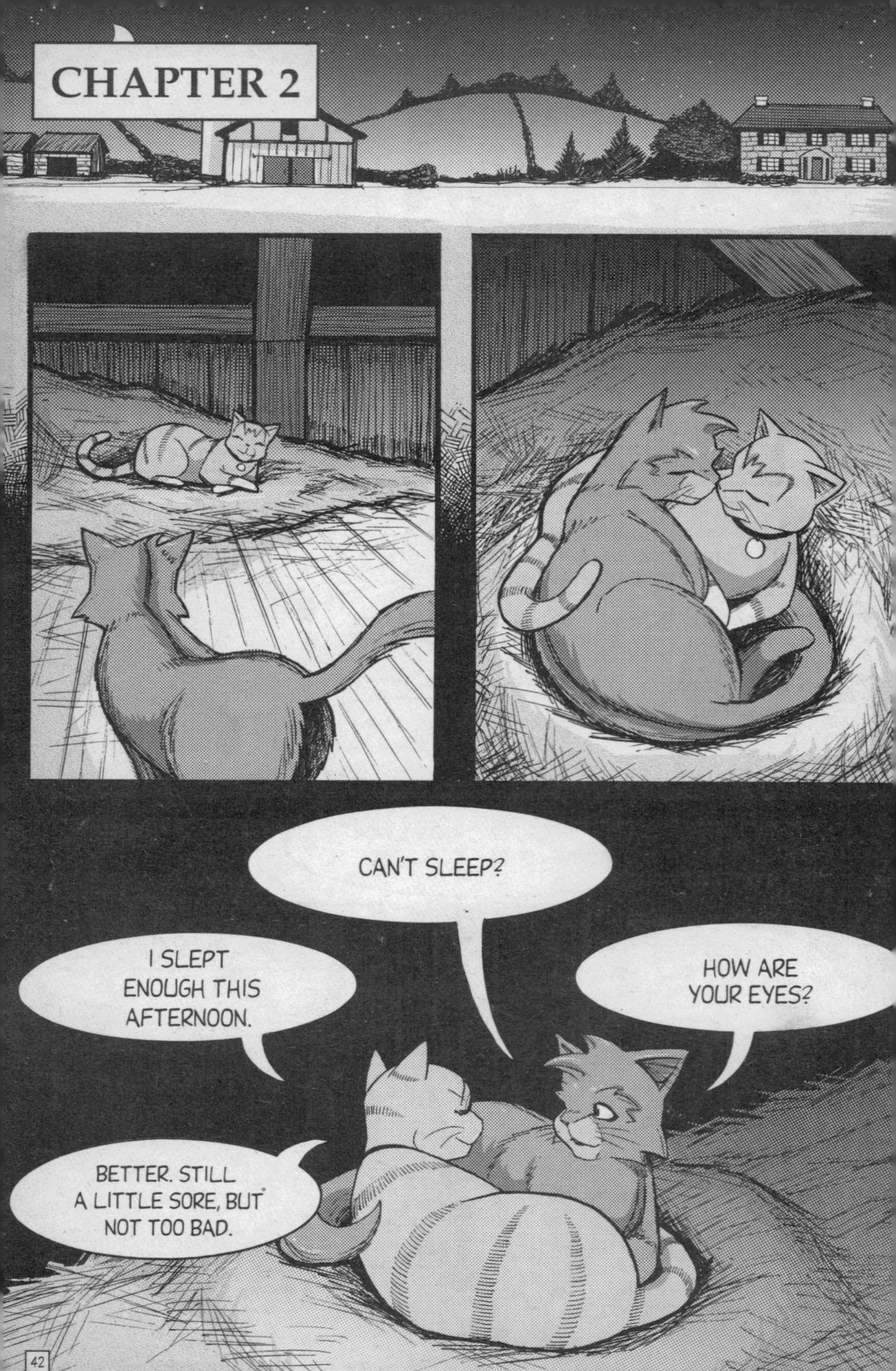
CHAPTER 2
CAN'T SLEEP?
I SLEPT ENOUGH THIS AFTERNOON.
HOW ARE YOUR EYES?
BETTER. STILL A LITTLE SORE, BUT NOT TOO BAD.

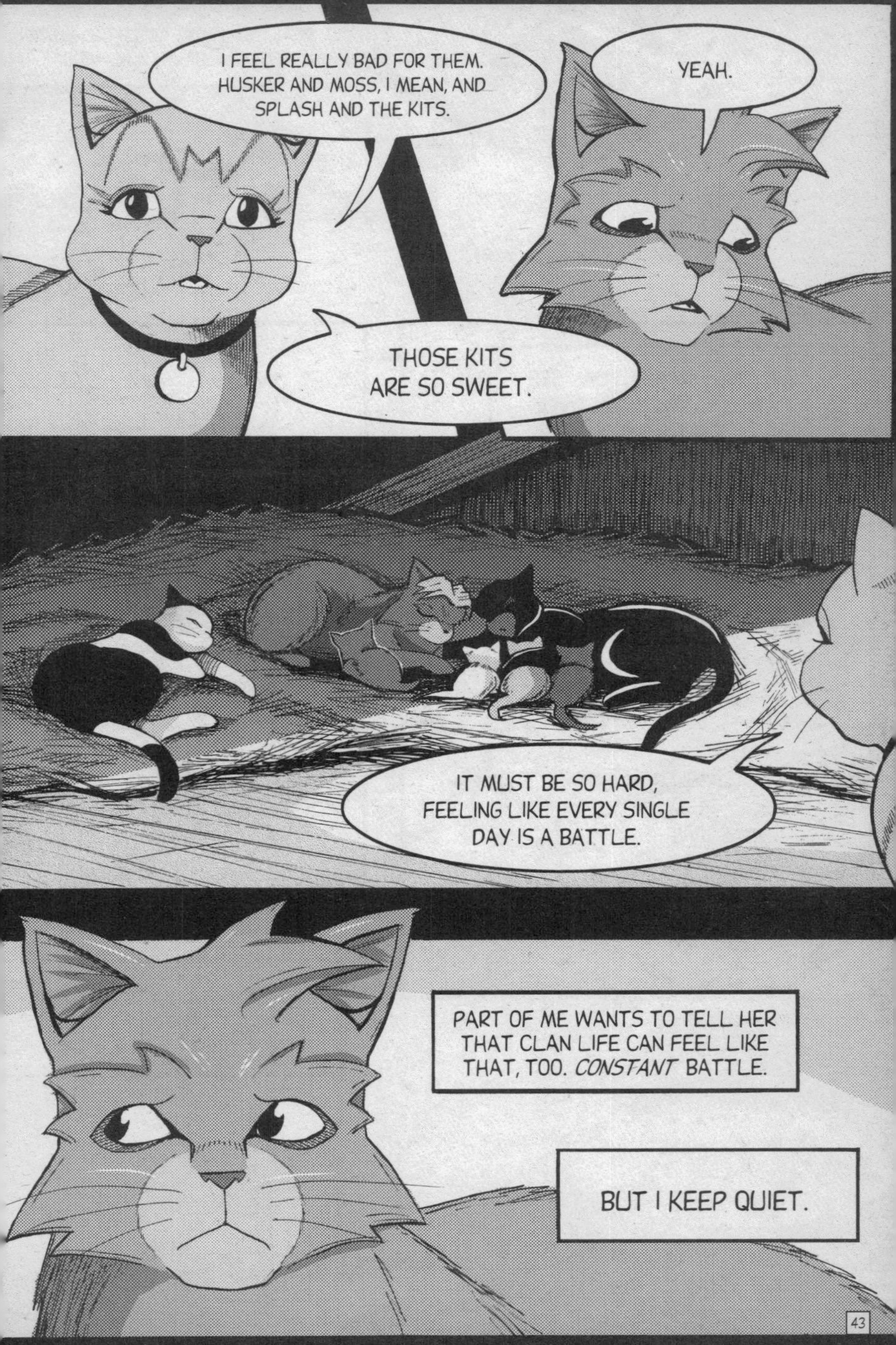
I FEEL REALLY BAD FOR THEM. HUSKER AND MOSS, I MEAN, AND SPLASH AND THE KITS.
YEAH.
THOSE KITS ARE SO SWEET.
IT MUST BE SO HARD, FEELING LIKE EVERY SINGLE DAY IS A BATTLE.
PART OF ME WANTS TO TELL HER THAT CLAN LIFE CAN FEEL LIKE THAT, TOO. *CONSTANT* BATTLE.
BUT I KEEP QUIET.

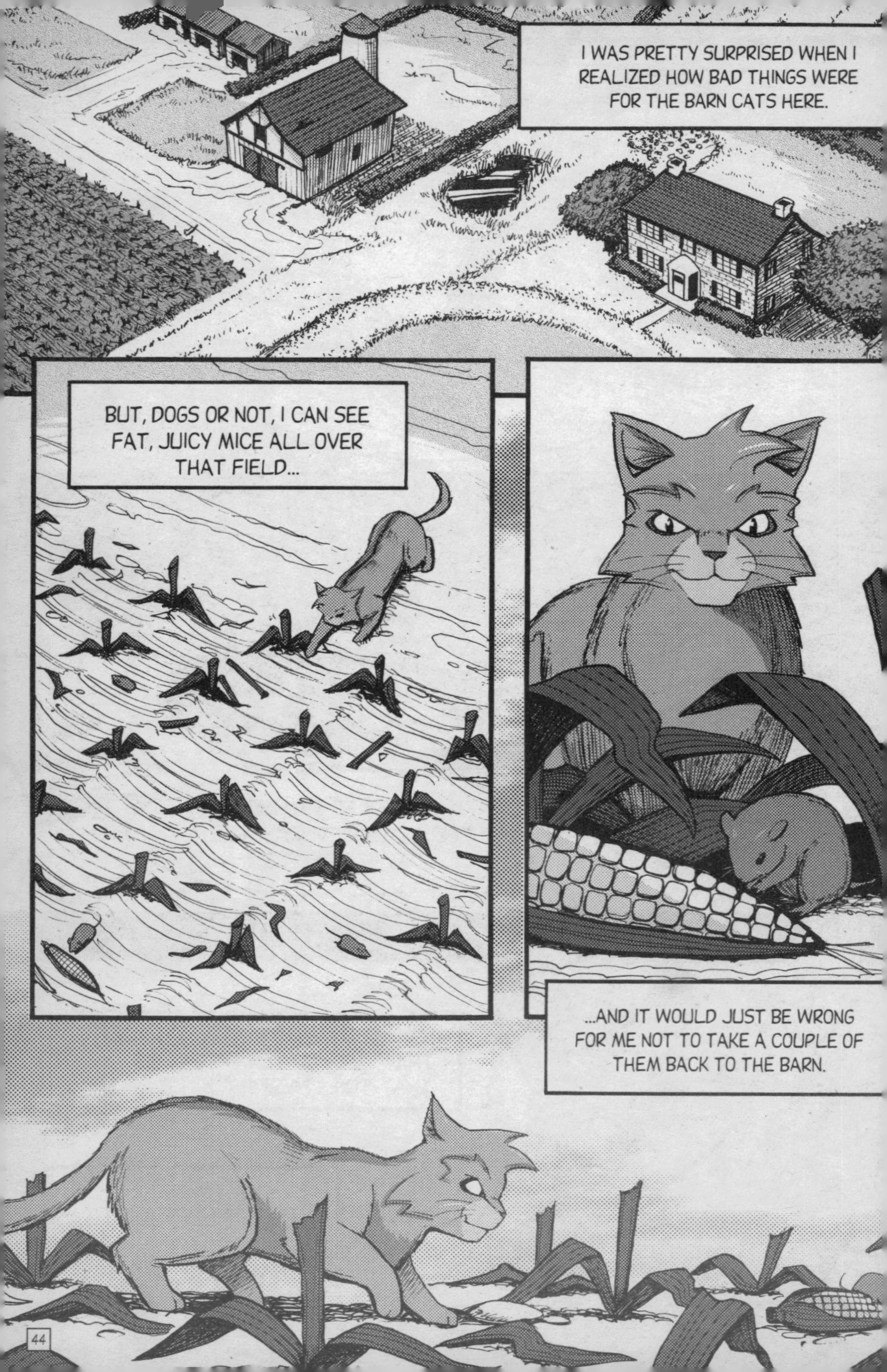
I WAS PRETTY SURPRISED WHEN I REALIZED HOW BAD THINGS WERE FOR THE BARN CATS HERE.
BUT, DOGS OR NOT, I CAN SEE FAT, JUICY MICE ALL OVER THAT FIELD...
...AND IT WOULD JUST BE WRONG FOR ME NOT TO TAKE A COUPLE OF THEM BACK TO THE BARN.

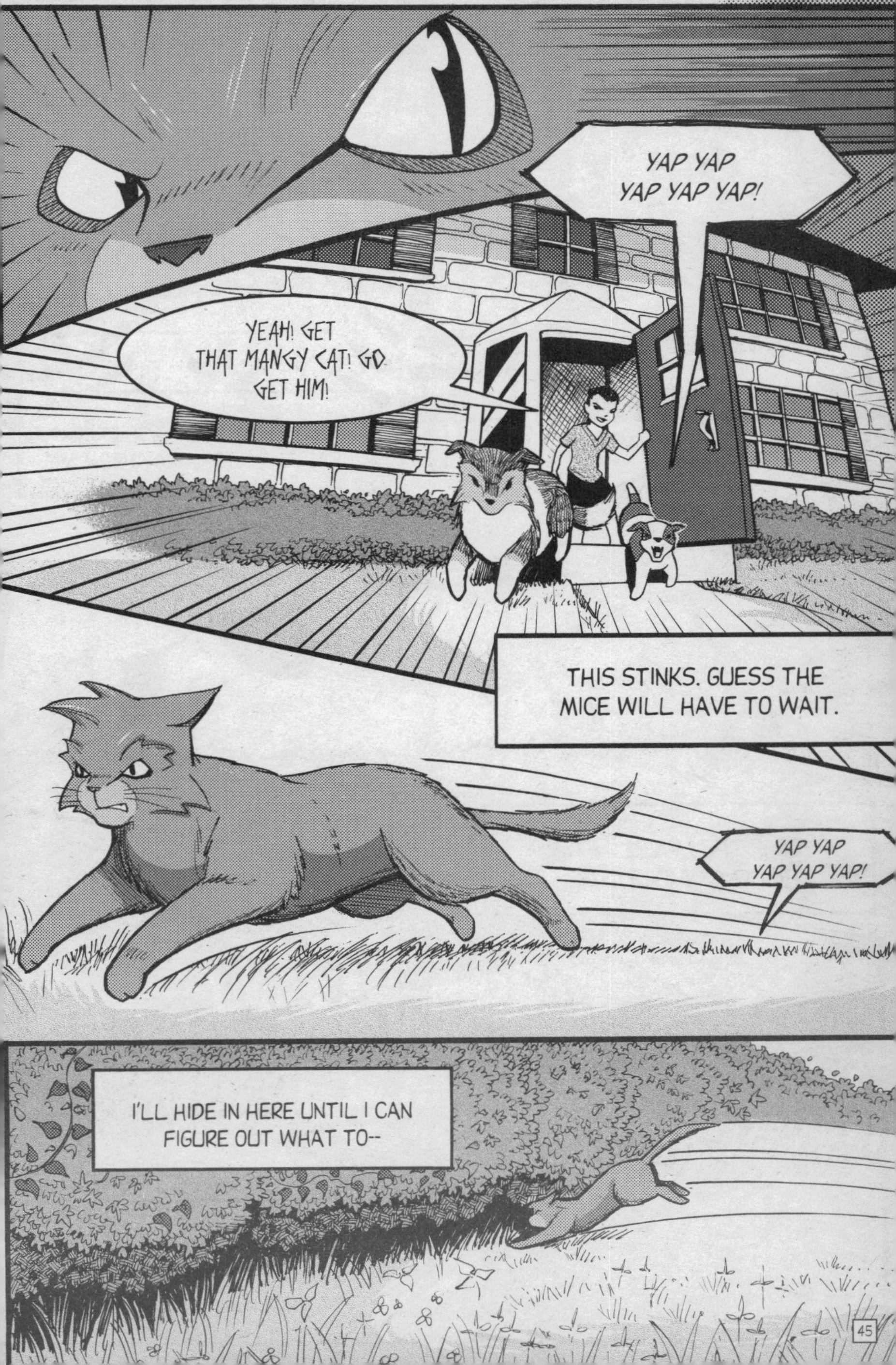
YAP YAP
YAP YAP YAP!
YEAH! GET
THAT MANGY CAT! GO
GET HIM!
THIS STINKS. GUESS THE
MICE WILL HAVE TO WAIT.
YAP YAP
YAP YAP YAP!
I'LL HIDE IN HERE UNTIL I CAN
FIGURE OUT WHAT TO--

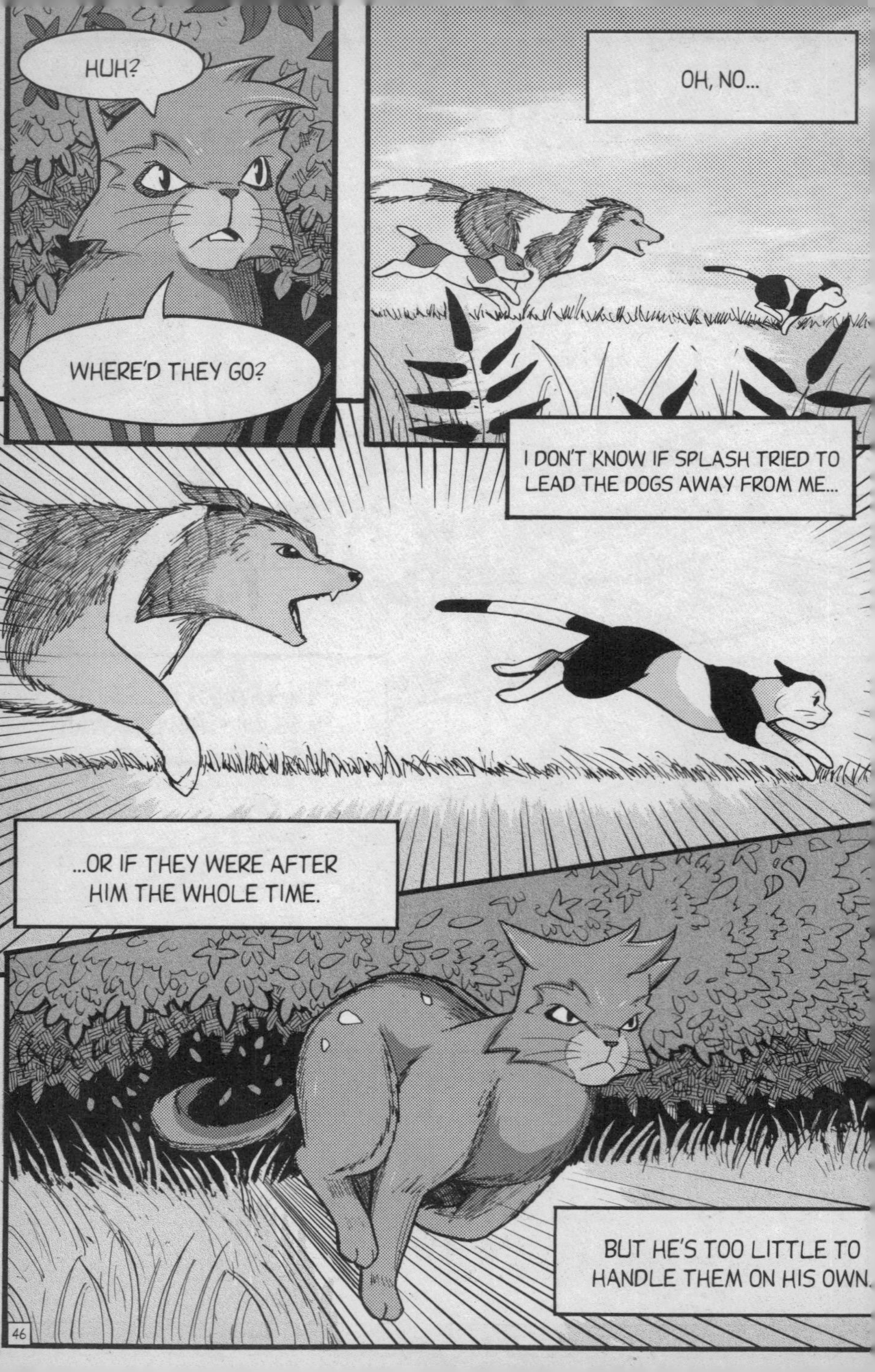
HUH?
WHERE'D THEY GO?
OH, NO...
I DON'T KNOW IF SPLASH TRIED TO LEAD THE DOGS AWAY FROM ME...
...OR IF THEY WERE AFTER HIM THE WHOLE TIME.
BUT HE'S TOO LITTLE TO HANDLE THEM ON HIS OWN.

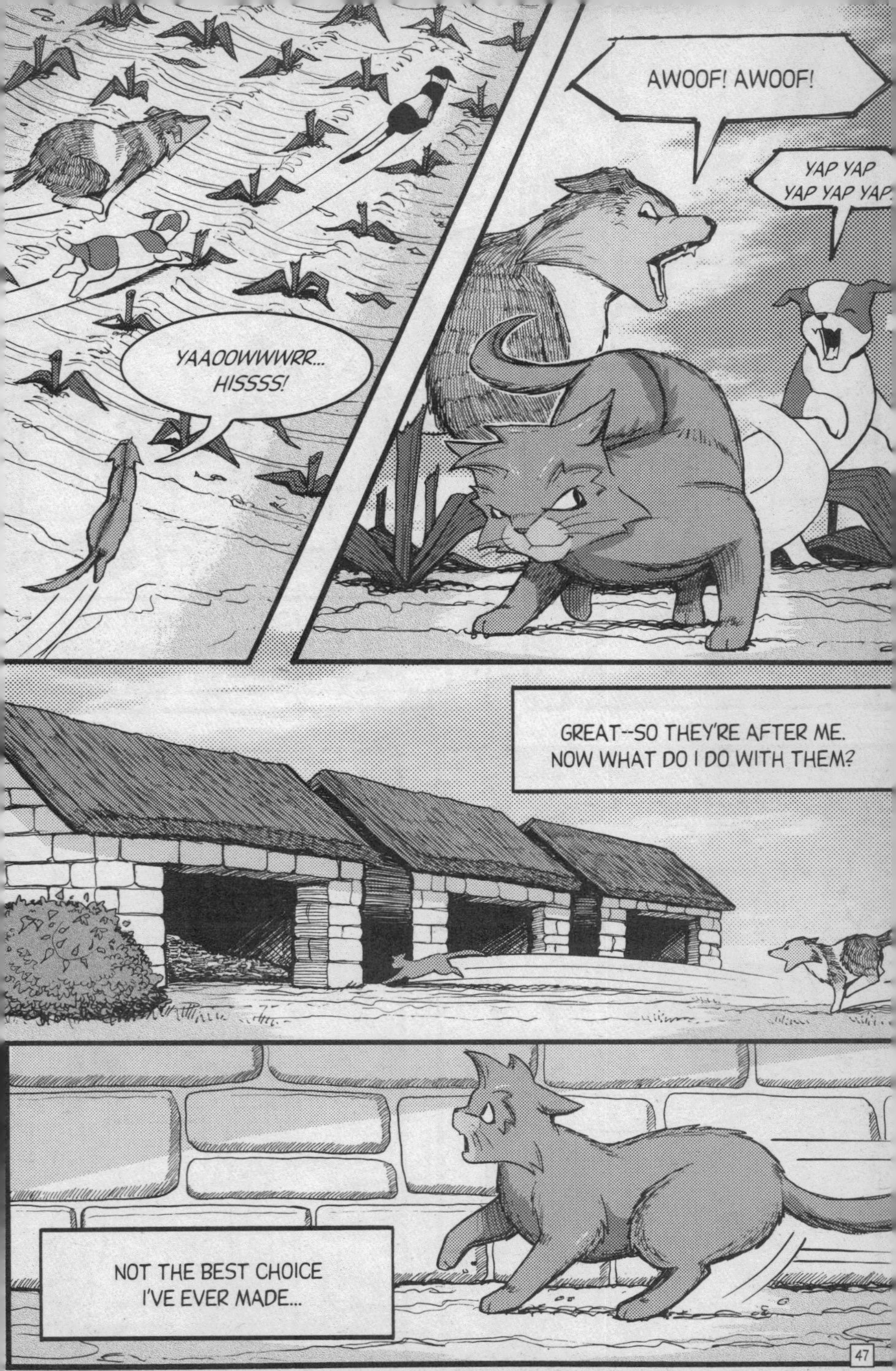
YAAOOWWWRR... HISSSS!
AWOOF! AWOOF!
YAP YAP YAP YAP YAP!
GREAT--SO THEY'RE AFTER ME. NOW WHAT DO I DO WITH THEM?
NOT THE BEST CHOICE I'VE EVER MADE...

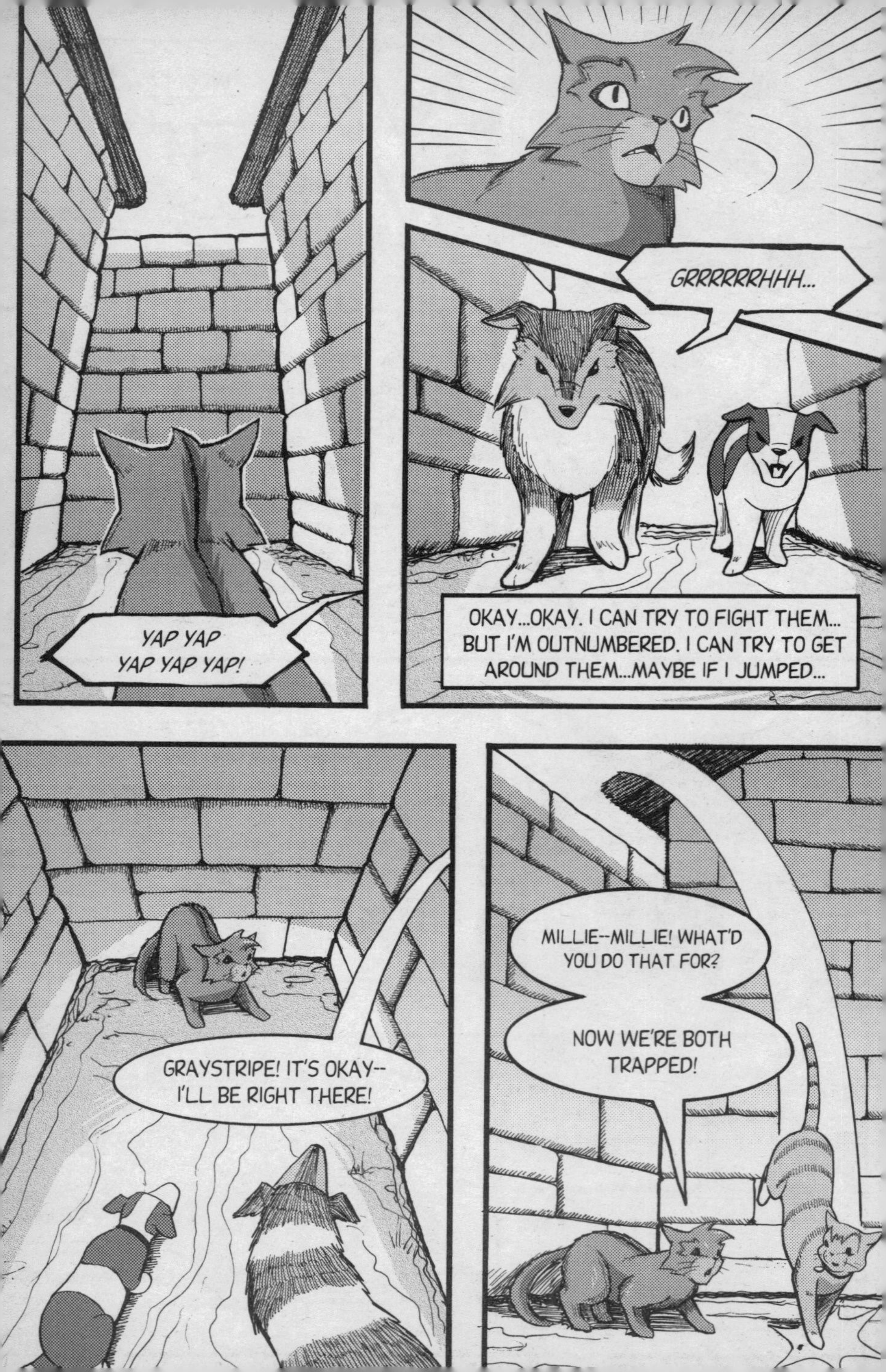
YAP YAP
YAP YAP YAP!
GRRRRRRHHH...
OKAY...OKAY. I CAN TRY TO FIGHT THEM... BUT I'M OUTNUMBERED. I CAN TRY TO GET AROUND THEM...MAYBE IF I JUMPED...
GRAYSTRIPE! IT'S OKAY-- I'LL BE RIGHT THERE!
MILLIE--MILLIE! WHAT'D YOU DO THAT FOR?
NOW WE'RE BOTH TRAPPED!

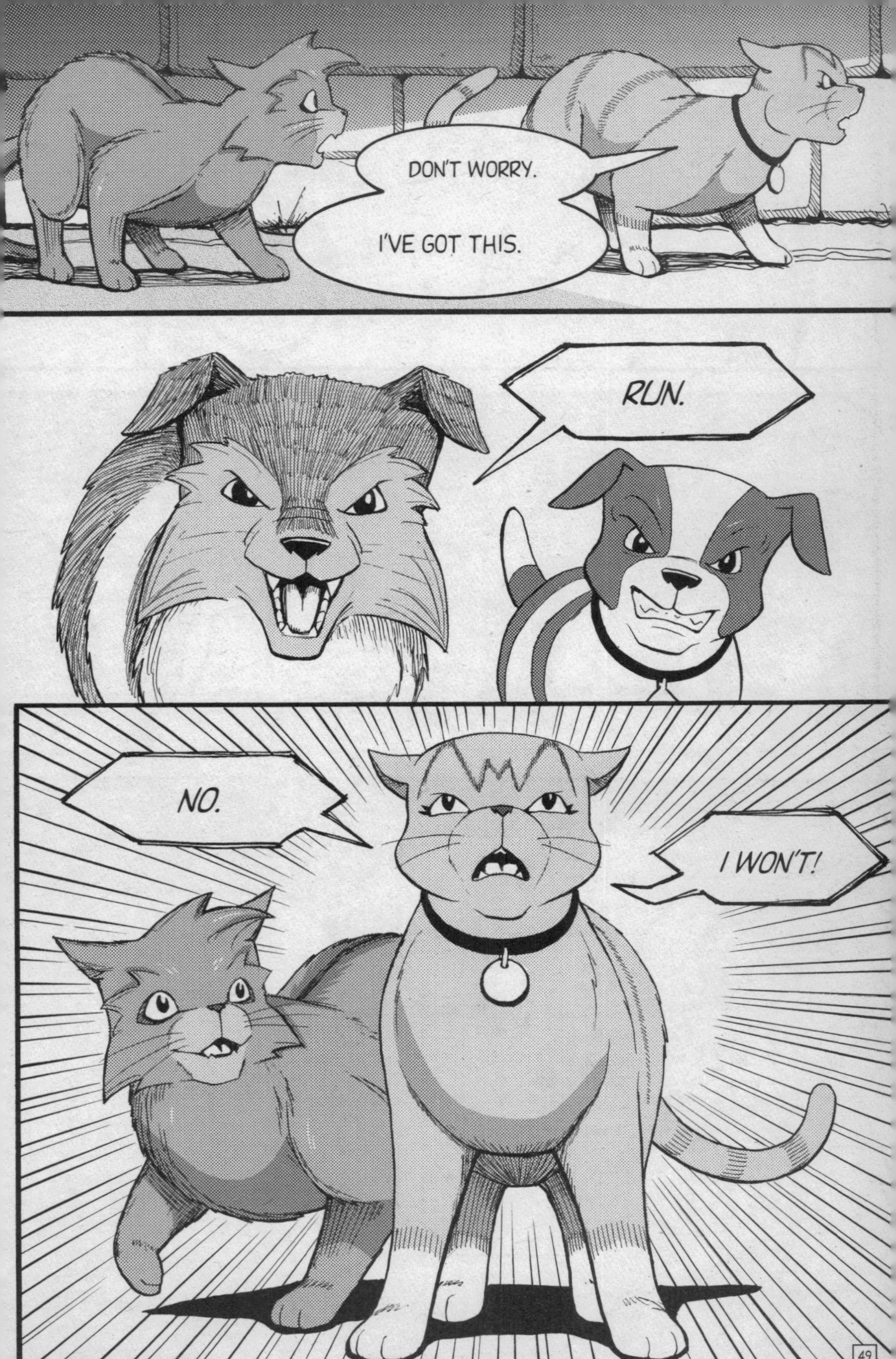
DON'T WORRY.
I'VE GOT THIS.
RUN.
NO.
I WON'T!

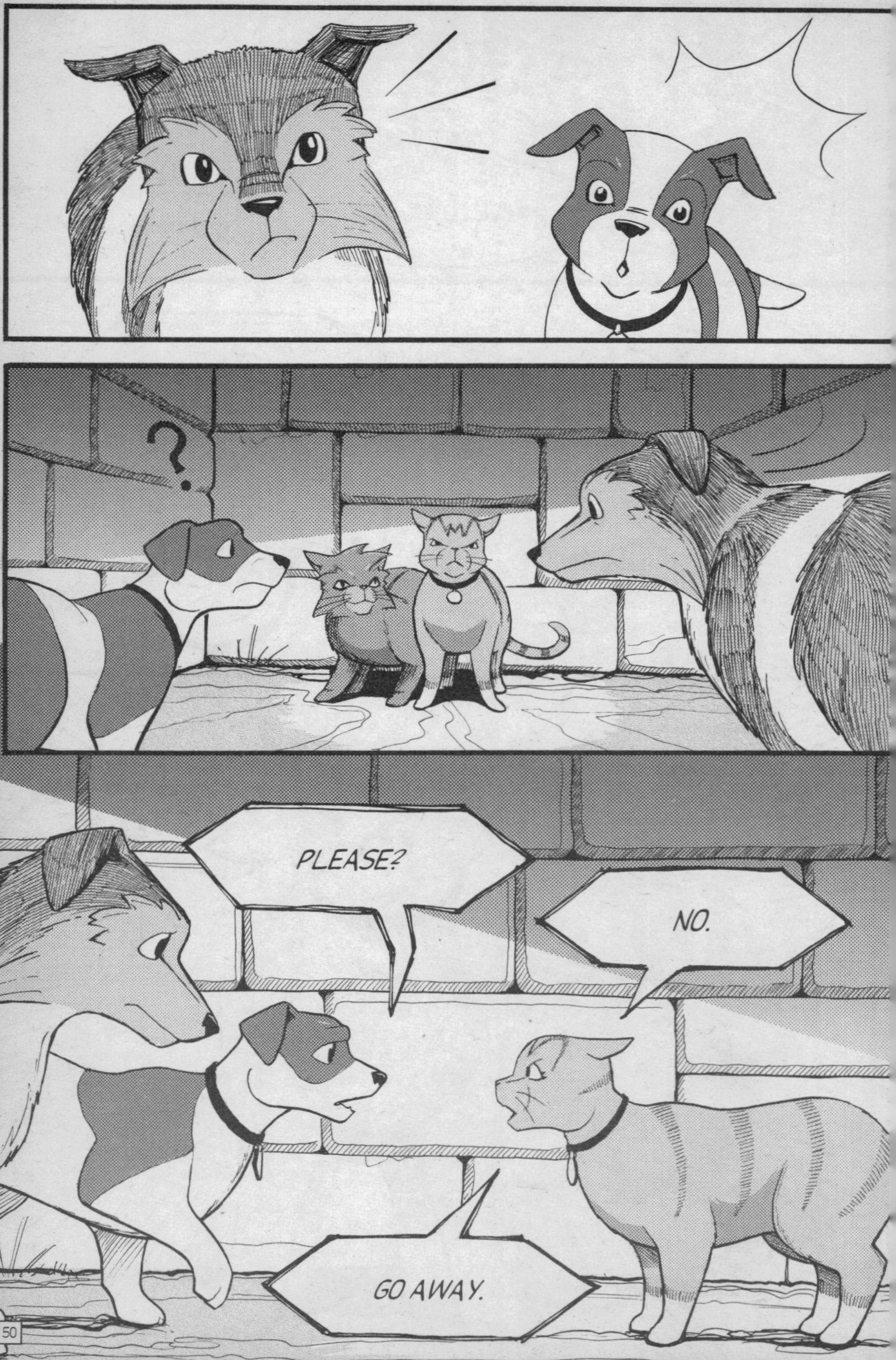
?
PLEASE?
NO.
GO AWAY.

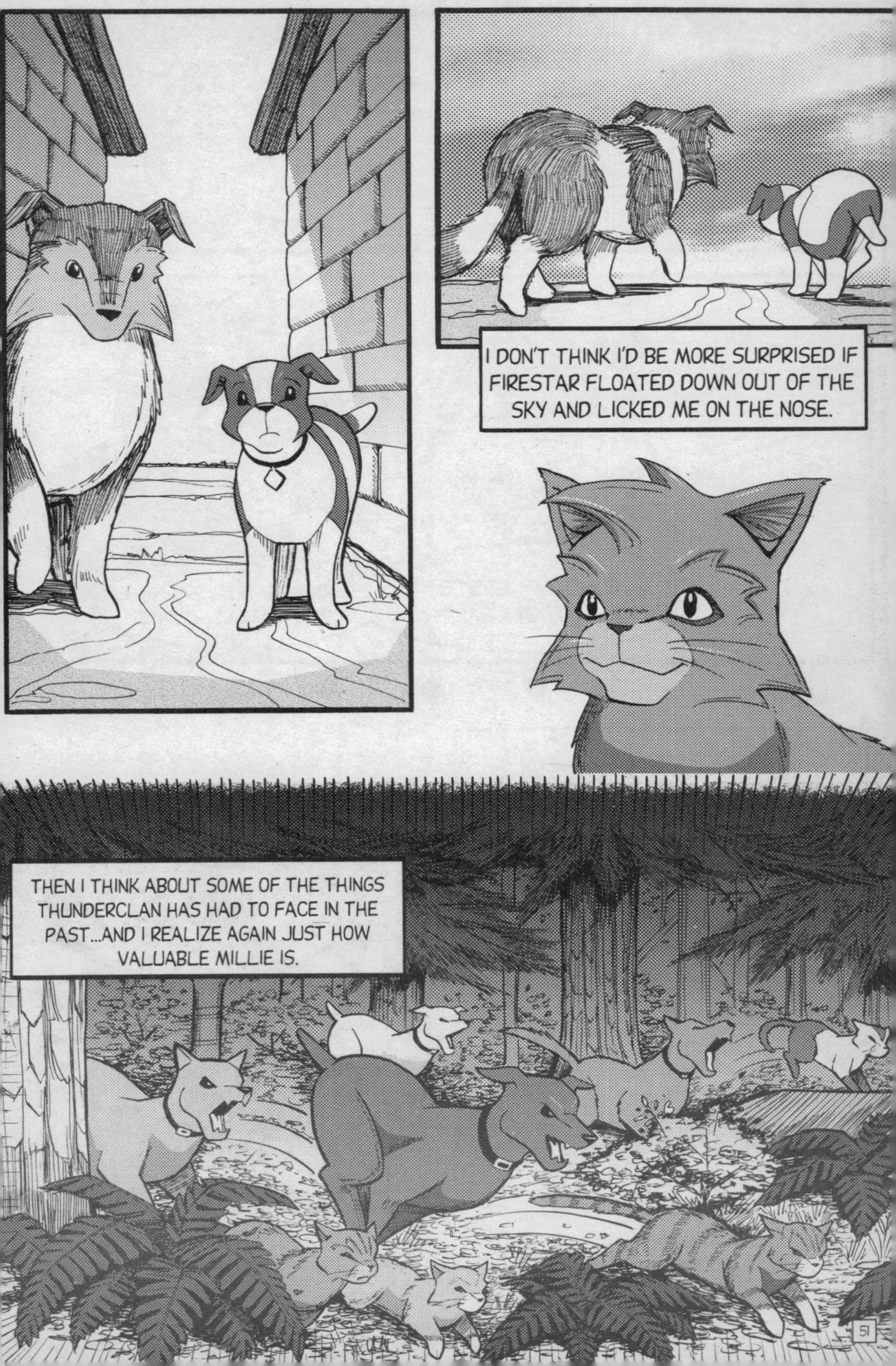
I DON'T THINK I'D BE MORE SURPRISED IF FIRESTAR FLOATED DOWN OUT OF THE SKY AND LICKED ME ON THE NOSE.
THEN I THINK ABOUT SOME OF THE THINGS THUNDERCLAN HAS HAD TO FACE IN THE PAST...AND I REALIZE AGAIN JUST HOW VALUABLE MILLIE IS.

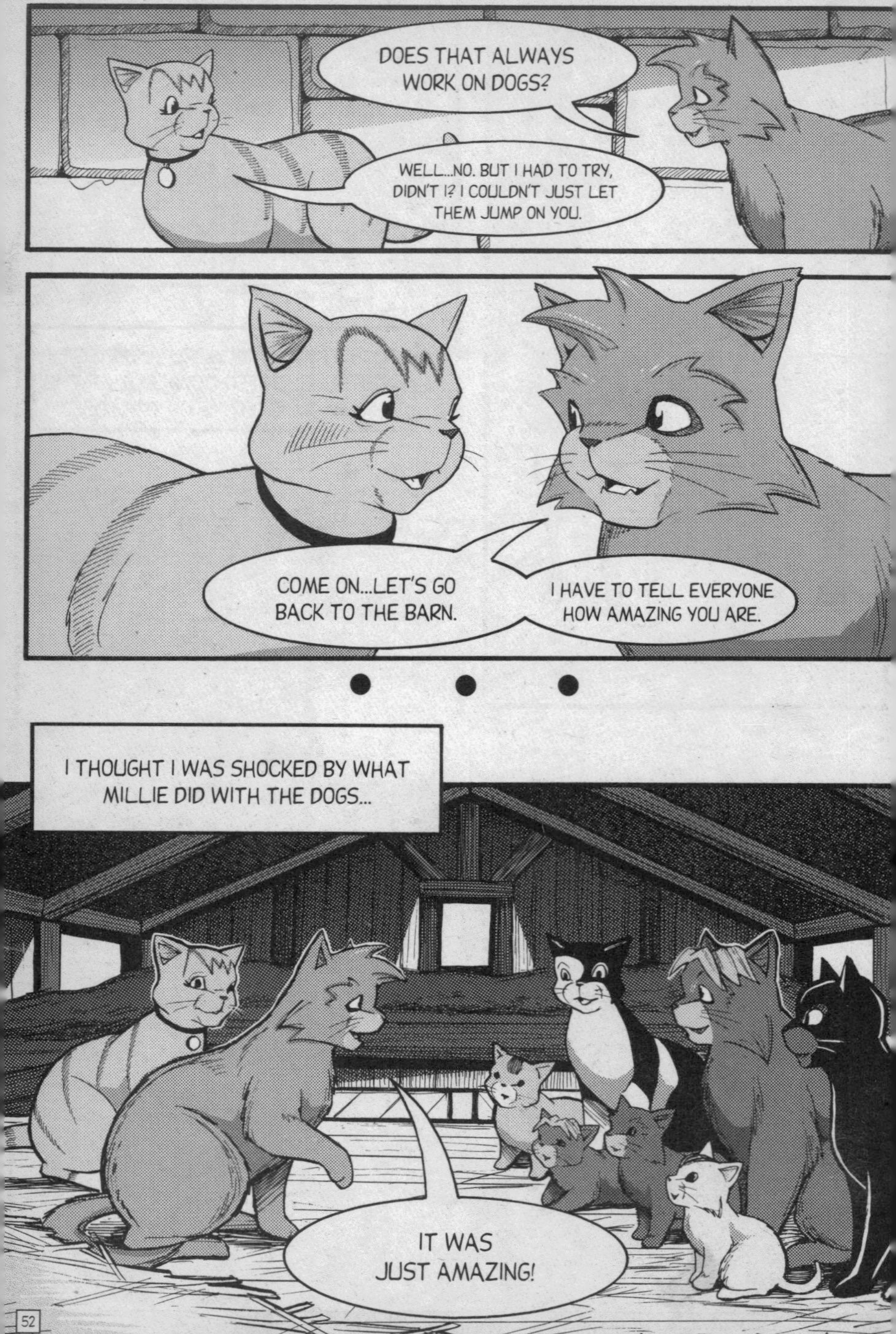

DOES THAT ALWAYS WORK ON DOGS?
WELL...NO. BUT I HAD TO TRY, DIDN'T I? I COULDN'T JUST LET THEM JUMP ON YOU.
COME ON...LET'S GO BACK TO THE BARN.
I HAVE TO TELL EVERYONE HOW AMAZING YOU ARE.
I THOUGHT I WAS SHOCKED BY WHAT MILLIE DID WITH THE DOGS...
IT WAS JUST AMAZING!

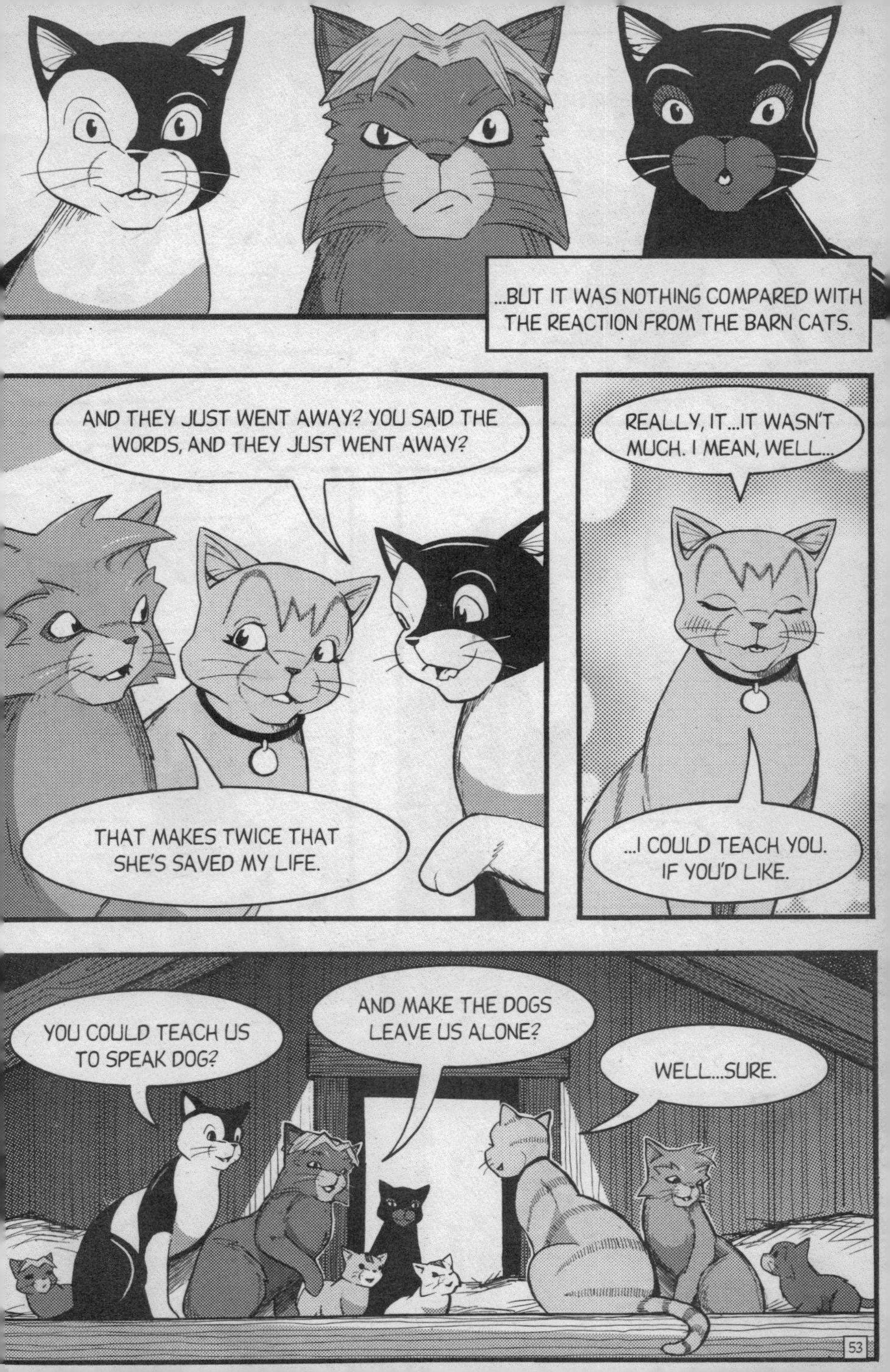
...BUT IT WAS NOTHING COMPARED WITH THE REACTION FROM THE BARN CATS.
AND THEY JUST WENT AWAY? YOU SAID THE WORDS, AND THEY JUST WENT AWAY?
THAT MAKES TWICE THAT SHE'S SAVED MY LIFE.
REALLY, IT...IT WASN'T MUCH. I MEAN, WELL...
...I COULD TEACH YOU. IF YOU'D LIKE.
YOU COULD TEACH US TO SPEAK DOG?
AND MAKE THE DOGS LEAVE US ALONE?
WELL...SURE.

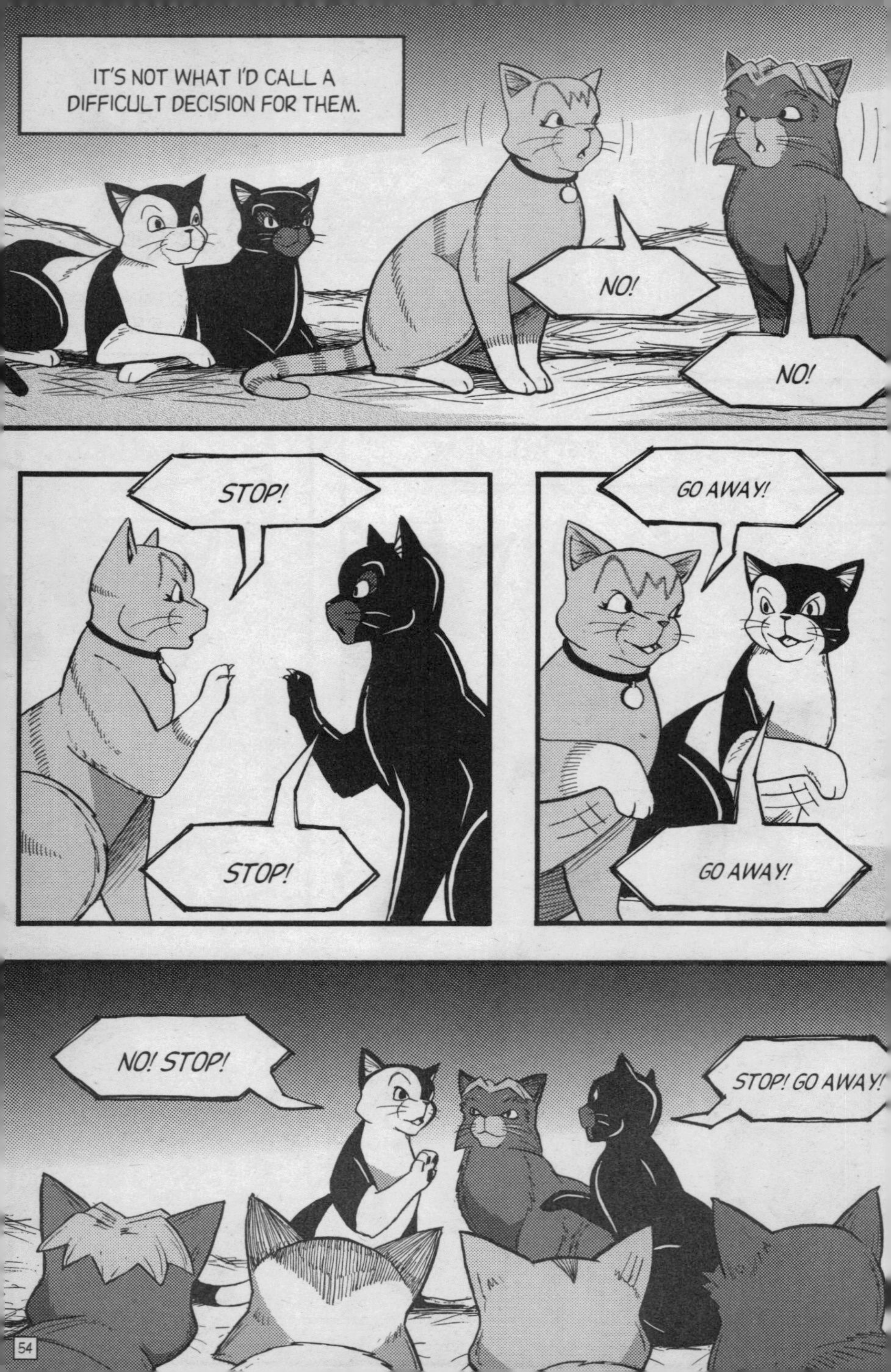
IT'S NOT WHAT I'D CALL A DIFFICULT DECISION FOR THEM.
NO!
NO!
STOP!
STOP!
GO AWAY!
GO AWAY!
NO! STOP!
STOP! GO AWAY!

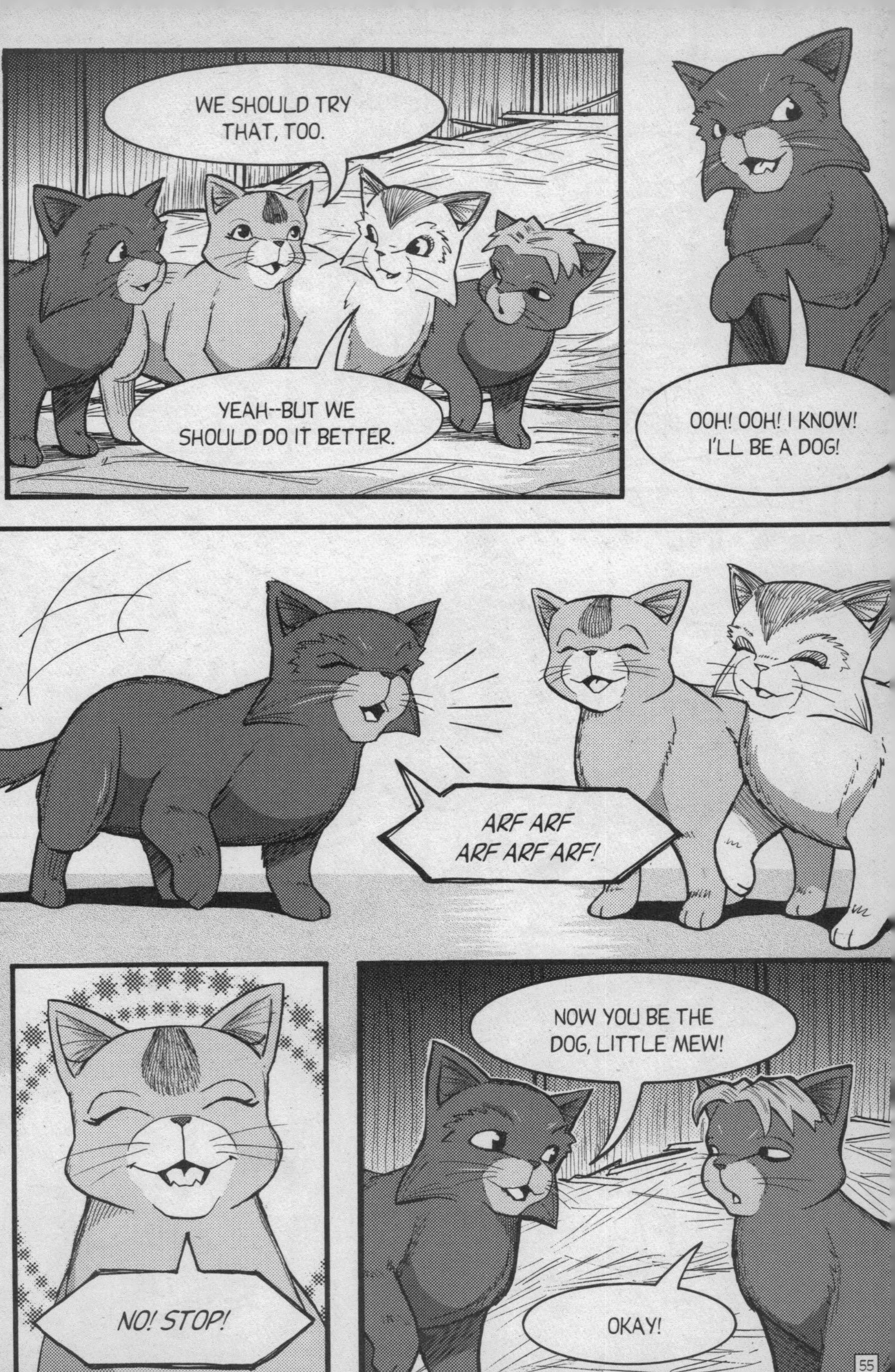
WE SHOULD TRY THAT, TOO.
YEAH--BUT WE SHOULD DO IT BETTER.
OOH! OOH! I KNOW! I'LL BE A DOG!
ARF ARF ARF ARF ARF!
NO! STOP!
NOW YOU BE THE DOG, LITTLE MEW!
OKAY!

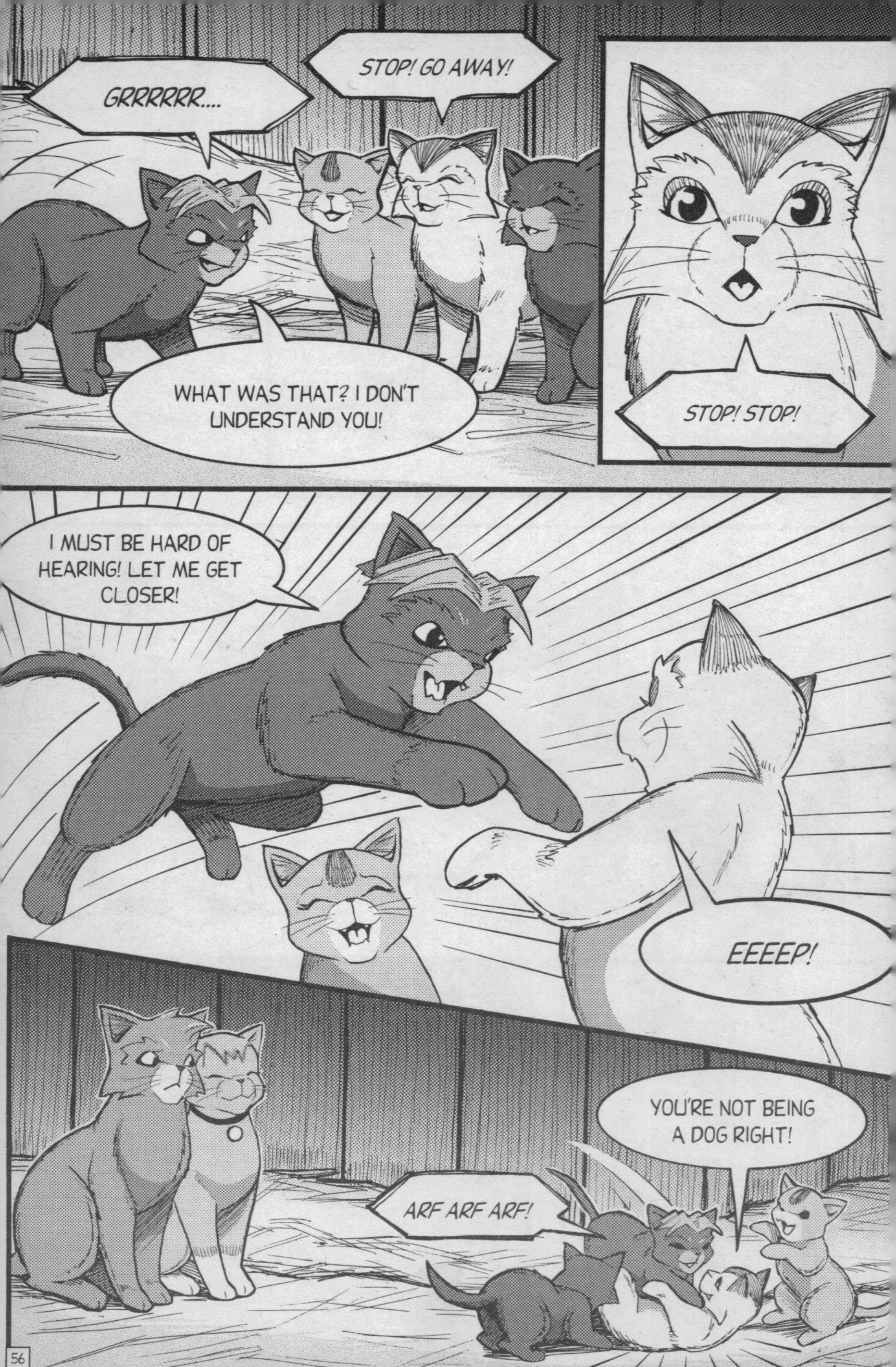
GRRRRRR....
STOP! GO AWAY!
WHAT WAS THAT? I DON'T UNDERSTAND YOU!
STOP! STOP!
I MUST BE HARD OF HEARING! LET ME GET CLOSER!
EEEEP!
YOU'RE NOT BEING A DOG RIGHT!
ARF ARF ARF!

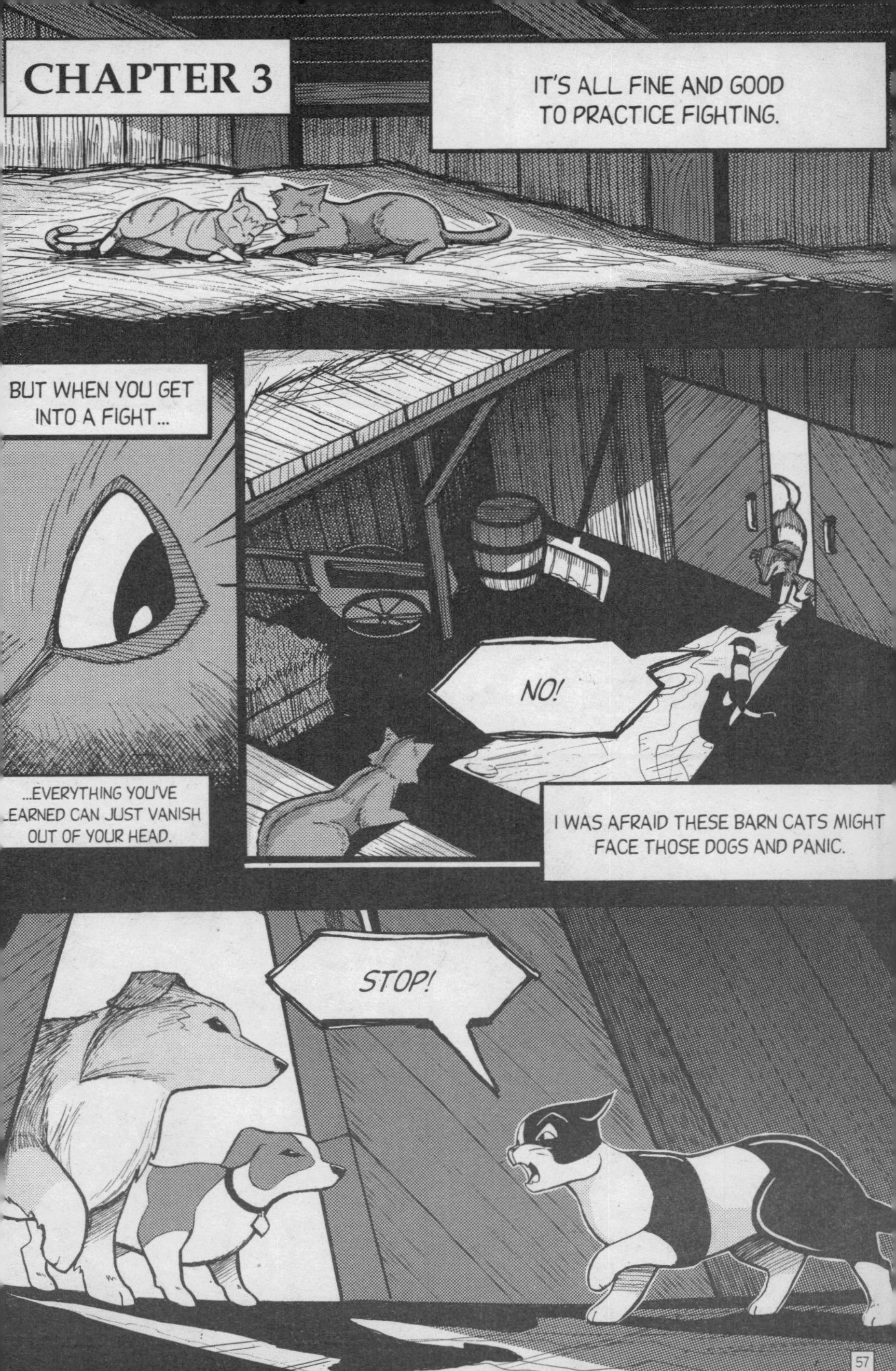
CHAPTER 3
IT'S ALL FINE AND GOOD TO PRACTICE FIGHTING.
BUT WHEN YOU GET INTO A FIGHT...
NO!
...EVERYTHING YOU'VE LEARNED CAN JUST VANISH OUT OF YOUR HEAD.
I WAS AFRAID THESE BARN CATS MIGHT FACE THOSE DOGS AND PANIC.
STOP!

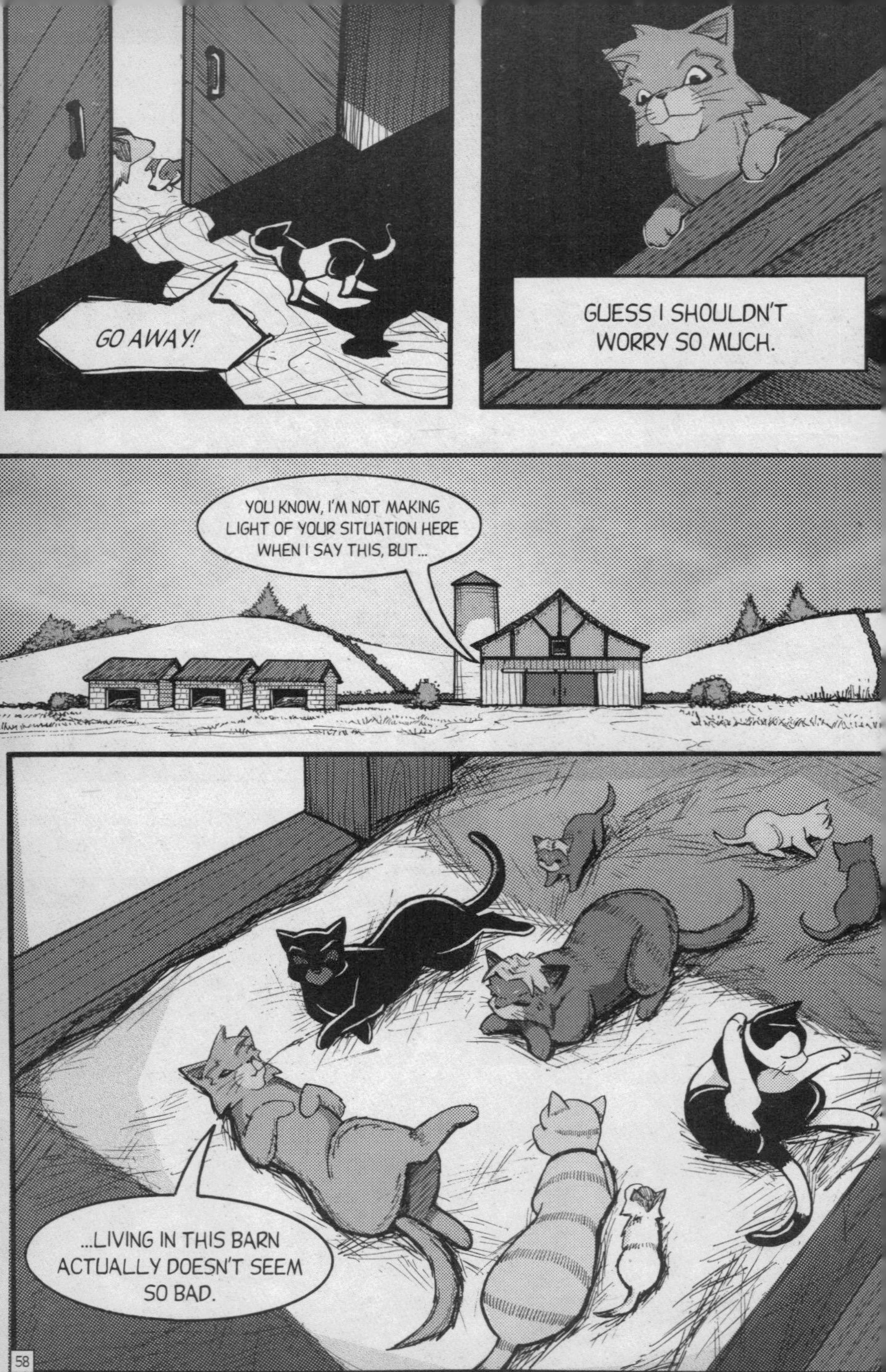
GO AWAY!
GUESS I SHOULDN'T WORRY SO MUCH.
YOU KNOW, I'M NOT MAKING LIGHT OF YOUR SITUATION HERE WHEN I SAY THIS, BUT...
...LIVING IN THIS BARN ACTUALLY DOESN'T SEEM SO BAD.

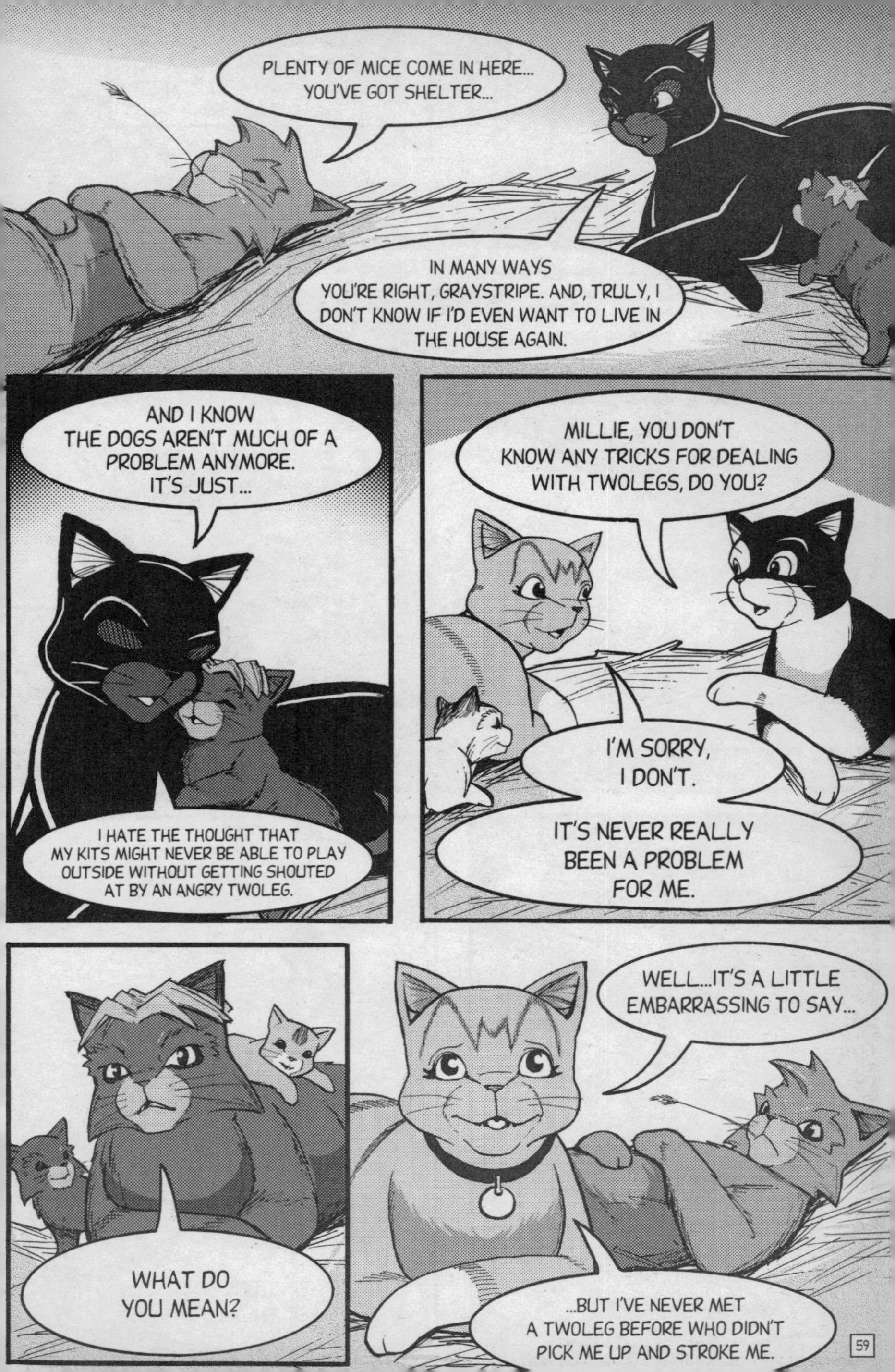
PLENTY OF MICE COME IN HERE... YOU'VE GOT SHELTER...
IN MANY WAYS YOU'RE RIGHT, GRAYSTRIPE. AND, TRULY, I DON'T KNOW IF I'D EVEN WANT TO LIVE IN THE HOUSE AGAIN.
AND I KNOW THE DOGS AREN'T MUCH OF A PROBLEM ANYMORE. IT'S JUST...
I HATE THE THOUGHT THAT MY KITS MIGHT NEVER BE ABLE TO PLAY OUTSIDE WITHOUT GETTING SHOUTED AT BY AN ANGRY TWOLEG.
MILLIE, YOU DON'T KNOW ANY TRICKS FOR DEALING WITH TWOLEGS, DO YOU?
I'M SORRY, I DON'T.
IT'S NEVER REALLY BEEN A PROBLEM FOR ME.
WHAT DO YOU MEAN?
WELL...IT'S A LITTLE EMBARRASSING TO SAY...
...BUT I'VE NEVER MET A TWOLEG BEFORE WHO DIDN'T PICK ME UP AND STROKE ME.

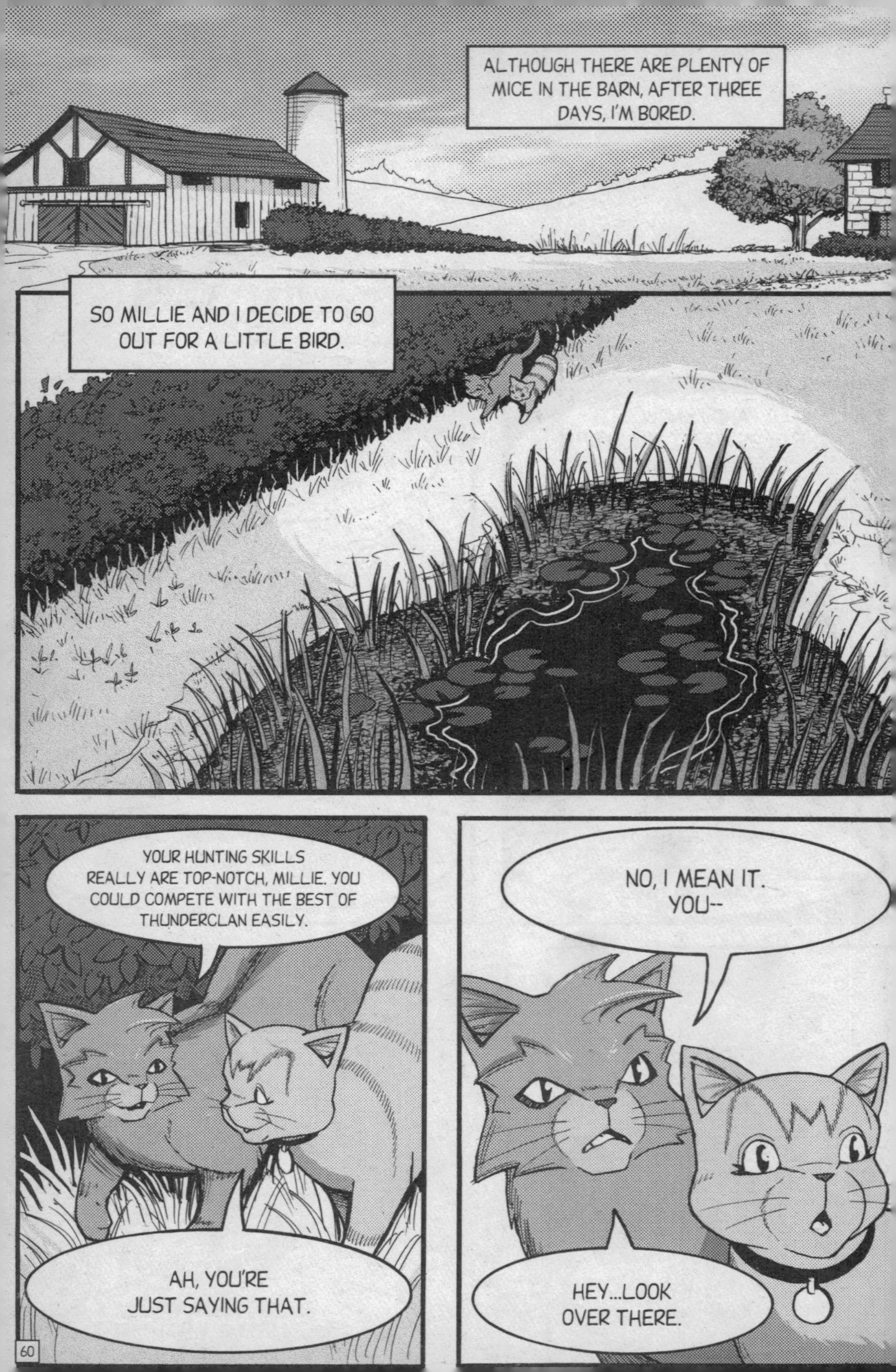
ALTHOUGH THERE ARE PLENTY OF MICE IN THE BARN, AFTER THREE DAYS, I'M BORED.
SO MILLIE AND I DECIDE TO GO OUT FOR A LITTLE BIRD.
YOUR HUNTING SKILLS REALLY ARE TOP-NOTCH, MILLIE. YOU COULD COMPETE WITH THE BEST OF THUNDERCLAN EASILY.
AH, YOU'RE JUST SAYING THAT.
NO, I MEAN IT. YOU--
HEY...LOOK OVER THERE.

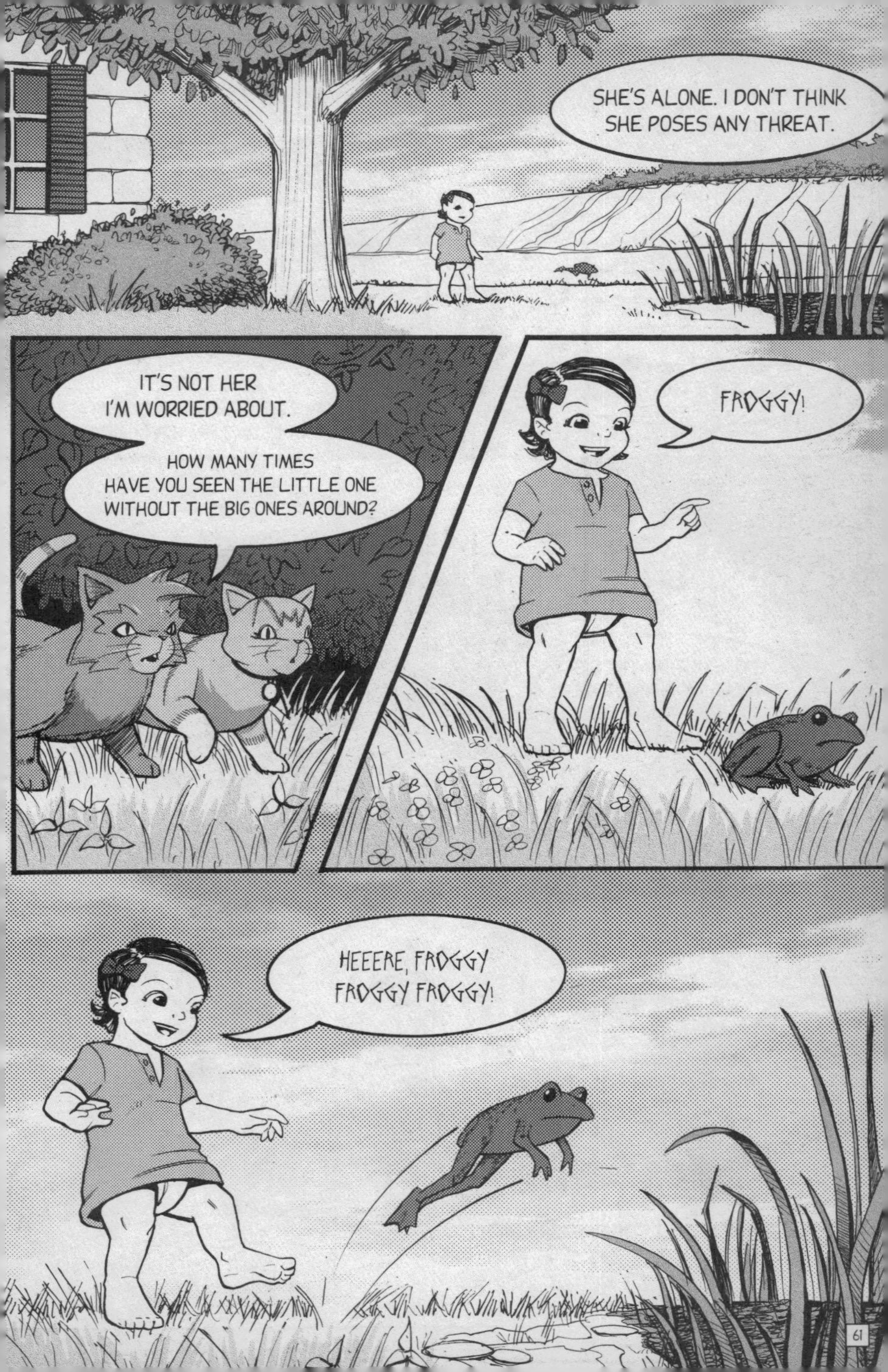
SHE'S ALONE. I DON'T THINK SHE POSES ANY THREAT.
IT'S NOT HER I'M WORRIED ABOUT.
HOW MANY TIMES HAVE YOU SEEN THE LITTLE ONE WITHOUT THE BIG ONES AROUND?
FROGGY!
HEEERE, FROGGY FROGGY FROGGY!

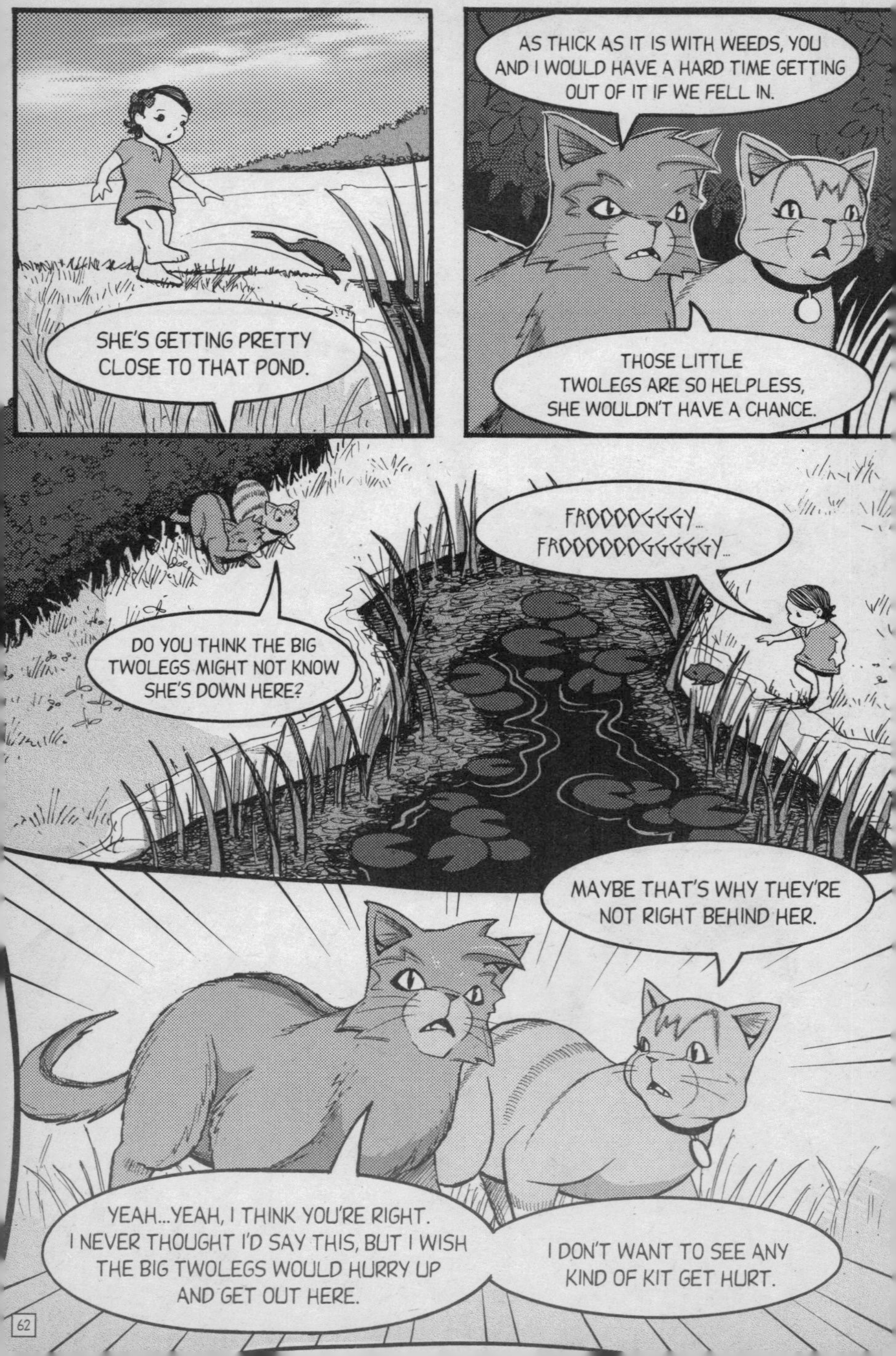

SHE'S GETTING PRETTY CLOSE TO THAT POND.
AS THICK AS IT IS WITH WEEDS, YOU AND I WOULD HAVE A HARD TIME GETTING OUT OF IT IF WE FELL IN.
THOSE LITTLE TWOLEGS ARE SO HELPLESS, SHE WOULDN'T HAVE A CHANCE.
FROOOOGGGY... FROOOOOOGGGGGY...
DO YOU THINK THE BIG TWOLEGS MIGHT NOT KNOW SHE'S DOWN HERE?
MAYBE THAT'S WHY THEY'RE NOT RIGHT BEHIND HER.
YEAH...YEAH, I THINK YOU'RE RIGHT. I NEVER THOUGHT I'D SAY THIS, BUT I WISH THE BIG TWOLEGS WOULD HURRY UP AND GET OUT HERE.
I DON'T WANT TO SEE ANY KIND OF KIT GET HURT.

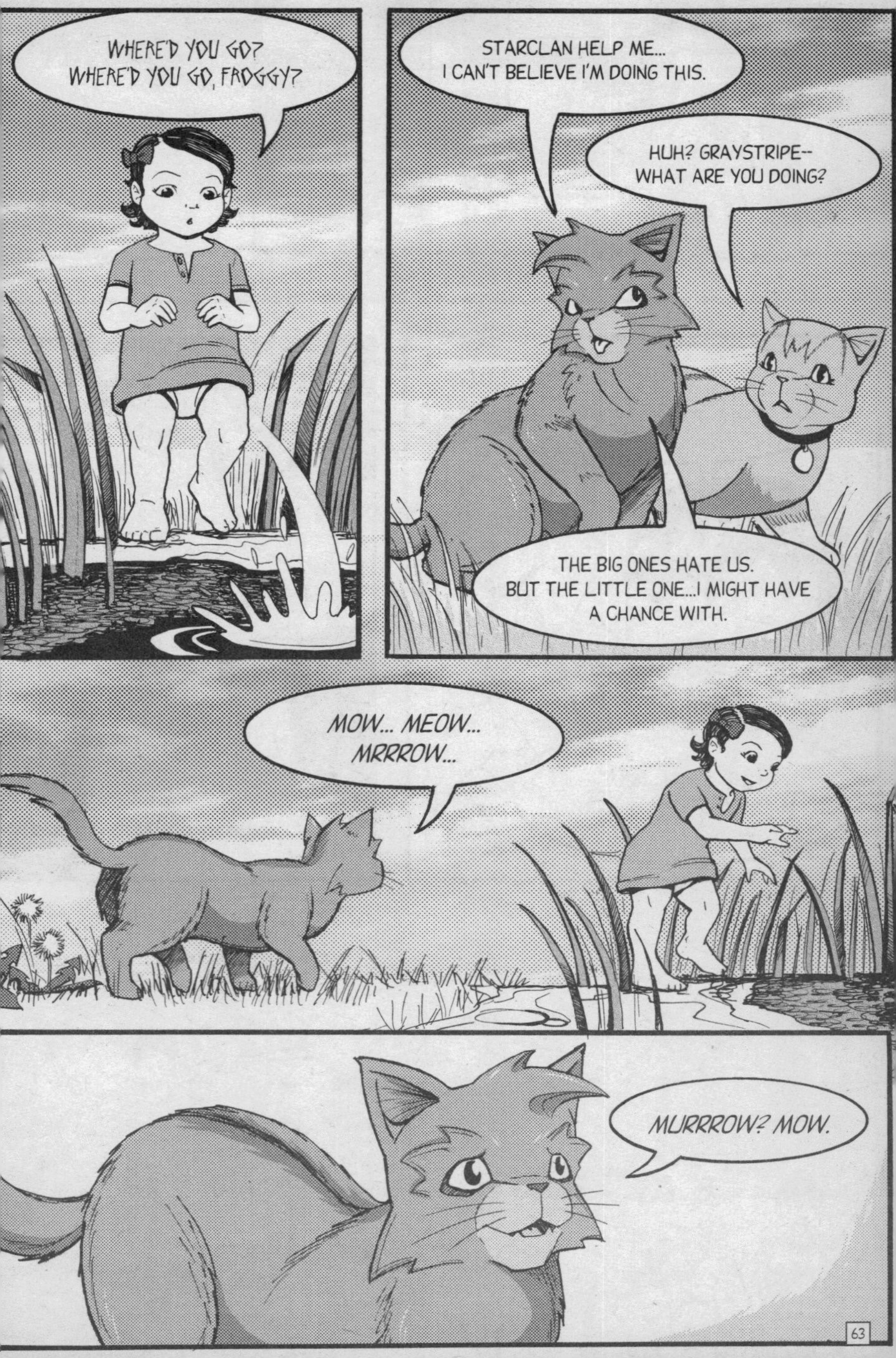
WHERE'D YOU GO?
WHERE'D YOU GO, FROGGY?
STARCLAN HELP ME... I CAN'T BELIEVE I'M DOING THIS.
HUH? GRAYSTRIPE-- WHAT ARE YOU DOING?
THE BIG ONES HATE US. BUT THE LITTLE ONE...I MIGHT HAVE A CHANCE WITH.
MOW... MEOW... MRRROW...
MURRROW? MOW.

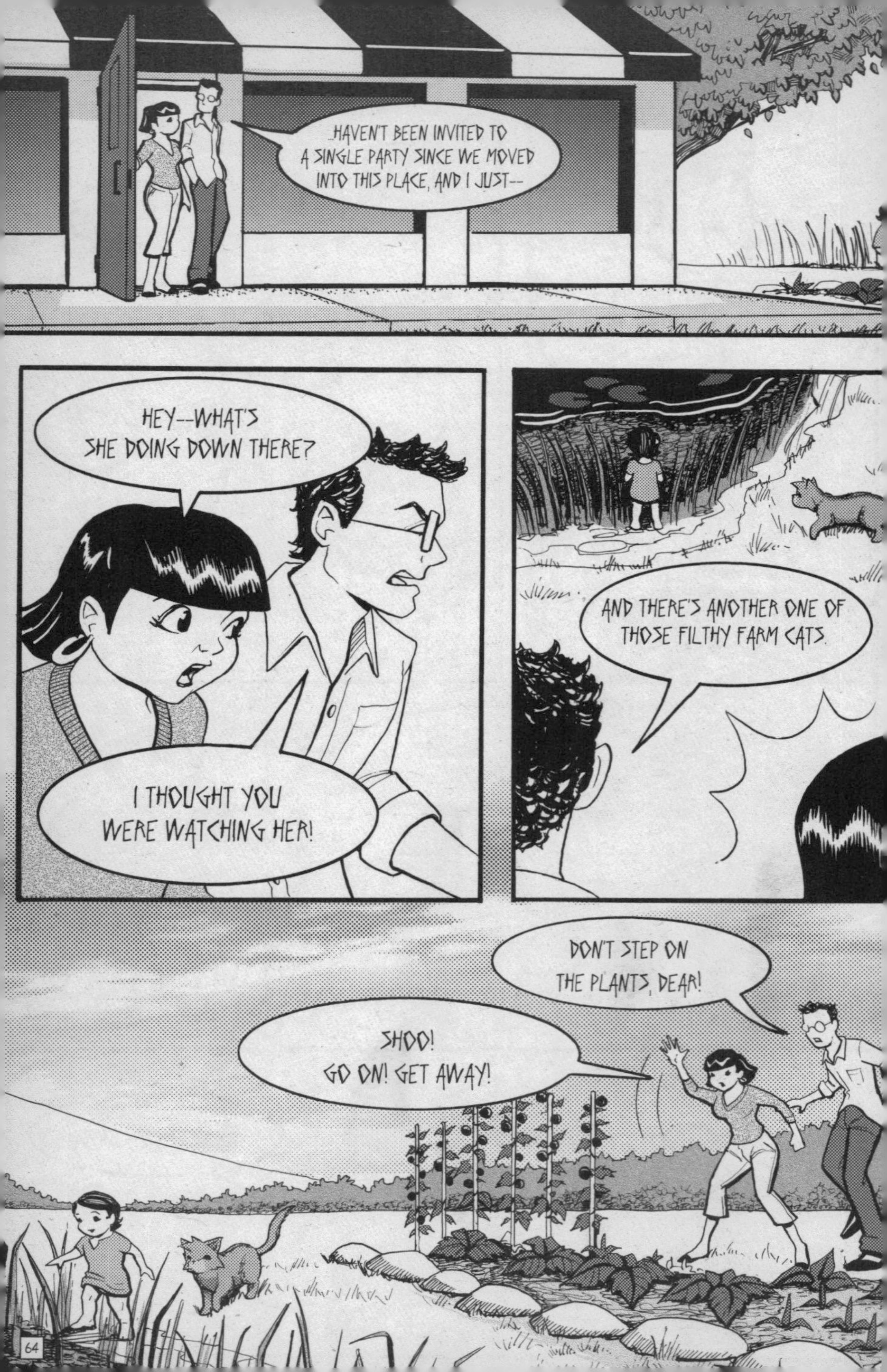
...HAVEN'T BEEN INVITED TO A SINGLE PARTY SINCE WE MOVED INTO THIS PLACE, AND I JUST--
HEY--WHAT'S SHE DOING DOWN THERE?
I THOUGHT YOU WERE WATCHING HER!
AND THERE'S ANOTHER ONE OF THOSE FILTHY FARM CATS.
DON'T STEP ON THE PLANTS, DEAR!
SHOO! GO ON! GET AWAY!

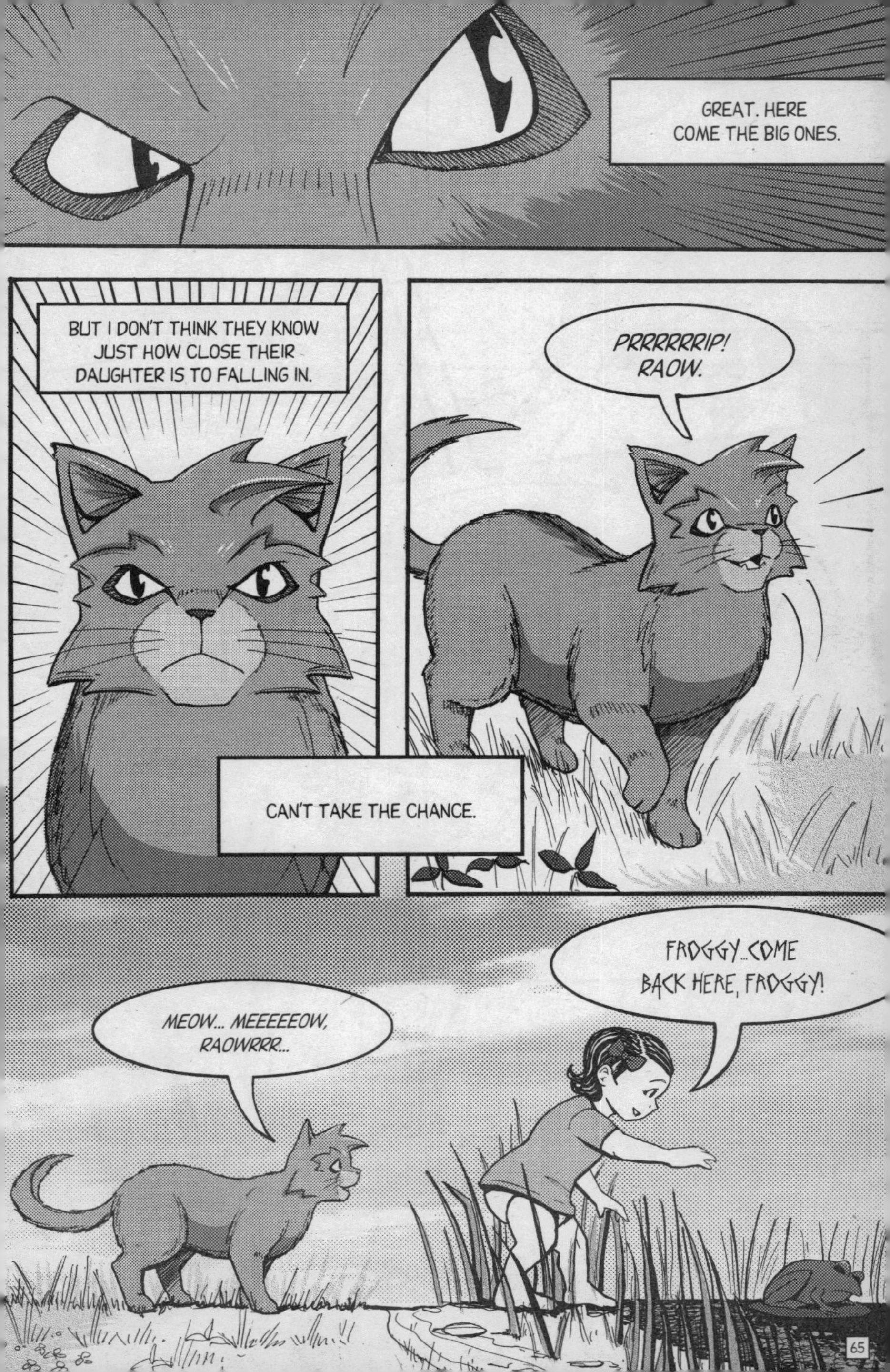
GREAT. HERE COME THE BIG ONES.
BUT I DON'T THINK THEY KNOW JUST HOW CLOSE THEIR DAUGHTER IS TO FALLING IN.
PRRRRRRIP! RAOW.
CAN'T TAKE THE CHANCE.
FROGGY...COME BACK HERE, FROGGY!
MEOW... MEEEEEOW, RAOWRRR...

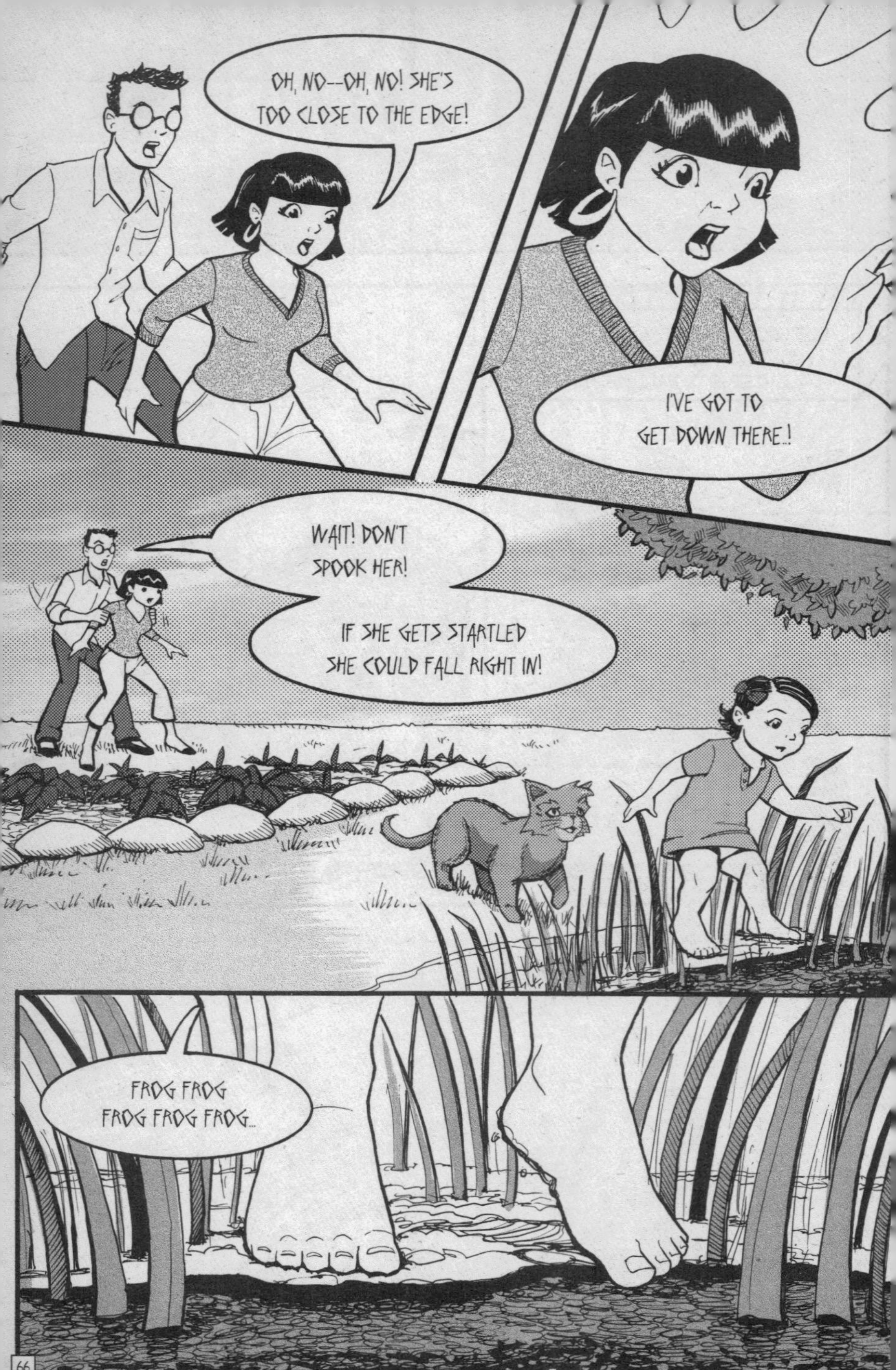
OH, NO--OH, NO! SHE'S TOO CLOSE TO THE EDGE!
I'VE GOT TO GET DOWN THERE..!
WAIT! DON'T SPOOK HER!
IF SHE GETS STARTLED SHE COULD FALL RIGHT IN!
FROG FROG FROG FROG FROG...

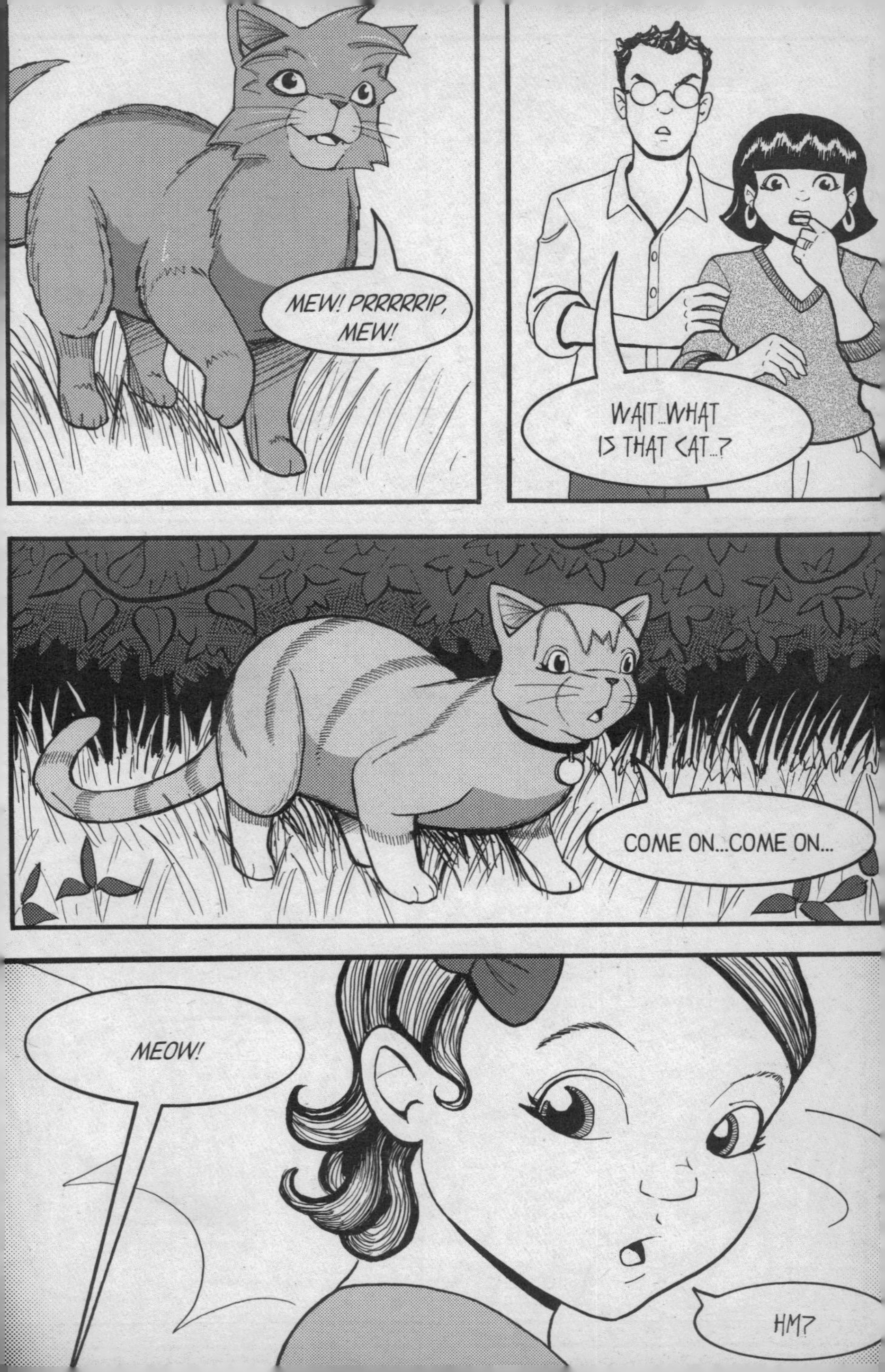
MEW! PRRRRRIP, MEW!
WAIT...WHAT IS THAT CAT...?
COME ON...COME ON...
MEOW!
HM?

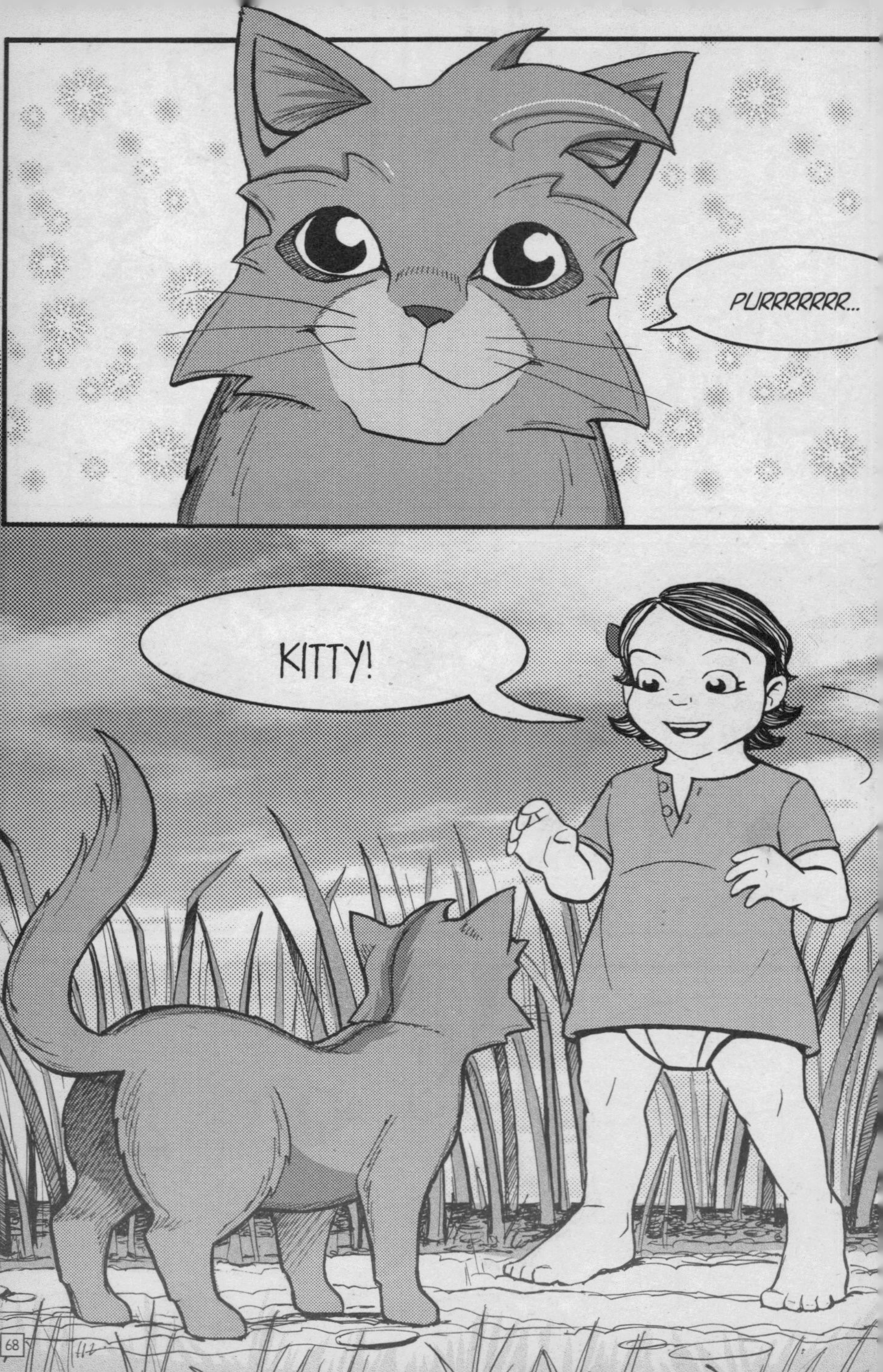
PURRRRRRR...
KITTY!

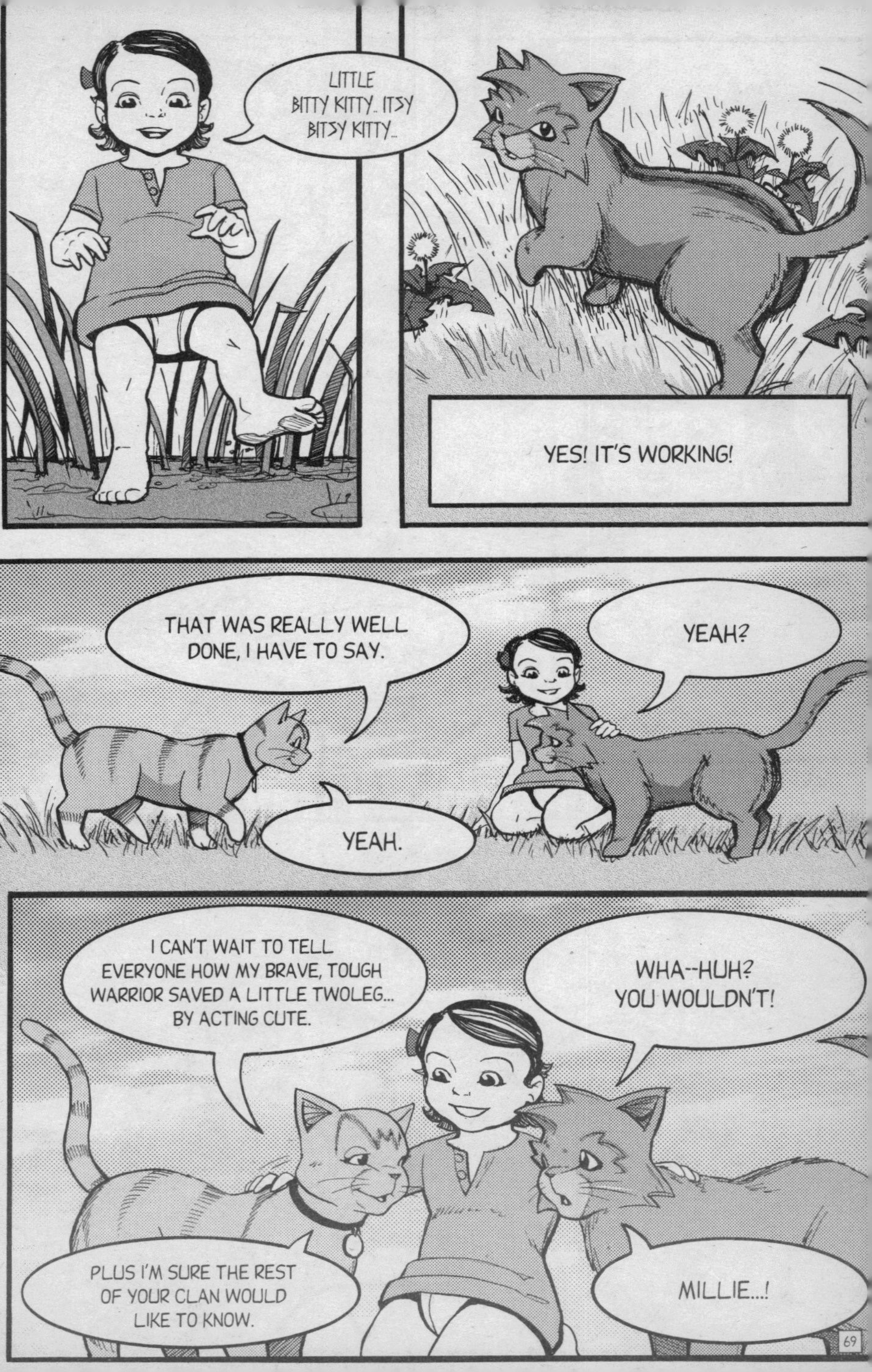
LITTLE BITTY KITTY.. ITSY BITSY KITTY...
YES! IT'S WORKING!
THAT WAS REALLY WELL DONE, I HAVE TO SAY.
YEAH?
YEAH.
I CAN'T WAIT TO TELL EVERYONE HOW MY BRAVE, TOUGH WARRIOR SAVED A LITTLE TWOLEG... BY ACTING CUTE.
WHA--HUH? YOU WOULDN'T!
PLUS I'M SURE THE REST OF YOUR CLAN WOULD LIKE TO KNOW.
MILLIE...!

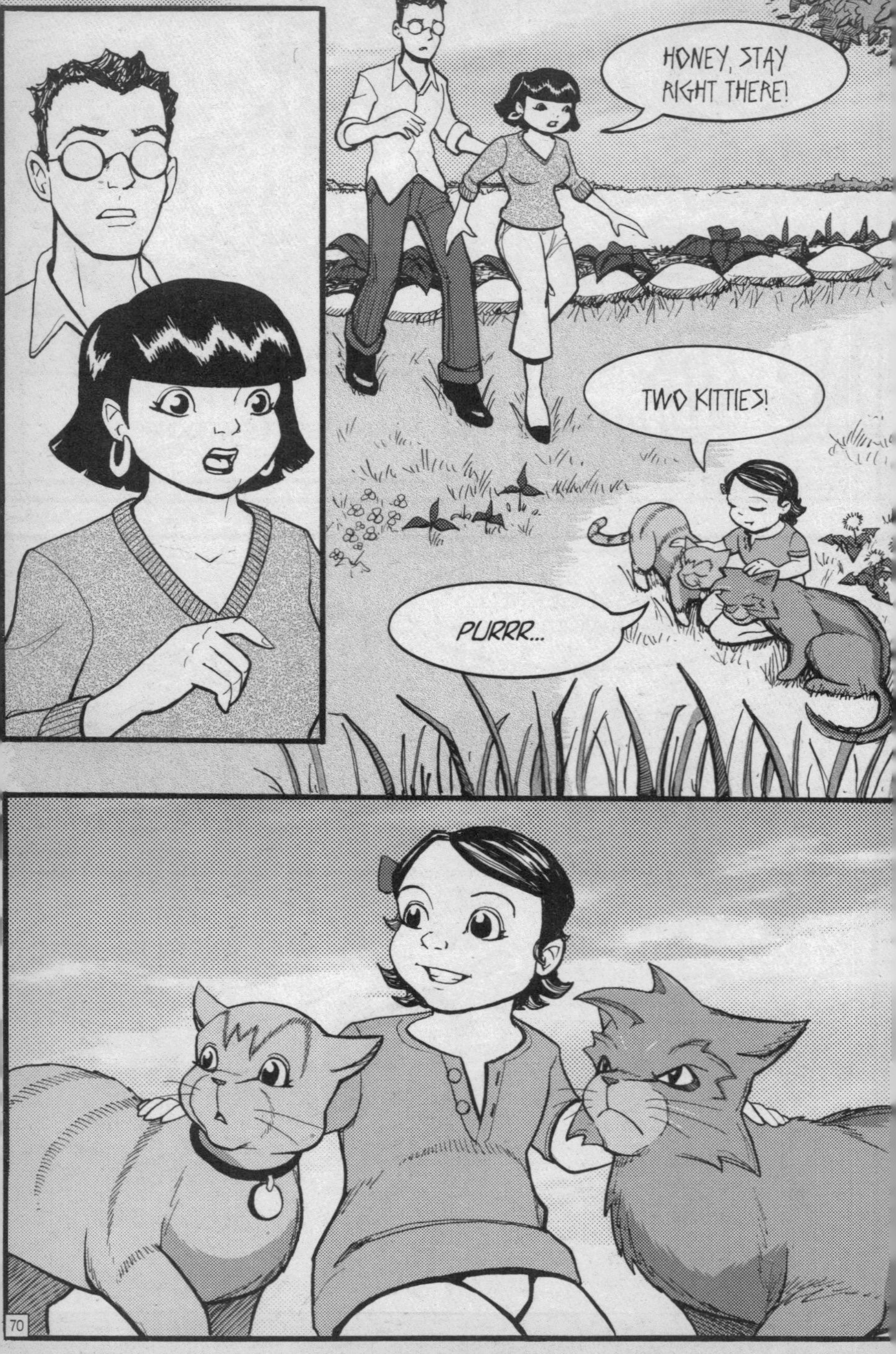
HONEY, STAY RIGHT THERE!
TWO KITTIES!
PURRR...

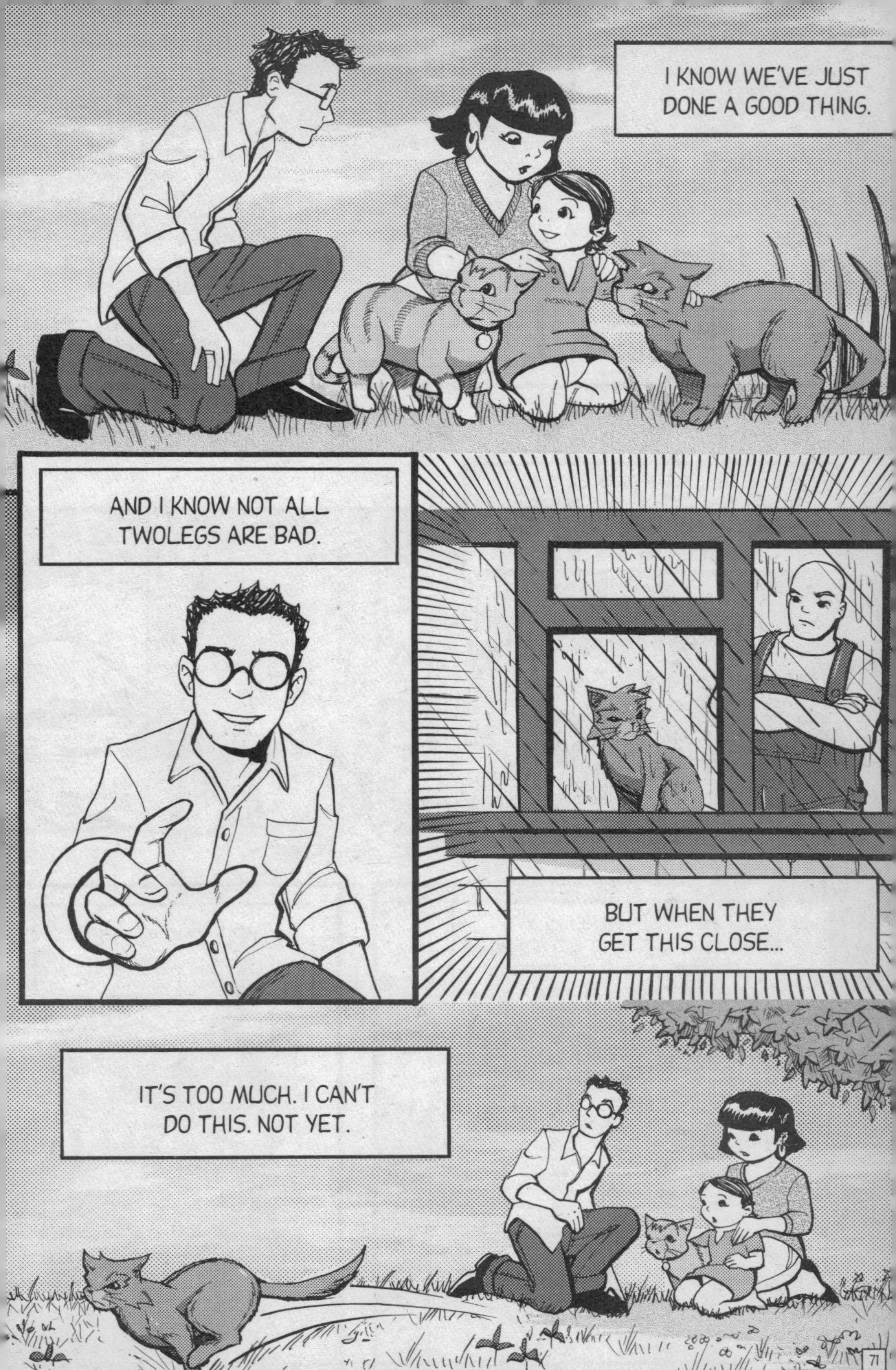
I KNOW WE'VE JUST DONE A GOOD THING.
AND I KNOW NOT ALL TWOLEGS ARE BAD.
BUT WHEN THEY GET THIS CLOSE...
IT'S TOO MUCH. I CAN'T DO THIS. NOT YET.

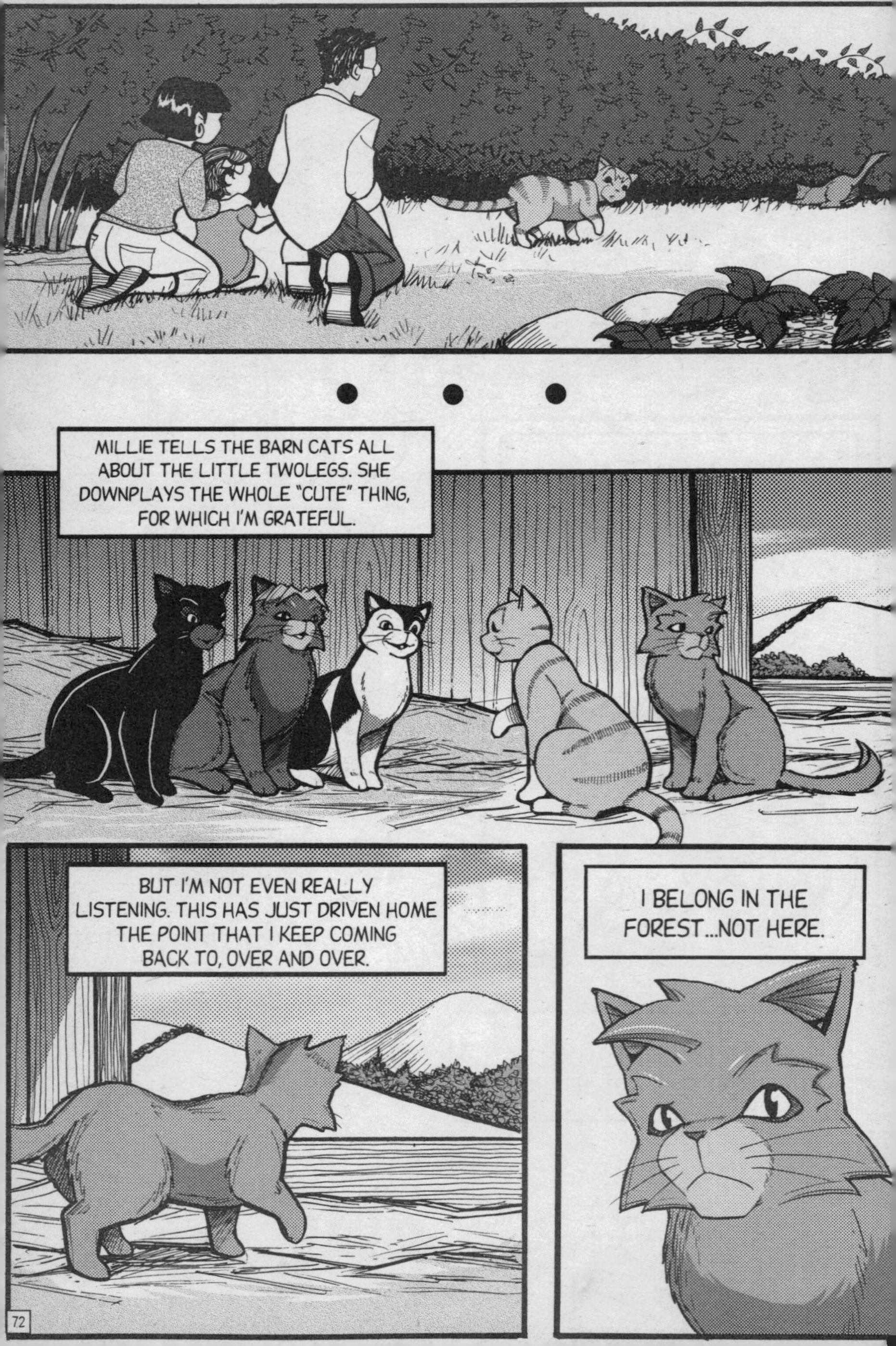

MILLIE TELLS THE BARN CATS ALL ABOUT THE LITTLE TWOLEGS. SHE DOWNPLAYS THE WHOLE "CUTE" THING, FOR WHICH I'M GRATEFUL.
BUT I'M NOT EVEN REALLY LISTENING. THIS HAS JUST DRIVEN HOME THE POINT THAT I KEEP COMING BACK TO, OVER AND OVER.
I BELONG IN THE FOREST...NOT HERE.

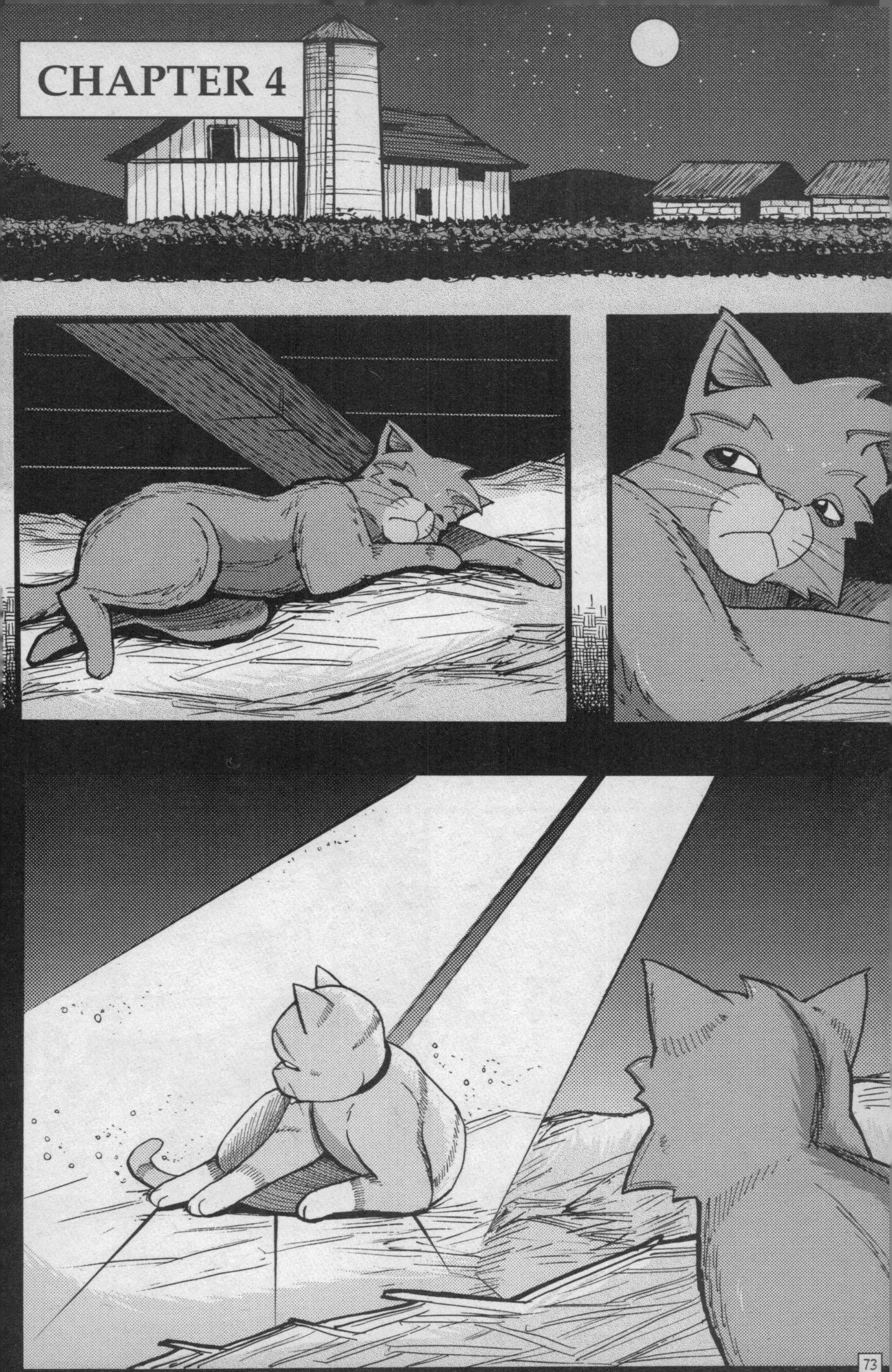
CHAPTER 4

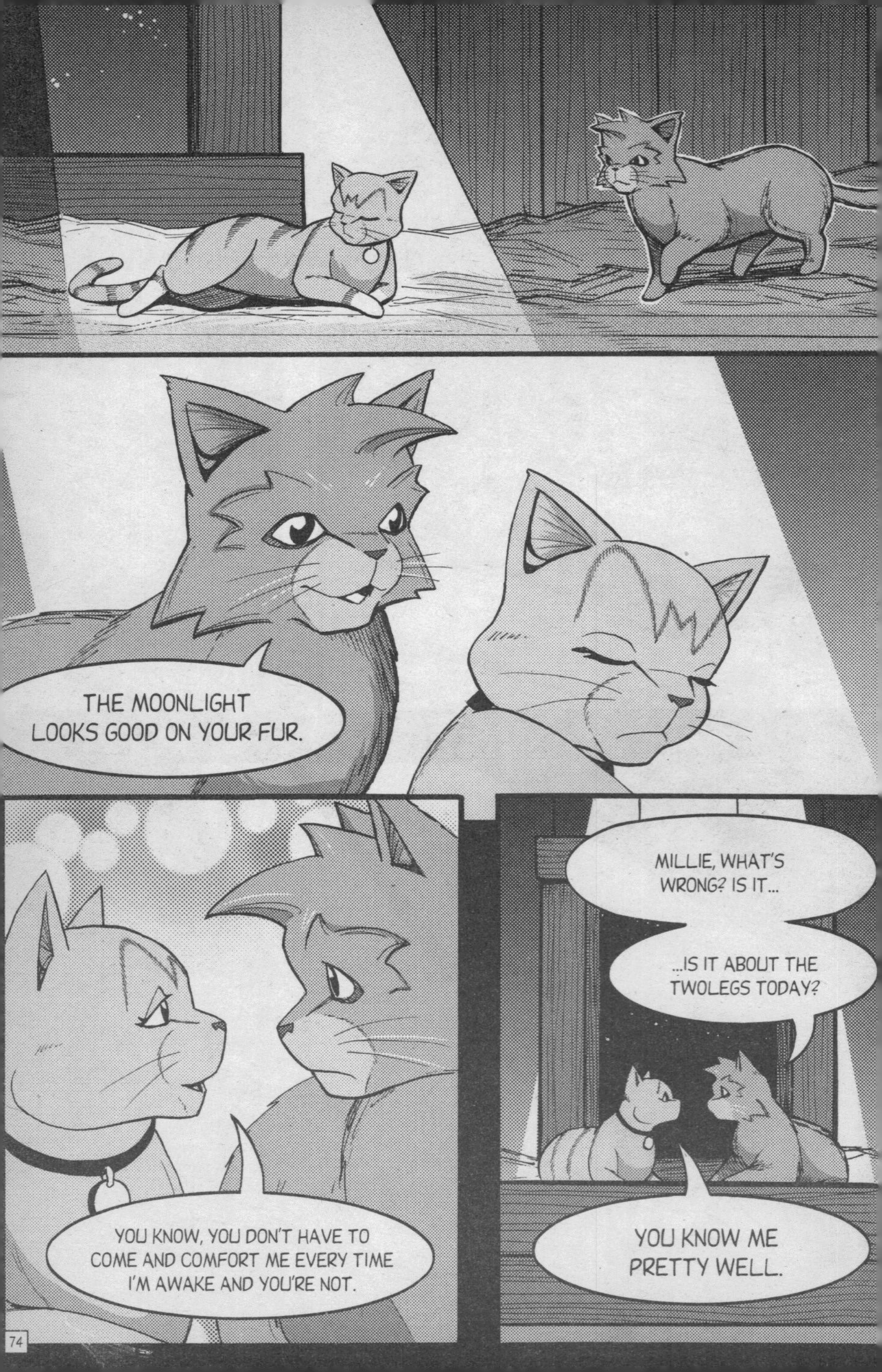
THE MOONLIGHT LOOKS GOOD ON YOUR FUR.
YOU KNOW, YOU DON'T HAVE TO COME AND COMFORT ME EVERY TIME I'M AWAKE AND YOU'RE NOT.
MILLIE, WHAT'S WRONG? IS IT...
...IS IT ABOUT THE TWOLEGS TODAY?
YOU KNOW ME PRETTY WELL.

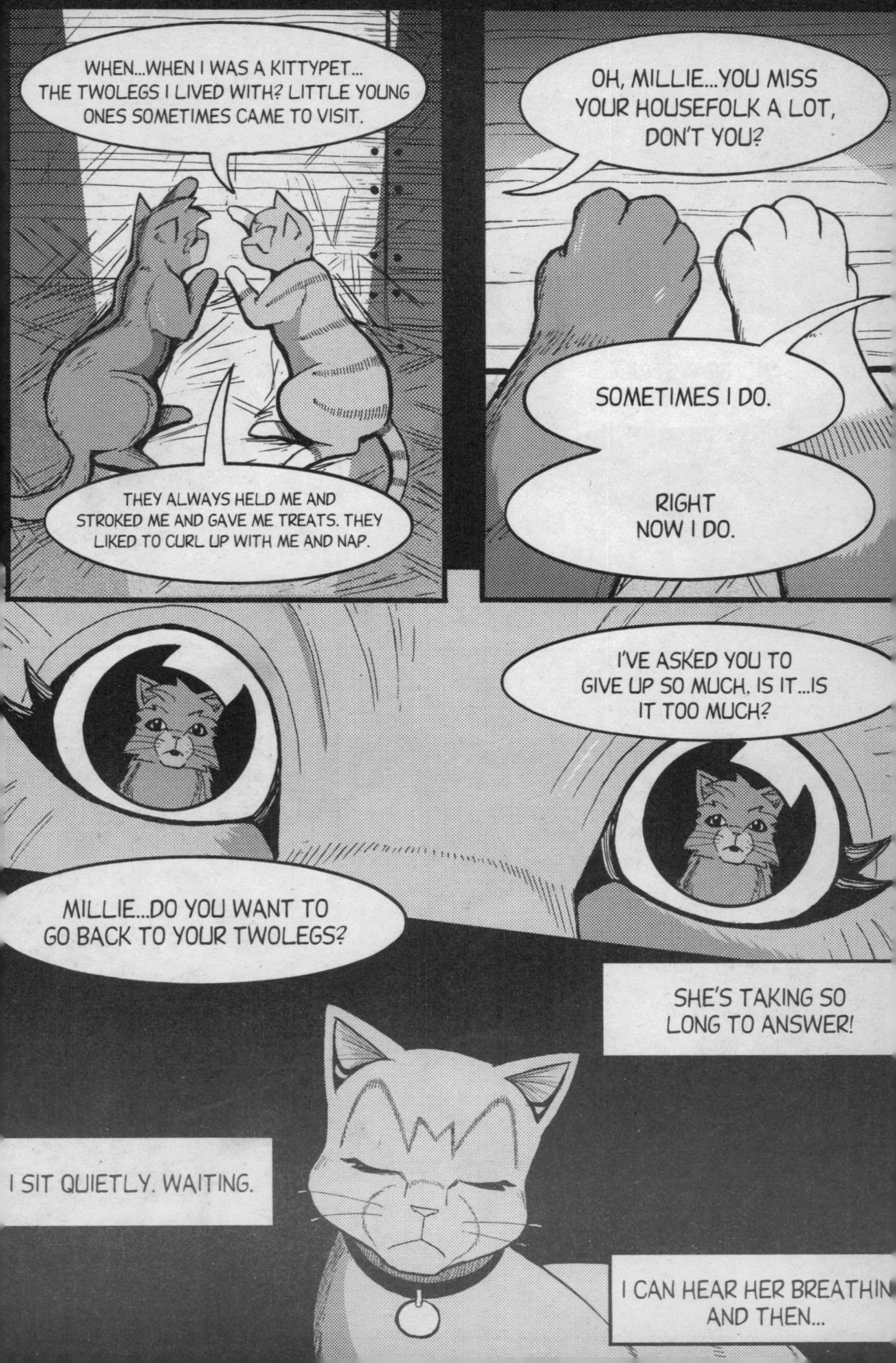
WHEN...WHEN I WAS A KITTYPET... THE TWOLEGS I LIVED WITH? LITTLE YOUNG ONES SOMETIMES CAME TO VISIT.
THEY ALWAYS HELD ME AND STROKED ME AND GAVE ME TREATS. THEY LIKED TO CURL UP WITH ME AND NAP.
OH, MILLIE...YOU MISS YOUR HOUSEFOLK A LOT, DON'T YOU?
SOMETIMES I DO.
RIGHT NOW I DO.
I'VE ASKED YOU TO GIVE UP SO MUCH. IS IT...IS IT TOO MUCH?
MILLIE...DO YOU WANT TO GO BACK TO YOUR TWOLEGS?
SHE'S TAKING SO LONG TO ANSWER!
I SIT QUIETLY. WAITING.
I CAN HEAR HER BREATHIN
AND THEN...

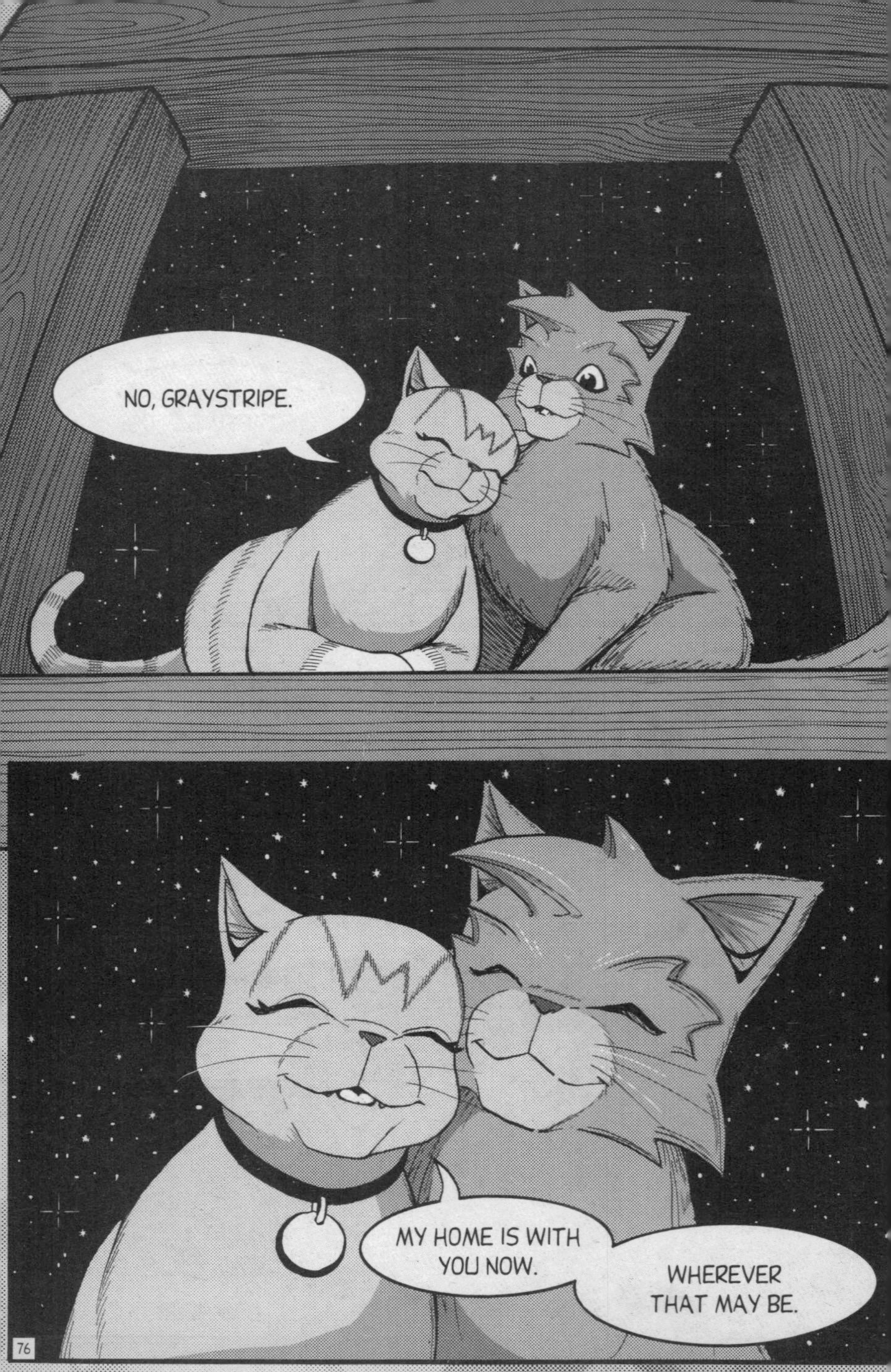
NO, GRAYSTRIPE.
MY HOME IS WITH YOU NOW.
WHEREVER THAT MAY BE.

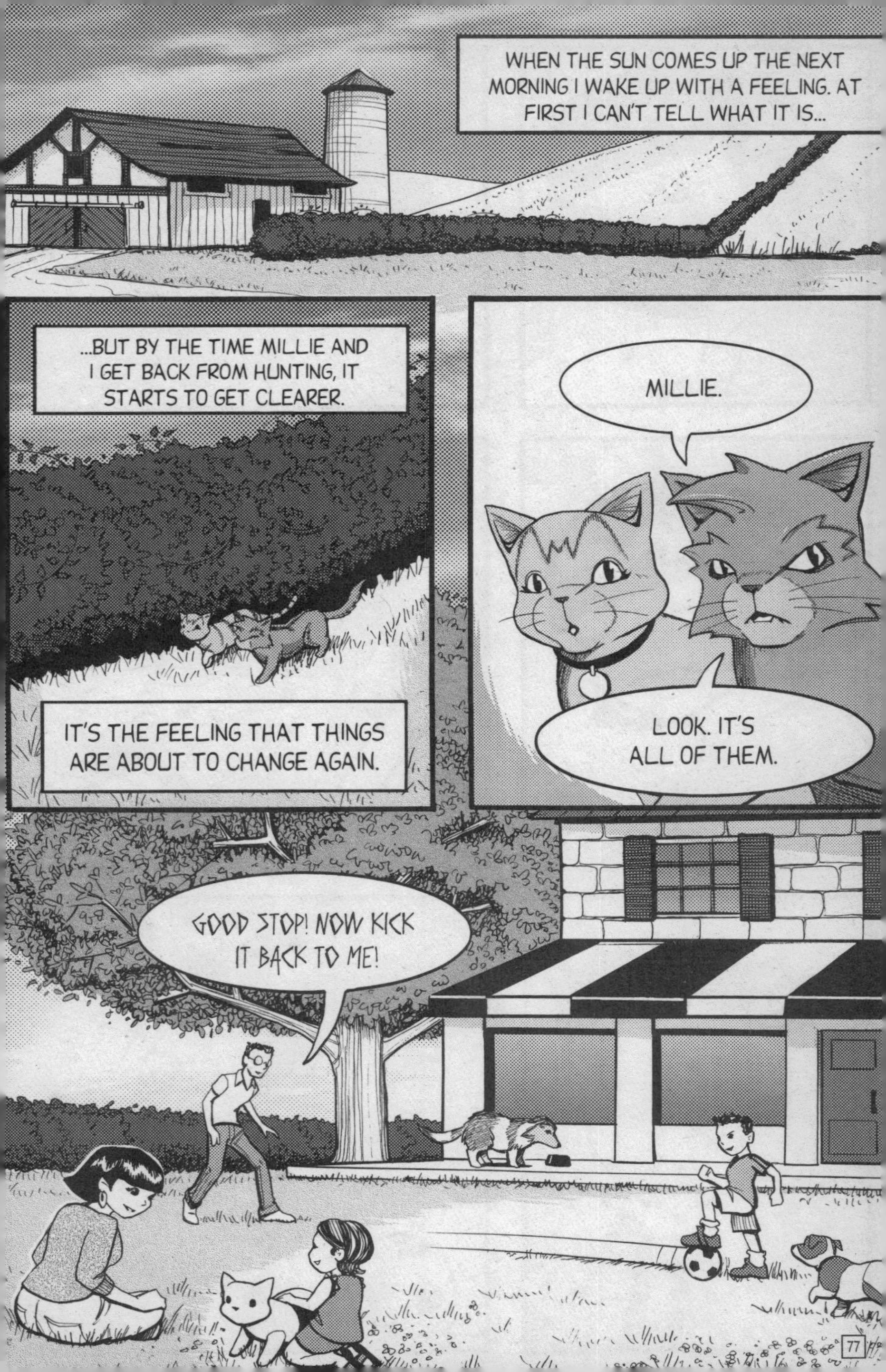
WHEN THE SUN COMES UP THE NEXT MORNING I WAKE UP WITH A FEELING. AT FIRST I CAN'T TELL WHAT IT IS...
...BUT BY THE TIME MILLIE AND I GET BACK FROM HUNTING, IT STARTS TO GET CLEARER.
IT'S THE FEELING THAT THINGS ARE ABOUT TO CHANGE AGAIN.
MILLIE.
LOOK. IT'S ALL OF THEM.
GOOD STOP! NOW KICK IT BACK TO ME!

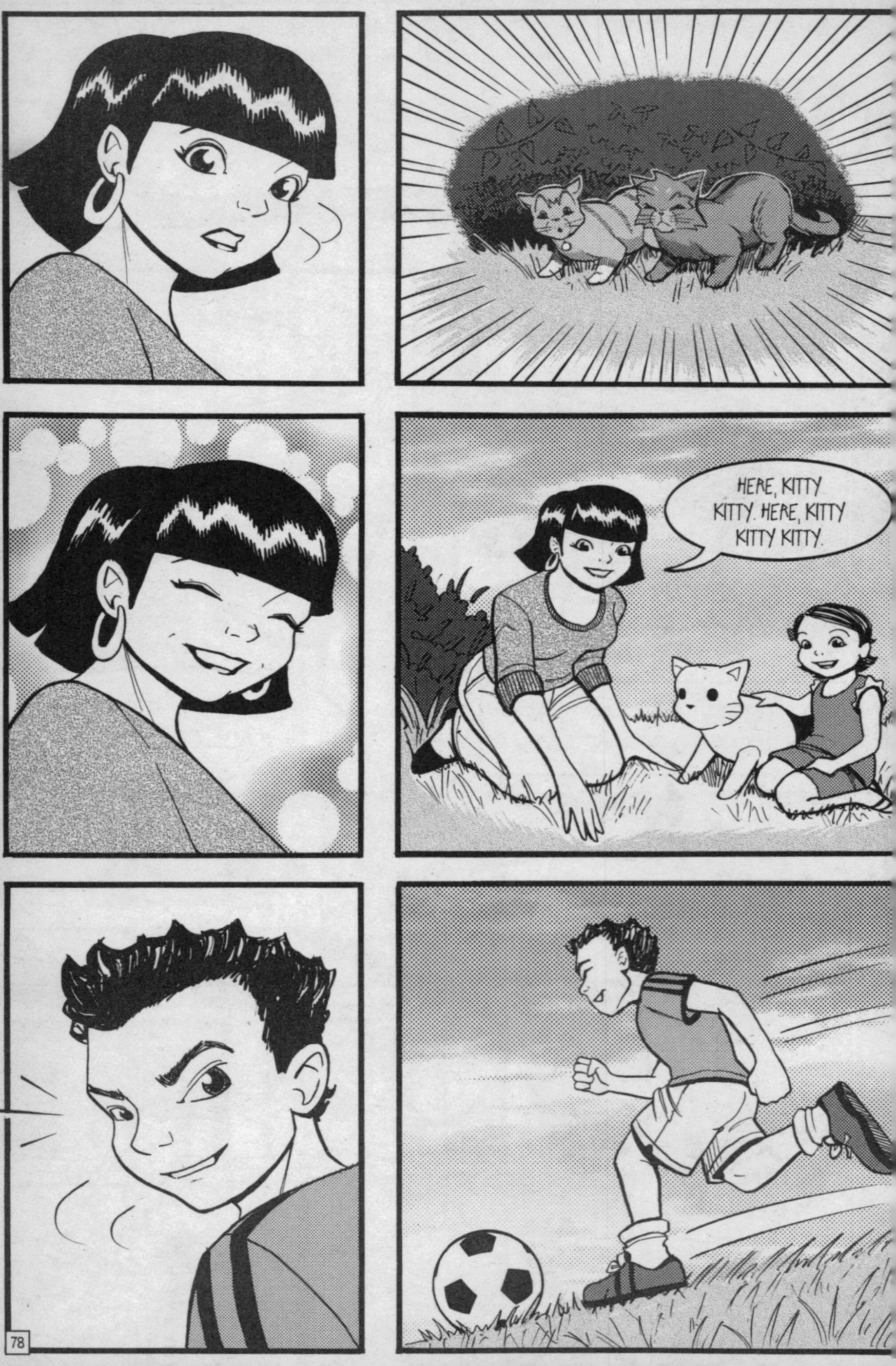
HERE, KITTY KITTY. HERE, KITTY KITTY KITTY.

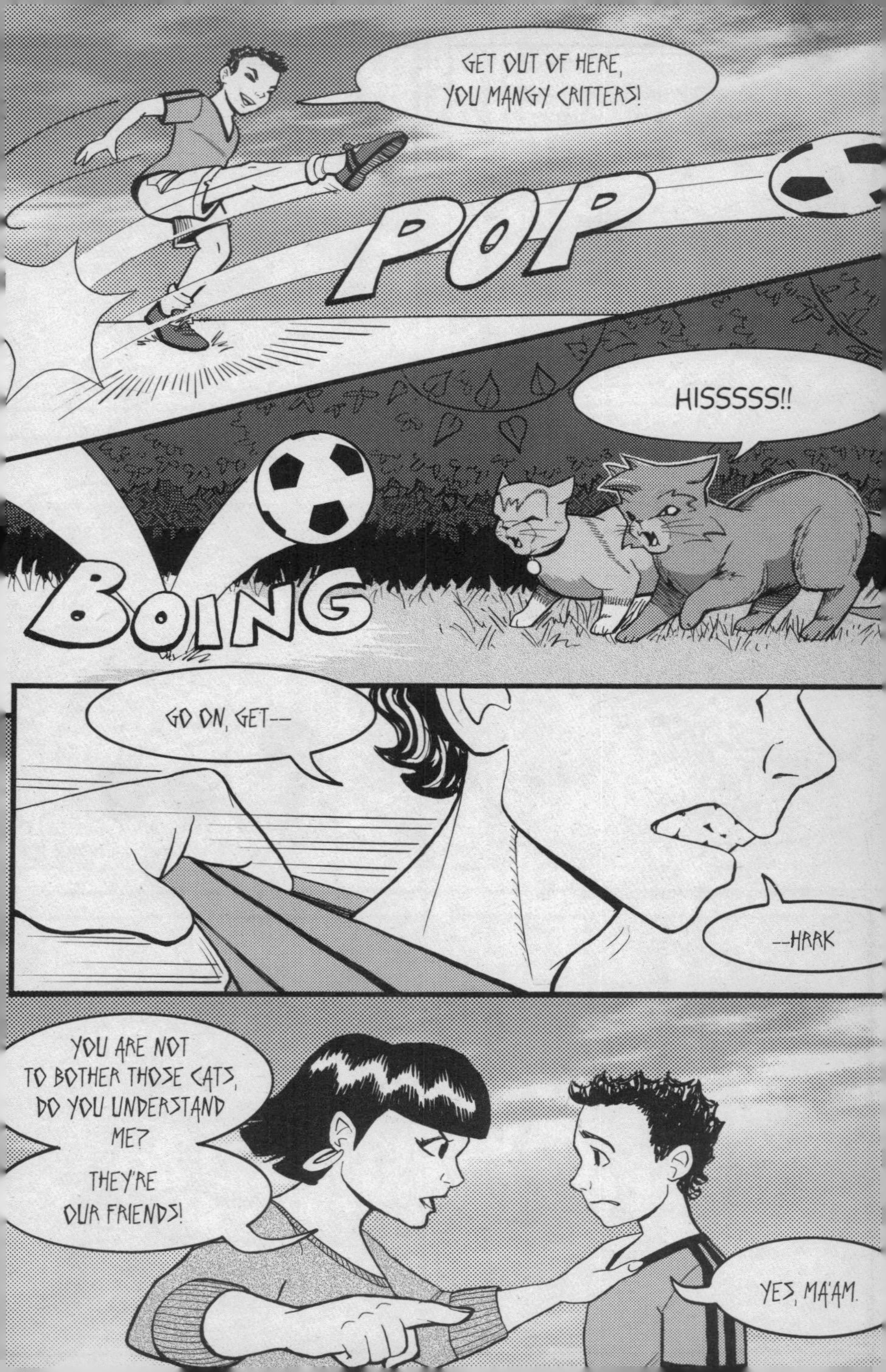
GET OUT OF HERE, YOU MANGY CRITTERS!
POP
HISSSSS!!
BOING
GO ON, GET--
--HRRK
YOU ARE NOT TO BOTHER THOSE CATS, DO YOU UNDERSTAND ME?
THEY'RE OUR FRIENDS!
YES, MA'AM.

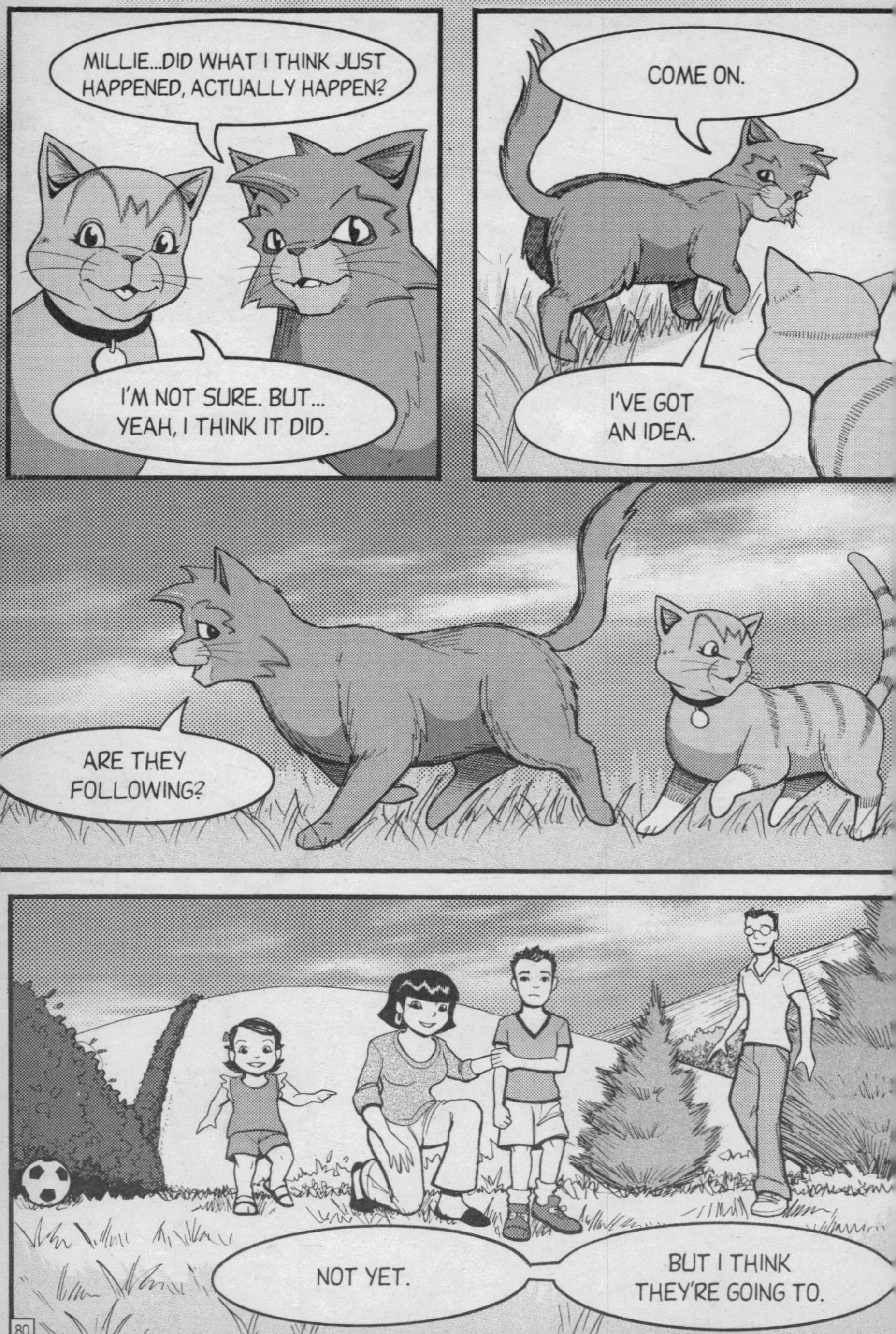
MILLIE...DID WHAT I THINK JUST HAPPENED, ACTUALLY HAPPEN?
I'M NOT SURE. BUT... YEAH, I THINK IT DID.
COME ON.
I'VE GOT AN IDEA.
ARE THEY FOLLOWING?
NOT YET.
BUT I THINK THEY'RE GOING TO.

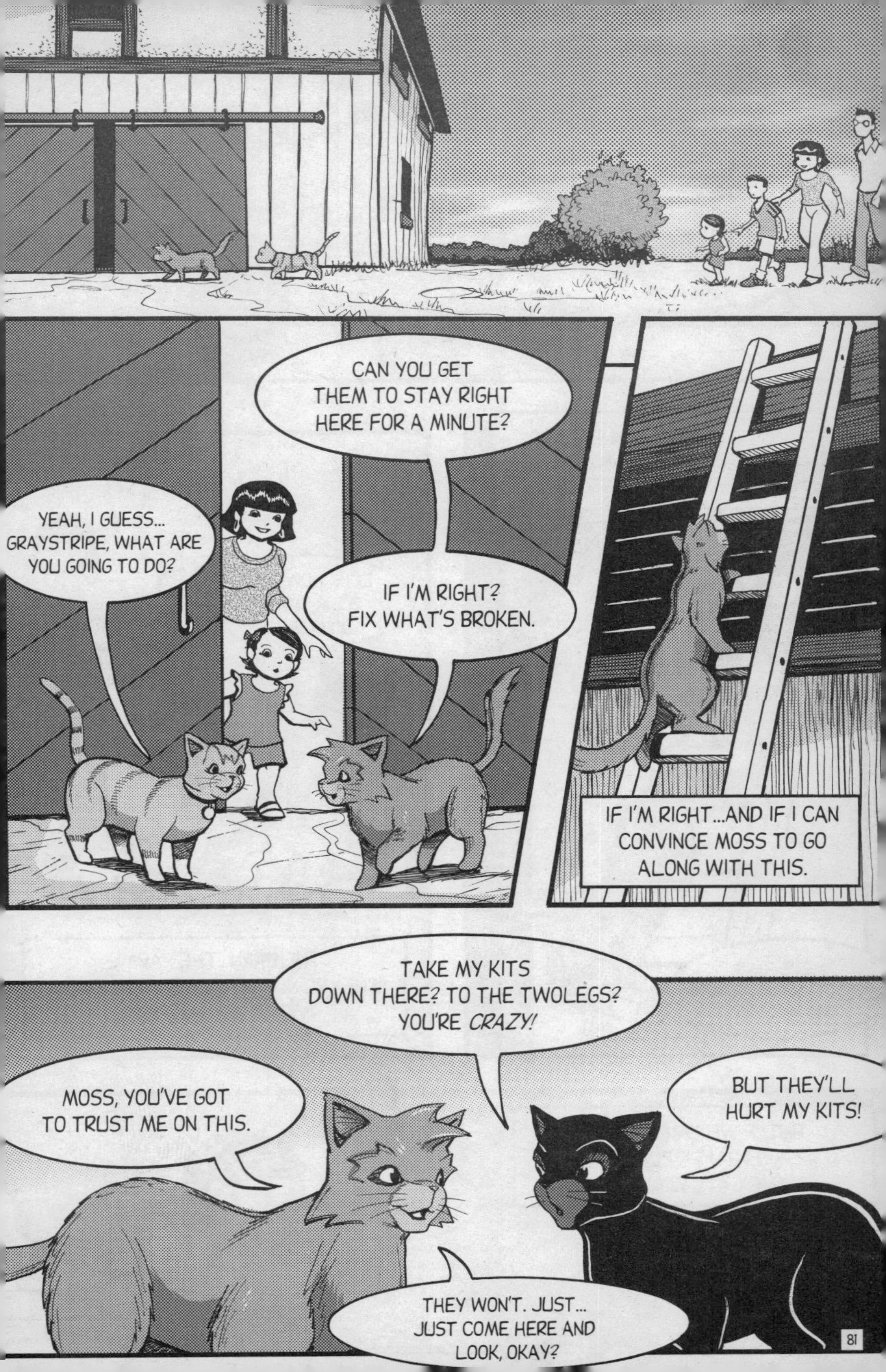
CAN YOU GET THEM TO STAY RIGHT HERE FOR A MINUTE?
YEAH, I GUESS... GRAYSTRIPE, WHAT ARE YOU GOING TO DO?
IF I'M RIGHT? FIX WHAT'S BROKEN.
IF I'M RIGHT...AND IF I CAN CONVINCE MOSS TO GO ALONG WITH THIS.
TAKE MY KITS DOWN THERE? TO THE TWOLEGS? YOU'RE *CRAZY!*
MOSS, YOU'VE GOT TO TRUST ME ON THIS.
BUT THEY'LL HURT MY KITS!
THEY WON'T. JUST... JUST COME HERE AND LOOK, OKAY?

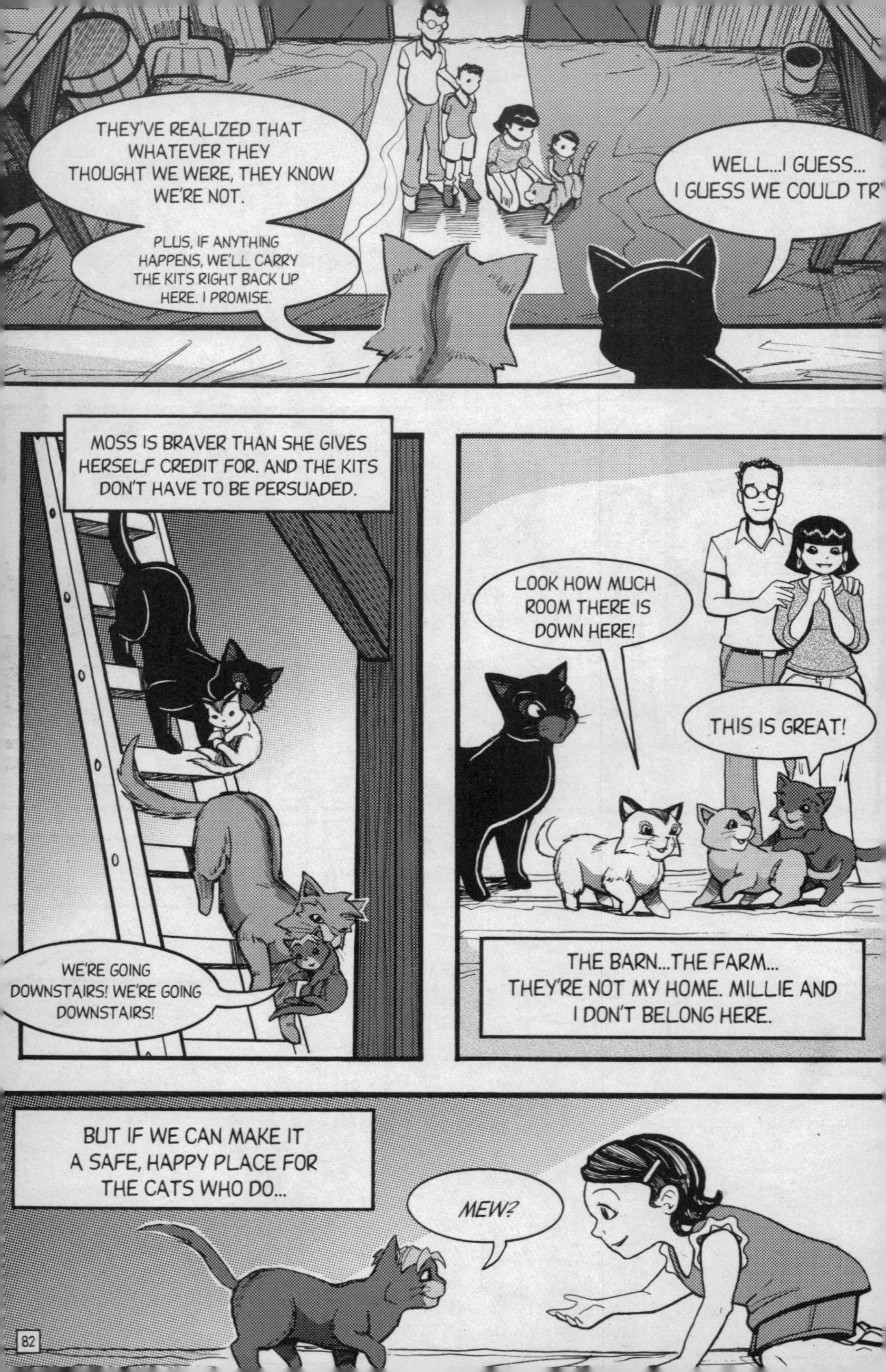
THEY'VE REALIZED THAT WHATEVER THEY THOUGHT WE WERE, THEY KNOW WE'RE NOT.
PLUS, IF ANYTHING HAPPENS, WE'LL CARRY THE KITS RIGHT BACK UP HERE. I PROMISE.
WELL...I GUESS... I GUESS WE COULD TR
MOSS IS BRAVER THAN SHE GIVES HERSELF CREDIT FOR. AND THE KITS DON'T HAVE TO BE PERSUADED.
WE'RE GOING DOWNSTAIRS! WE'RE GOING DOWNSTAIRS!
LOOK HOW MUCH ROOM THERE IS DOWN HERE!
THIS IS GREAT!
THE BARN...THE FARM... THEY'RE NOT MY HOME. MILLIE AND I DON'T BELONG HERE.
BUT IF WE CAN MAKE IT A SAFE, HAPPY PLACE FOR THE CATS WHO DO...
MEW?

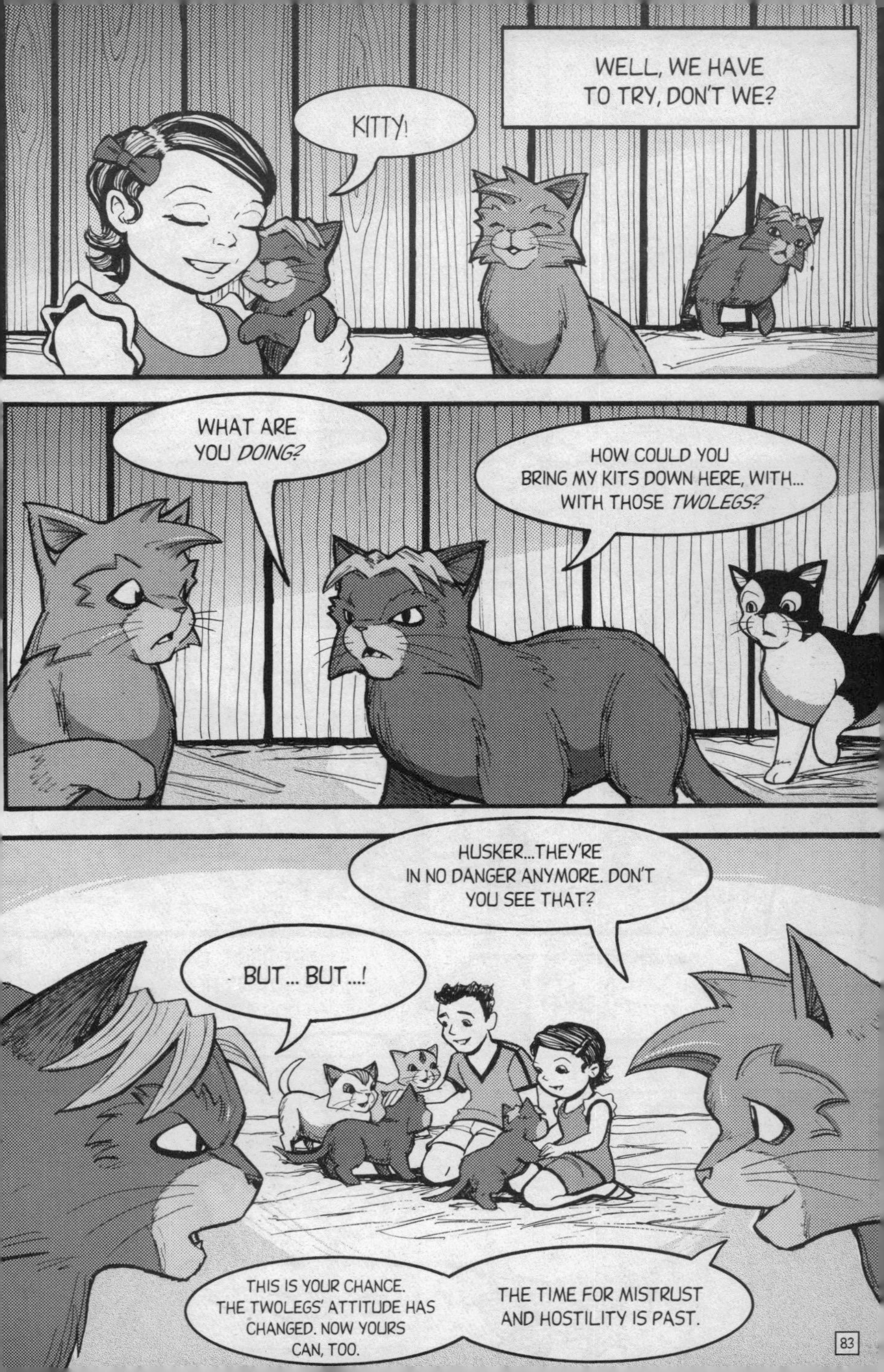
WELL, WE HAVE TO TRY, DON'T WE?
KITTY!
WHAT ARE YOU *DOING?*
HOW COULD YOU BRING MY KITS DOWN HERE, WITH... WITH THOSE *TWOLEGS?*
HUSKER...THEY'RE IN NO DANGER ANYMORE. DON'T YOU SEE THAT?
BUT... BUT...!
THIS IS YOUR CHANCE. THE TWOLEGS' ATTITUDE HAS CHANGED. NOW YOURS CAN, TOO.
THE TIME FOR MISTRUST AND HOSTILITY IS PAST.

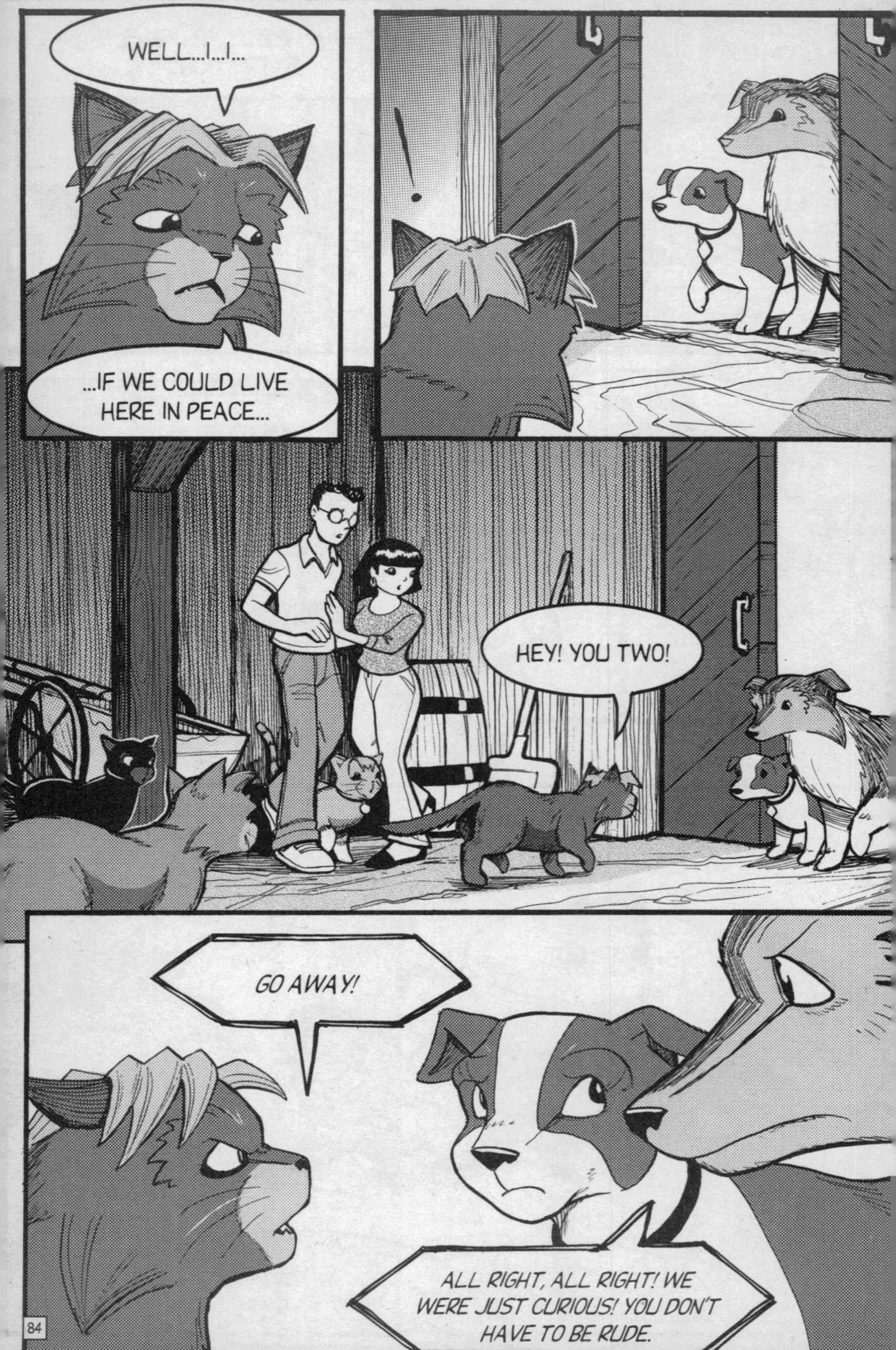
WELL...I...I...
...IF WE COULD LIVE HERE IN PEACE...
!
HEY! YOU TWO!
GO AWAY!
ALL RIGHT, ALL RIGHT! WE WERE JUST CURIOUS! YOU DON'T HAVE TO BE RUDE.

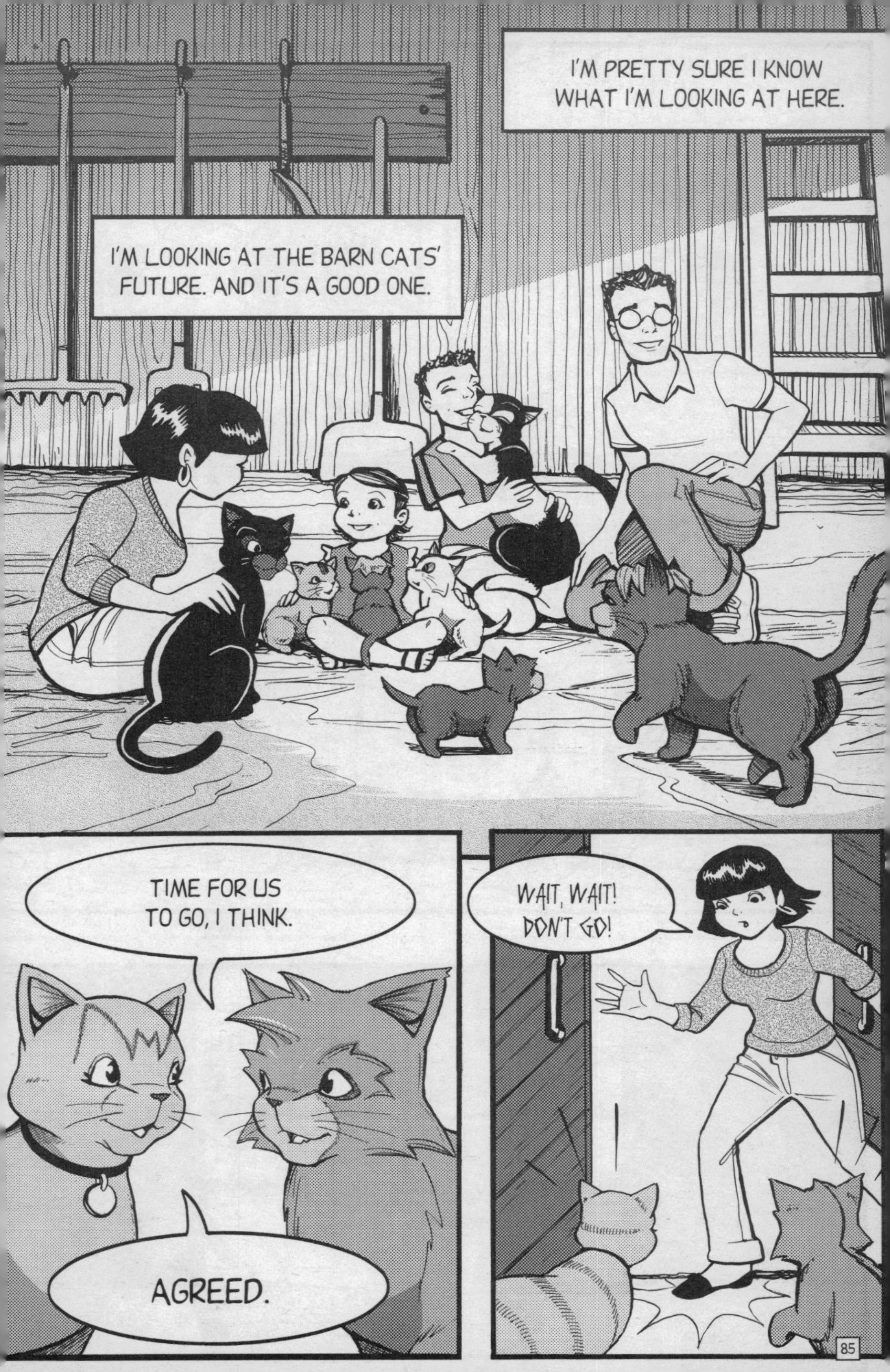
I'M PRETTY SURE I KNOW WHAT I'M LOOKING AT HERE.
I'M LOOKING AT THE BARN CATS' FUTURE. AND IT'S A GOOD ONE.
TIME FOR US TO GO, I THINK.
AGREED.
WAIT, WAIT! DON'T GO!

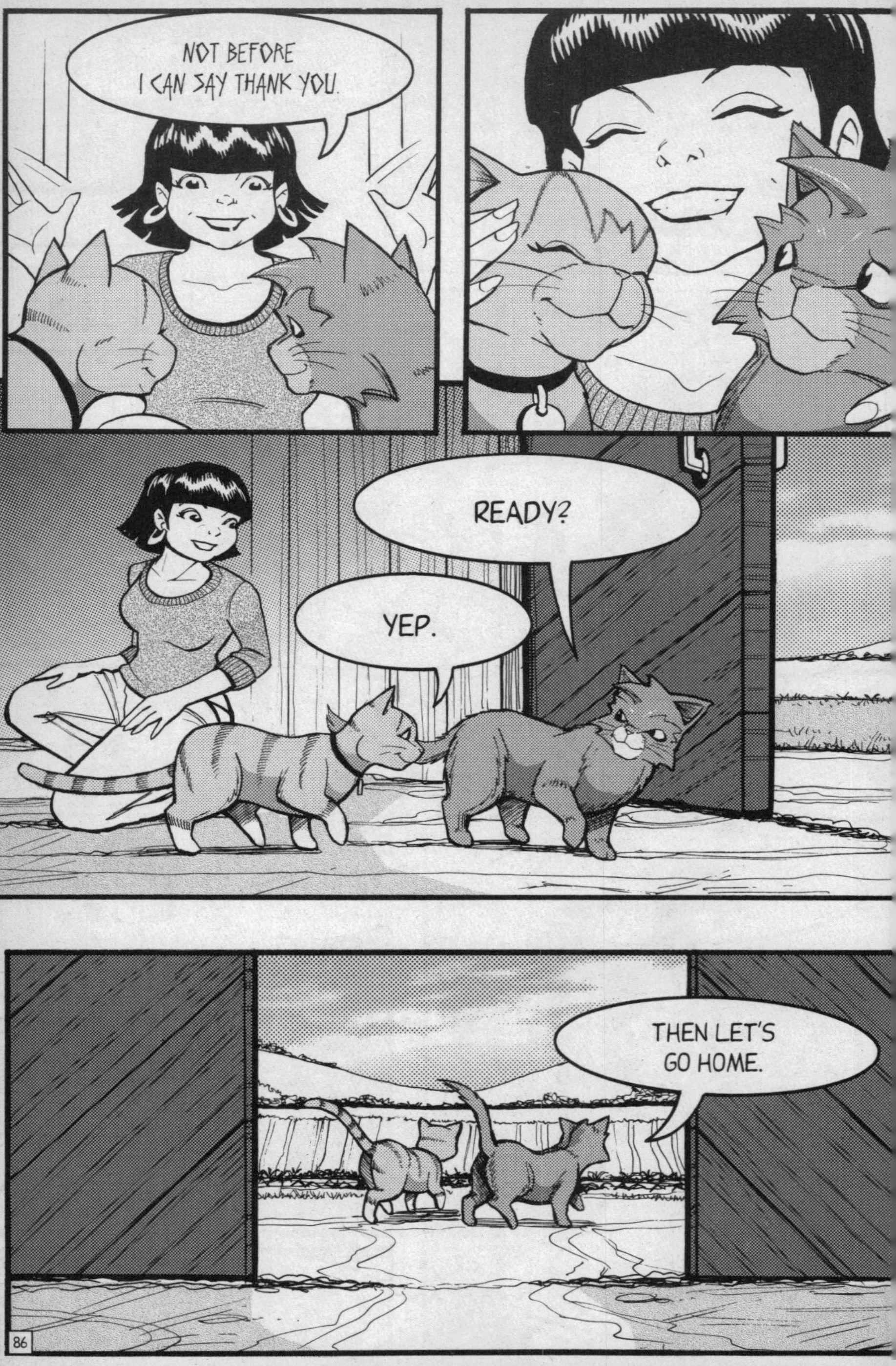
NOT BEFORE I CAN SAY THANK YOU.
READY?
YEP.
THEN LET'S GO HOME.

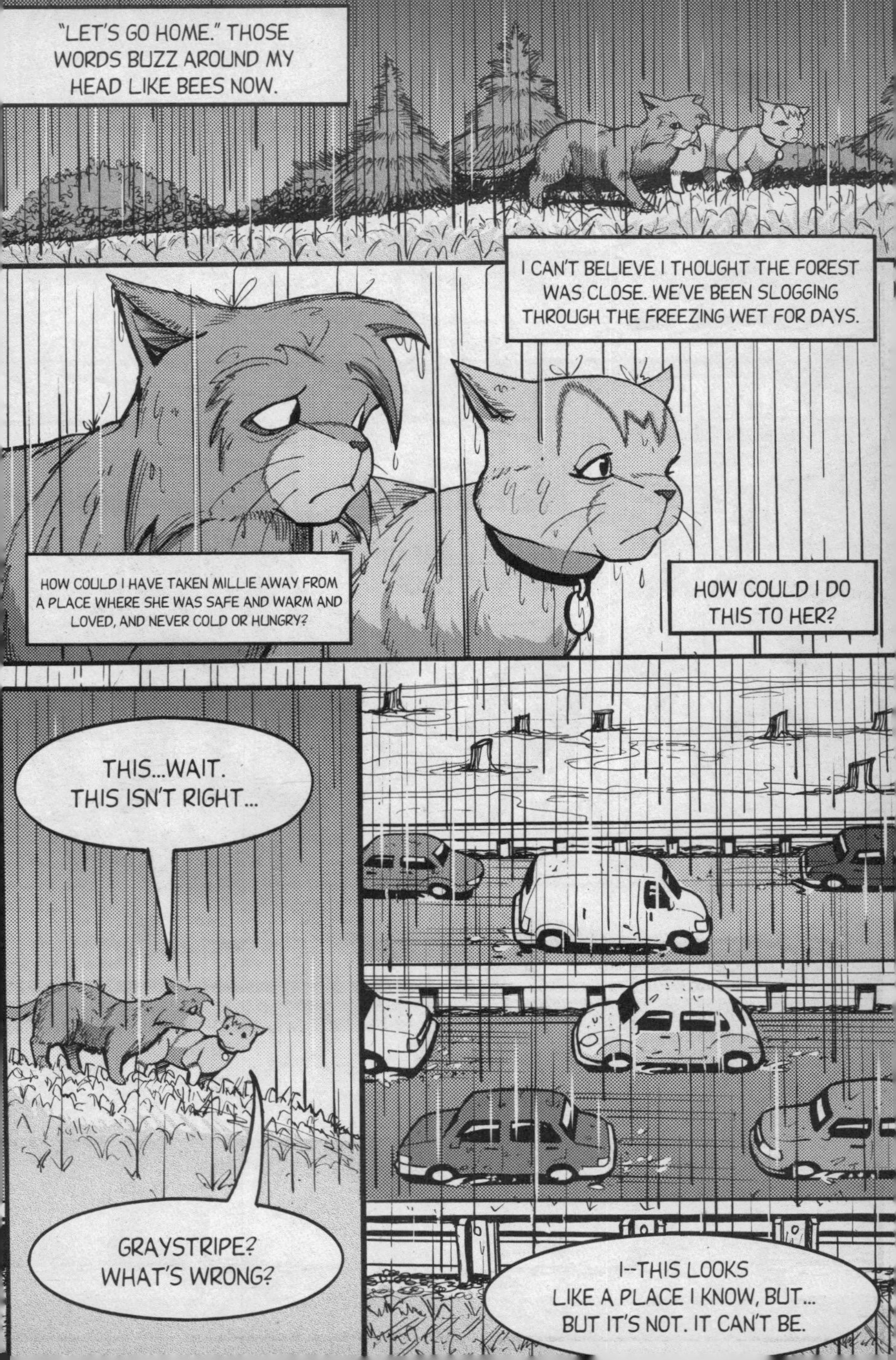
"LET'S GO HOME." THOSE WORDS BUZZ AROUND MY HEAD LIKE BEES NOW.
I CAN'T BELIEVE I THOUGHT THE FOREST WAS CLOSE. WE'VE BEEN SLOGGING THROUGH THE FREEZING WET FOR DAYS.
HOW COULD I HAVE TAKEN MILLIE AWAY FROM A PLACE WHERE SHE WAS SAFE AND WARM AND LOVED, AND NEVER COLD OR HUNGRY?
HOW COULD I DO THIS TO HER?
THIS...WAIT. THIS ISN'T RIGHT...
GRAYSTRIPE? WHAT'S WRONG?
I--THIS LOOKS LIKE A PLACE I KNOW, BUT... BUT IT'S NOT. IT CAN'T BE.

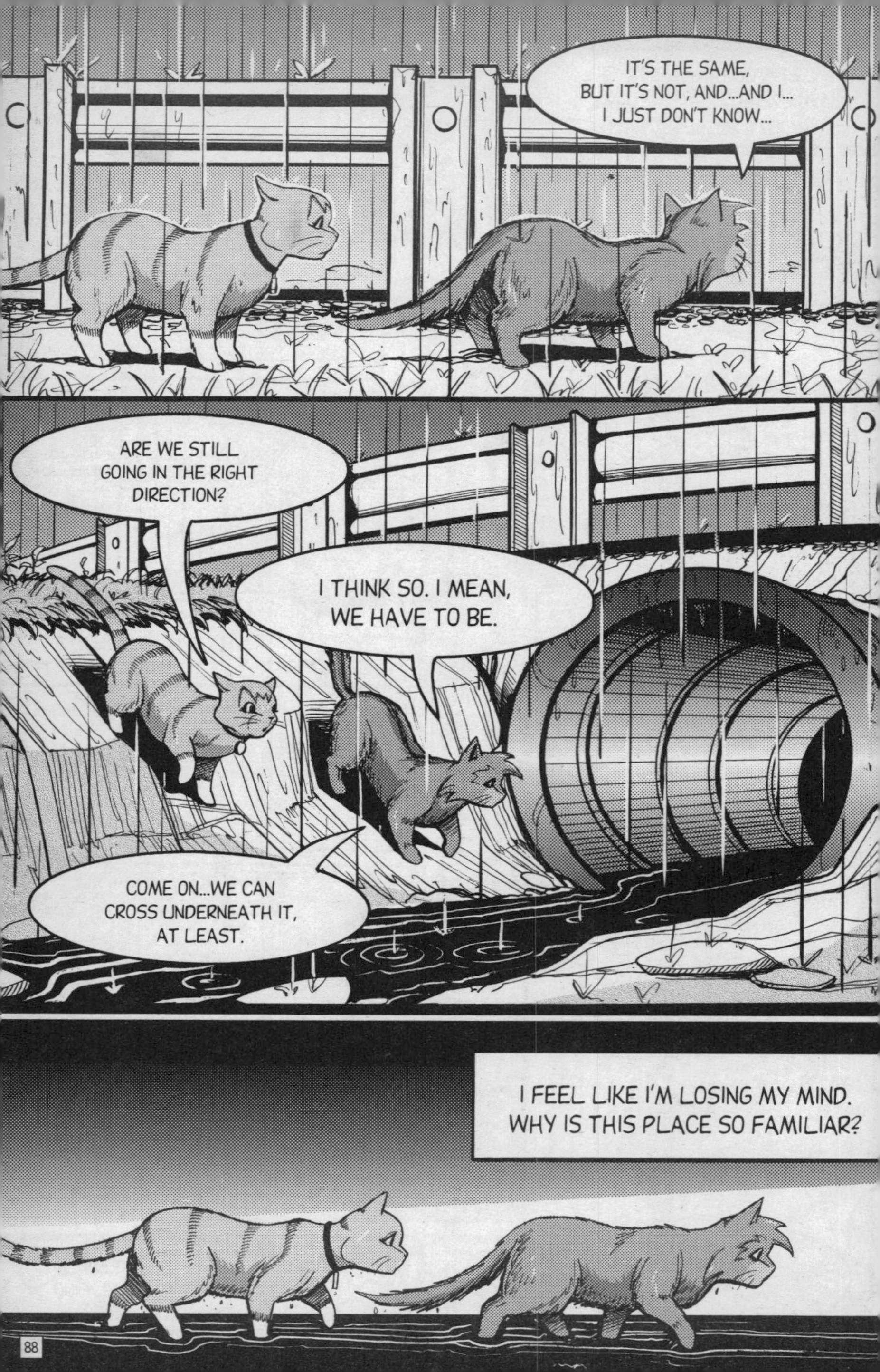
IT'S THE SAME, BUT IT'S NOT, AND...AND I... I JUST DON'T KNOW...
ARE WE STILL GOING IN THE RIGHT DIRECTION?
I THINK SO. I MEAN, WE HAVE TO BE.
COME ON...WE CAN CROSS UNDERNEATH IT, AT LEAST.
I FEEL LIKE I'M LOSING MY MIND. WHY IS THIS PLACE SO FAMILIAR?

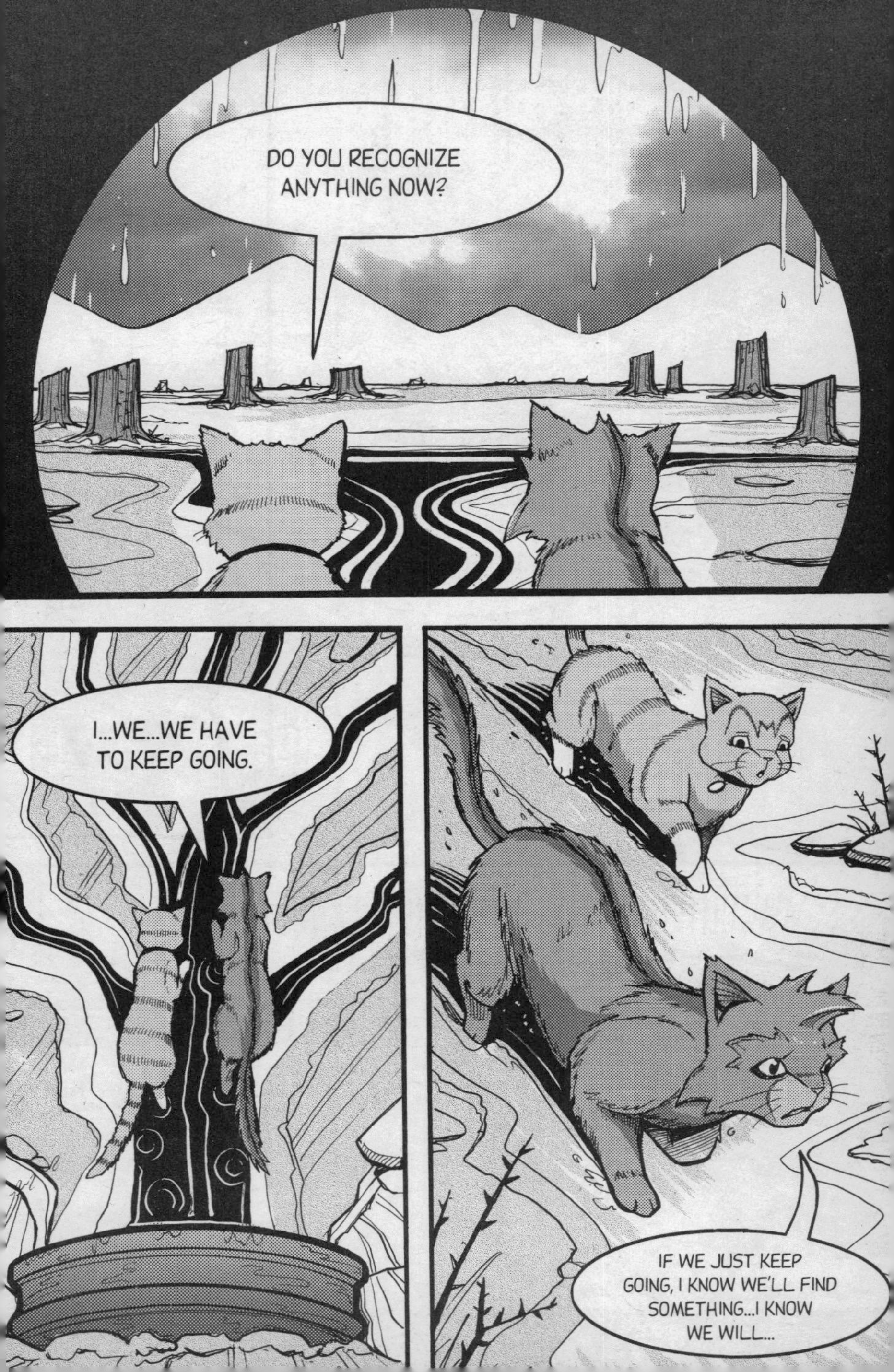
DO YOU RECOGNIZE ANYTHING NOW?
I...WE...WE HAVE TO KEEP GOING.
IF WE JUST KEEP GOING, I KNOW WE'LL FIND SOMETHING...I KNOW WE WILL...

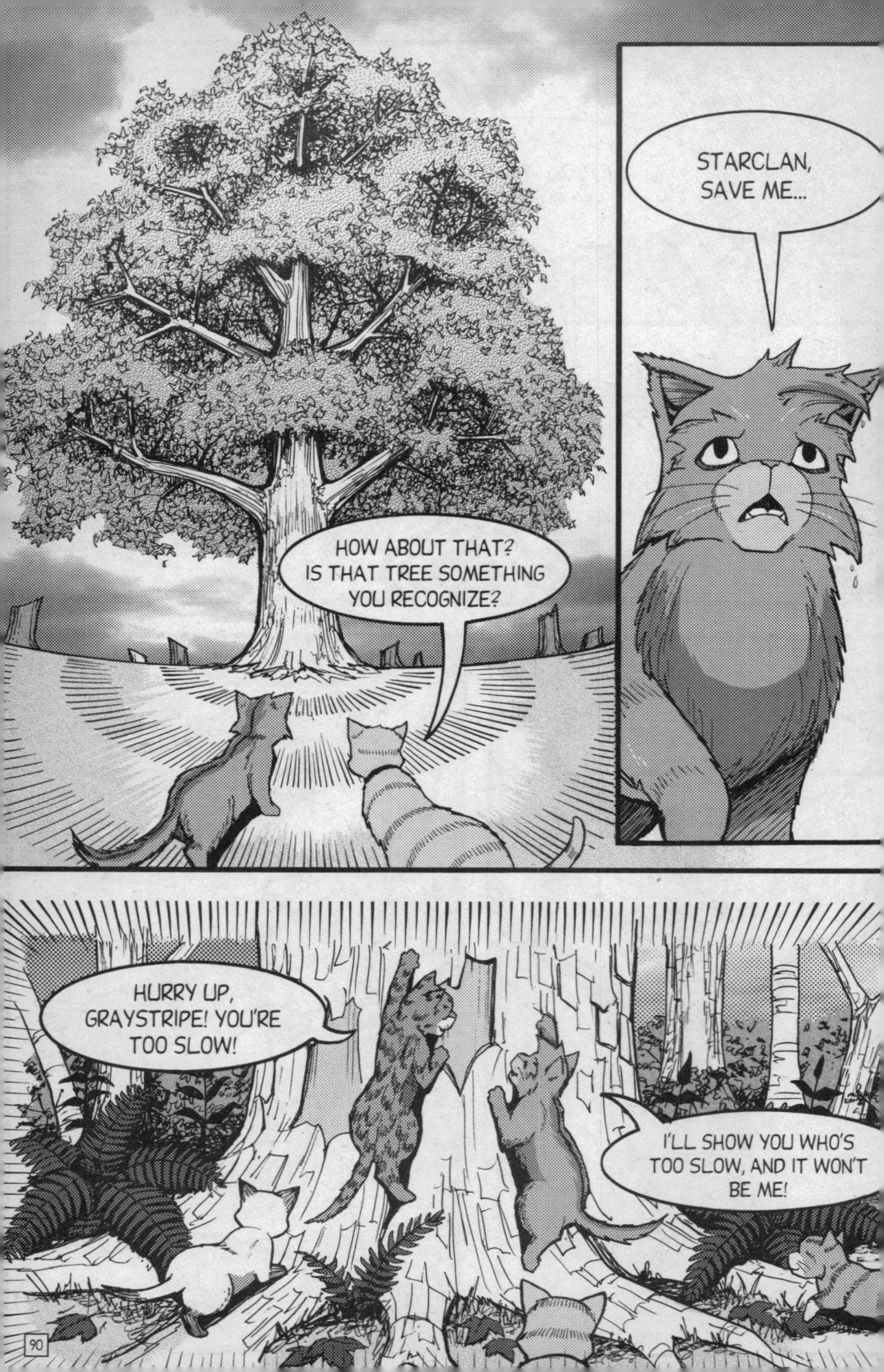
HOW ABOUT THAT? IS THAT TREE SOMETHING YOU RECOGNIZE?
STARCLAN, SAVE ME...
HURRY UP, GRAYSTRIPE! YOU'RE TOO SLOW!
I'LL SHOW YOU WHO'S TOO SLOW, AND IT WON'T BE ME!

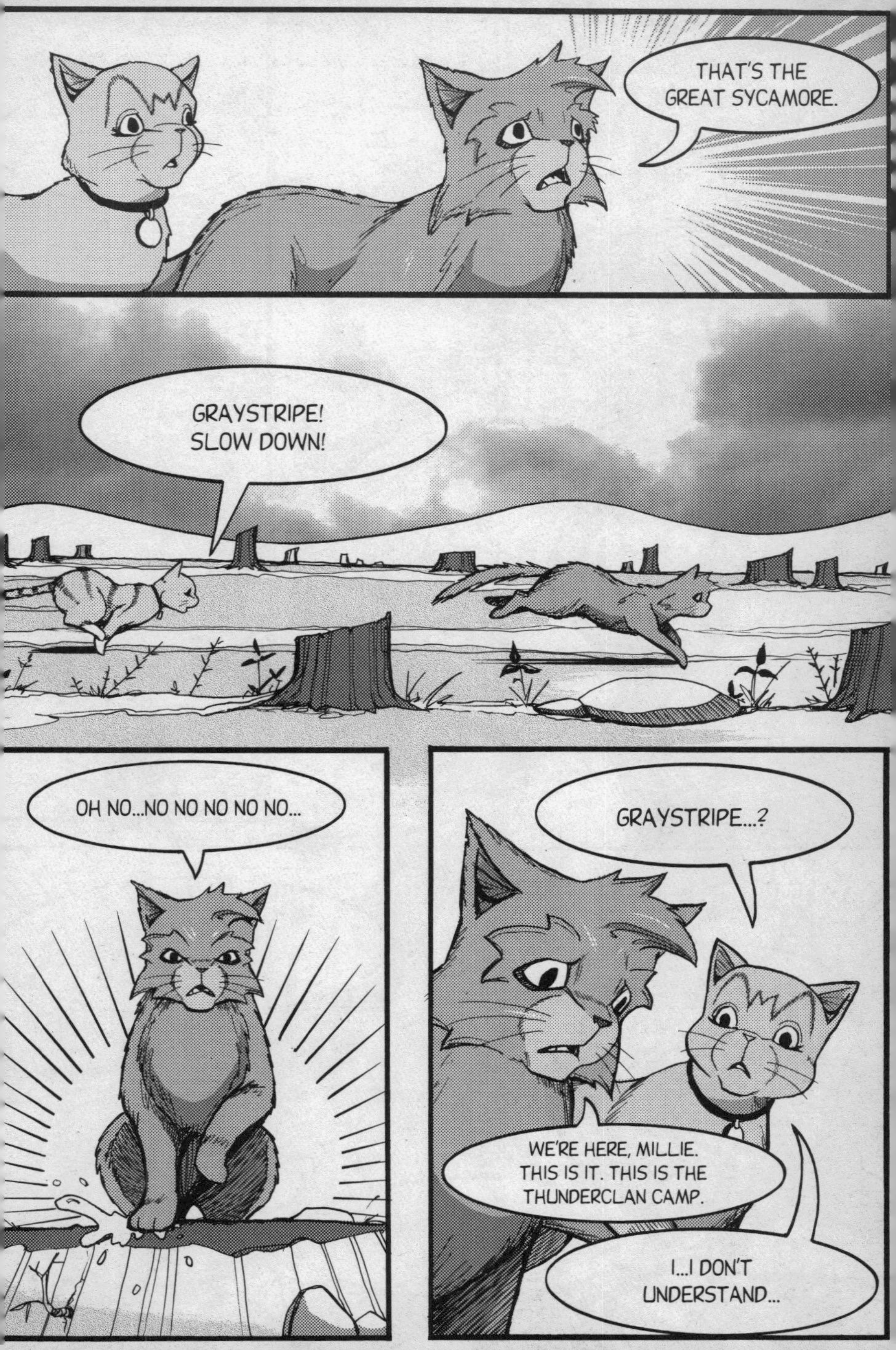
THAT'S THE GREAT SYCAMORE.
GRAYSTRIPE! SLOW DOWN!
OH NO...NO NO NO NO NO...
GRAYSTRIPE...?
WE'RE HERE, MILLIE. THIS IS IT. THIS IS THE THUNDERCLAN CAMP.
I...I DON'T UNDERSTAND...

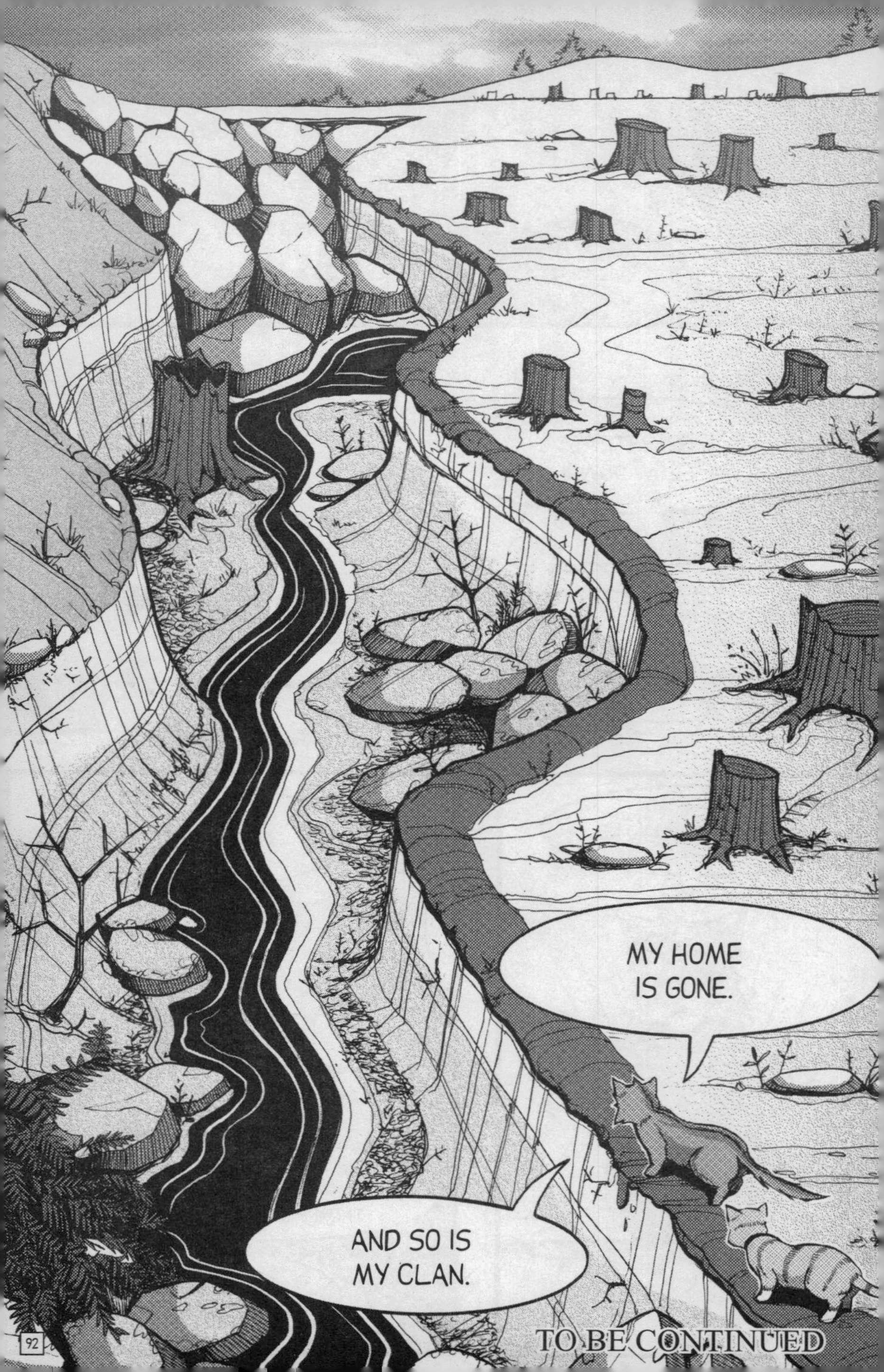
MY HOME IS GONE.
AND SO IS MY CLAN.
TO BE CONTINUED

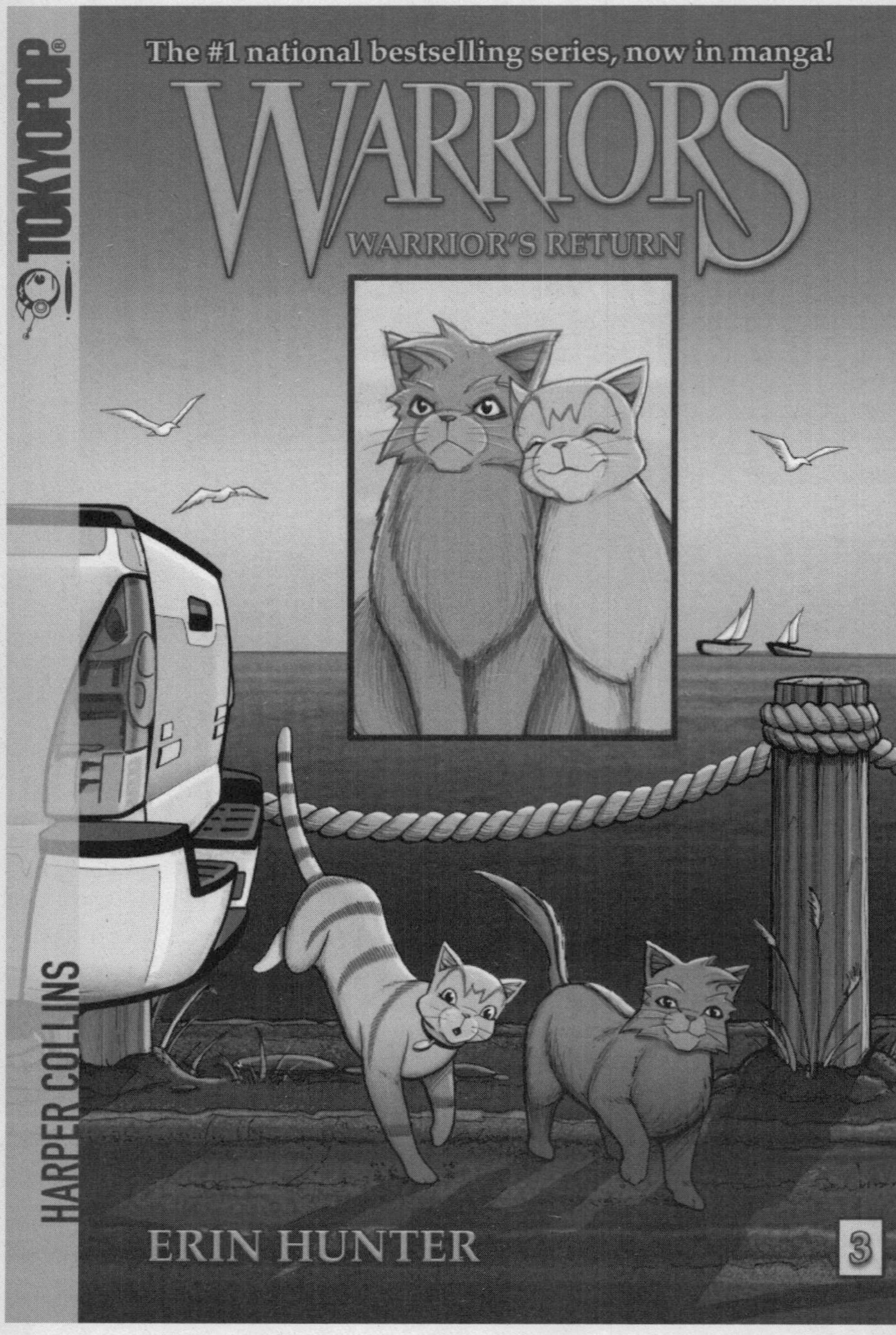

TOKYOPOP
The #1 national bestselling series, now in manga!
WARRIORS
WARRIOR'S RETURN
HARPER COLLINS
ERIN HUNTER
3

KEEP WATCH FOR

WARRIORS

VOLUME 3

WARRIOR'S RETURN

Graystripe and Millie have finally found ThunderClan's old territory, but Twoleg monsters have devastated the forest and Graystripe fears that all of his Clanmates have been killed, or captured by Twolegs. Millie insists that they keep looking, and an old friend helps point the two cats on the path that the Clans followed many moons ago. But danger still lurks around every turn, and Graystripe worries that he and Millie are lost on an impossible journey.

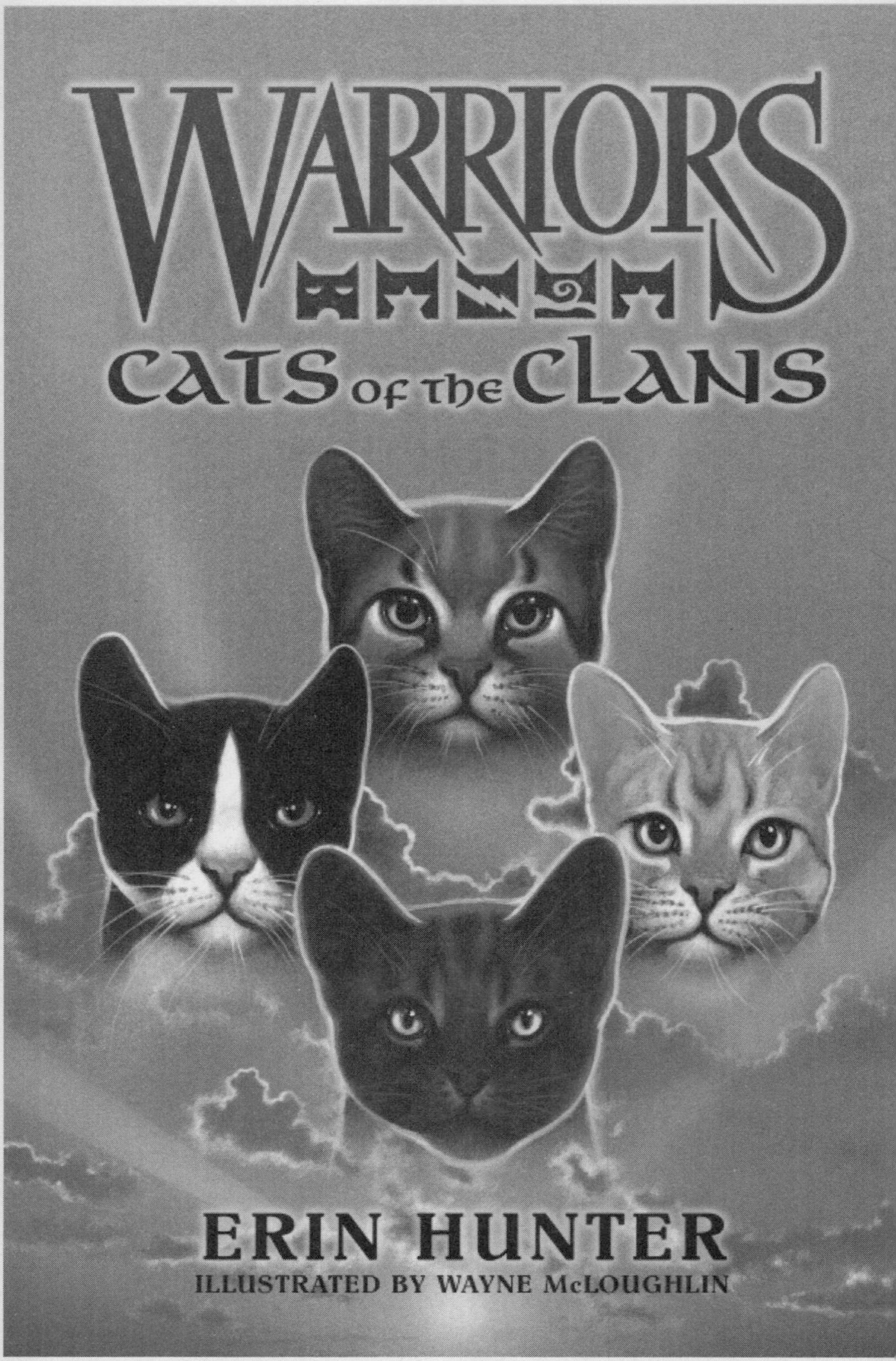
WARRIORS
CATS of the CLANS
ERIN HUNTER
ILLUSTRATED BY WAYNE McLOUGHLIN

MEET THE CLANS' HEROES IN

WARRIORS
CATS of the CLANS

Hear the stories of the great warriors as they've never
been told before! Chock-full of visual treats and
captivating details, including full-color illustrations and
in-depth biographies of important cats from all four
Clans, from fierce Clan leaders to wise medicine cats to
the most mischievous kits.

GO DEEP INSIDE THE CLANS WITH

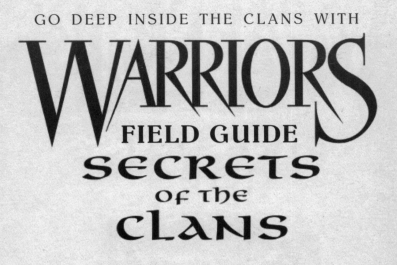

WARRIORS
FIELD GUIDE
SECRETS
OF THE
CLANS

Explore the warrior Clan camps with an insiders-
only tour guided by a warrior cat. Find out the secrets
of how an apprentice learns to fight, hunt, and live
by the warrior code. Understand the lore of healing
herbs passed down from one medicine cat to another.
Discover the never-before-revealed myths, legends,
and mystical origins of the warrior Clans.

THE NATIONAL BESTSELLING SERIES

WARRIORS
SUPER EDITION

FIRESTAR'S QUEST

The greatest adventure ever for ThunderClan's hero.

ERIN HUNTER

WARRIORS

SUPER EDITION

FIRESTAR'S QUEST

TURN THE PAGE FOR A PEEK
AT THUNDERCLAN'S LEADER
FIRESTAR'S GREATEST
ADVENTURE EVER!

Firestar slid around the edge of a hazel thicket and paused to taste the air. The moon was nearly full, and he could see that he was close to where the stream followed the border with ShadowClan. He could hear its faint gurgling, and picked up traces of the ShadowClan scent markers.

The flame-colored tomcat allowed himself a soft purr of satisfaction. He had been leader of ThunderClan for three seasons, and he felt as if he knew every tree, every bramble bush, every tiny path left by mice and voles throughout his territory. Since the fearsome battle when the forest Clans had joined together to drive out BloodClan and their murderous leader, Scourge, there had been peace, and the long days of newleaf and greenleaf had brought plentiful prey.

But Firestar knew that somewhere in the tranquil night an attacker was lurking. He made himself concentrate, all his senses alert. He caught the scent of mouse and rabbit, the green scent of grass and leaves, and very faintly the reek of the distant Thunderpath. But there was something else. Something he couldn't identify.

He raised his head, drawing the breeze over his scent

glands. At the same instant, a clump of bracken waved wildly, and a dark shape erupted from the middle of the curling fronds. Startled, Firestar spun to face it, but before he could raise his paws to defend himself the shape landed heavily on his shoulders, knocking him to the ground.

Summoning all his strength, Firestar rolled onto his back and brought up his hind paws to thrust his attacker away. Above him he could make out broad, muscular shoulders, a massive head with dark tabby markings, the glint of amber eyes. . . .

Firestar gritted his teeth and battered even harder with his hind paws. A forepaw lashed out toward him and he flinched, waiting for the strike.

Suddenly the weight that pinned him down vanished as the tabby cat sprang away with a yowl of triumph. "You didn't know I was there, did you?" he meowed. "Go on, Firestar, admit it. You had no idea."

Firestar staggered to his paws, shaking grass seeds and scraps of moss from his pelt. "Bramblepaw, you great lump! You've squashed me as flat as a leaf."

"I know." Bramblepaw's eyes gleamed. "If you'd really been a ShadowClan invader, you would be crow-food by now."

"So I would." Firestar touched his apprentice on the shoulder with the tip of his tail. "You did very well, especially disguising your scent like that."

"I rolled in a clump of damp ferns as soon as I left camp," Bramblepaw explained. He suddenly looked anxious. "Was my assessment okay, Firestar?"

Firestar hesitated, struggling to push away the memory of Bramblepaw's bloodthirsty father, Tigerstar. When he looked at the young apprentice, it was too easy to recall the same broad shoulders, dark tabby fur, and amber eyes that belonged to the cat who had been ready to murder and betray his own Clanmates to make himself leader.

"Firestar?" Bramblepaw prompted.

Firestar shook off the clinging cobwebs of the past. "Yes, Bramblepaw, of course. No cat could have done better."

"Thanks, Firestar!" Bramblepaw's amber eyes shone and his tail went straight up in the air. As they turned toward the ThunderClan camp, he glanced back at the ShadowClan border. "Do you think Tawnypaw will be near the end of her apprentice training, too?"

Bramblepaw's sister, Tawnypaw, had been born in ThunderClan, but she had never felt at home there. She was too sensitive to the mistrust of cats who couldn't forget that she was Tigerstar's daughter. When her father had become leader of ShadowClan, she had left ThunderClan to be with him. Firestar always felt that he had failed her, and he knew how much Bramblepaw missed her.

"I don't know how they do these things in ShadowClan," he meowed carefully, "but Tawnypaw started her training at the same time as you, so she should be ready for her warrior ceremony by now."

"I hope so," Bramblepaw mewed. "I know she'll be a great warrior."

"You both will," Firestar told him.

On their way back to camp, Firestar felt as if every shadowy hollow, every clump of fern or bramble thicket, could be hiding the gleam of amber eyes. Whatever Tigerstar's crimes, he had been proud of his son and daughter, and his death had been particularly dreadful, with all nine lives ripped away at once by Scourge's sharpened claws. Was the massive tabby watching them now? Not from StarClan, for Firestar had never seen him in his dreams; the ThunderClan medicine cat, Cinderpelt, had never reported meeting him when she shared tongues with StarClan, either. Could there be another place for coldhearted cats who had been ready to use the warrior code for their own dark ambitions? If there was such a shadowed path, Firestar hoped he would never have to walk it—nor his lively apprentice. Bramblepaw was bouncing through the grass beside him, excited as a kit; surely he had shaken off the legacy of his father?

As they slipped down the ravine toward the camp, Bramblepaw halted, his gaze serious. "Was my assessment *really* okay? Am I good enough—"

"To be a warrior?" Firestar guessed. "Yes, you are. We'll hold your ceremony tomorrow."

Bramblepaw dipped his head respectfully. "Thank you, Firestar," he mewed. "I won't let you down." His eyes blazed; he gave a sudden bound into the air and pelted down the rest of the ravine to wait by the entrance to the gorse tunnel. Firestar watched him, amused. He could still remember when he had felt as if he had too much energy to contain in his four paws, when he felt as if he could run through the forest forever.

"You'd better get some sleep," he warned as he joined his apprentice. "You'll have to sit vigil tomorrow night."

"If you're sure, Firestar . . ." Bramblepaw hesitated, working his claws in the sandy ground. "I could find you some fresh-kill first."

"No, go on," his leader told him. "You're so excited right now you wouldn't notice if a fox ate you."

Bramblepaw waved his tail and bundled through the gorse tunnel into the camp.

Firestar lingered outside the camp for a while, settling down on a flat rock with his tail curled around his paws. He could hear nothing but the faint rustle of leaves in the breeze, and the tiny scufflings of prey in the undergrowth.

The battle with BloodClan had cast its shadow over all the Clans; for more than a season after, every cat in the forest jumped at a cracking twig, and chased out strangers as if their lives depended on it. They were even scared of going too close to Twolegplace, in case any surviving members of BloodClan happened to be lurking there. But now, five moons later, ThunderClan was thriving. Tomorrow there would be a new warrior, and the apprentices Rainpaw, Sootpaw, and Sorrelpaw were all doing well after three moons of training. In time, they would be good warriors too—they were bound to be, considering who their father was. Every day they reminded Firestar of his first deputy, Whitestorm, who had died battling the vicious BloodClan deputy, Bone. He still grieved for the old white warrior.

His mind wrapped in memories of his old friend, it was a

moment before Firestar realized he could hear a faint sound: the footfalls of a cat stepping lightly through the undergrowth. He sprang to his paws, looking around, but he saw nothing.

He hardly had time to sit down before the noise came again. This time Firestar whipped his head around in time to glimpse the pale shape of a cat standing a little farther up the ravine.

Am I dreaming? Has Whitestorm left StarClan to come and visit me?

But this cat was smaller than Whitestorm and its fur was gray, patched with white. It stared straight at him, its eyes dark and earnest, as if it were trying to tell him something. Firestar had never seen it before. Could it be a rogue? Or worse—could BloodClan have recovered from their defeat and come back to invade the forest?

He sprang to his paws and raced up the ravine toward the strange cat. But as soon as he began to move, it vanished, and when he searched among the rocks he couldn't find it. There weren't even any pawmarks, but when he tasted the air there was a faint trace of an unfamiliar scent, almost swamped by the ThunderClan scents that came from the camp.

Slowly Firestar retraced his pawsteps and sat on the rock again. All his senses were alert now as he gazed into the shadows. But he saw nothing more of the strange gray cat.